"What do you want of me?" she said at last, her voice rising and cracking as if she fought to control it.

Symon spun her in his arms so she faced him. She gasped and managed to wedge her hands between them. Warmth radiated from her palms.

"Release me."

"Nay."

" 'Tis true? You are the Devil of Kilmartin?"

"I am Symon, Chief of Clan Lachlan." He pressed his fingers to his temple, physically forcing the returning stabs of pain back.

If he wanted to learn the truth of who this lass was and what had caused that strange, wonderful moment, he would have to act quickly, before he once more lost his grasp on reason. He must secure the lass until he could question her. Most likely, she was a witch, but he did not care. Anything that would dampen his madness, give him even a few extra moments of clarity, would strengthen his position with the clan.

"Where do you take me, *Devil*?"

He had to admire her courage, though her eyes showed the fear of a cornered animal. But he did not have time for pretty words to bend her to his wishes. The madness could crash around him again at any moment, and he must get her to safety before that happened. He could not guarantee she would live to see the next morn if he did not. And he desperately wished her to do so.

Symon released her arm and quickly scooped her over his shoulder.

11/29/02

For Marge —

The
Devil of
Kilmartin

Enjoy .

Laurin Wittig

Merry Christmas !

Laurin Wittig

J
JOVE BOOKS, NEW YORK

This is a work of fiction. Names, characters, places, and incidents either
are the product of the author's imagination or are used fictitiously,
and any resemblance to actual persons, living or dead, business
establishments, events, or locales is entirely coincidental.

THE DEVIL OF KILMARTIN

A Jove Book / published by arrangement with
the author

PRINTING HISTORY
Jove edition / September 2002

Visit our website at
www.penguinputnam.com

ISBN: 0-515-13421-X

A JOVE BOOK®
Jove Books are published by The Berkley Publishing Group,
a division of Penguin Putnam Inc.,
375 Hudson Street, New York, New York 10014.
JOVE and the "J" design
are trademarks belonging to Penguin Putnam Inc.

PRINTED IN THE UNITED STATES OF AMERICA

10   9   8   7   6   5   4   3   2   1

*This book is dedicated to the memory of my dad,
Joseph Wesley Watkins, III,
who taught me to love the music of language*

and

*to my husband, Dean,
the love of my life and my very own hero.*

Acknowledgments

It would be impossible to list all the wonderful people in my life who've helped me hone my craft and kept me laughing while I did it. However, there are a few who deserve special mention. Thanks to the members of Washington Romance Writers for all the shared knowledge, wisdom, and friendship over the years and to the amazing women who allow me to critique their work while they critique mine: Catherine Anderson, Lisa Arlt, Elizabeth Holcombe Fedorko, Courtney Henke, Karen Lee Smith, and my partner in plotting, Pamela Palmer Poulsen. Thanks also go to the sisterhood of the GH99er e-mail loop, the best support group any writer could ask for.

Jennifer Jackson and Kelly Sinanis get my huge thanks for guiding me through the publication of this book.

I'd especially like to thank my kids and my husband for making it possible for me to follow my dream, and my mom and stepdad, Jane Watkins and Ralph Kelly, for being eager chauffeurs during our adventure through Scotland.

chapter 1

Southwestern Highlands, Scotland
Spring 1307

Anger, pain, and grief fueled Elena Lamont's growing despair as she searched the torchlit chamber for the body of her cousin Ian. He was her last hope. He should be here, somewhere amongst the half score of her kinsmen lying bloodied on the rush-strewn floor. She shuddered as she moved between the pain-racked men. 'Twas an all too familiar sight since their chief, her father, had disappeared.

"Elena."

She saw a hand raised slightly and rushed to Ian, sinking to her knees at his side. The rough wool of her oldest gown quickly soaked up a pool of his blood. His face was gray, his eyes glassy.

"I see you did not parry fast enough again," she said, keeping her voice light as she carefully pulled a piece of bloody linen away from his chest. "The Devil will not deal so lightly with you next time." She swallowed a gasp as she revealed the pink-tinged bone of his ribs.

"Do not worry over me, lass," Ian said. " 'Tis too much this time."

"Shush, Ian. Save your breath. 'Tis for sure you'll be needing it when Isobel finds you've been hurt yet again." Blood oozed from the gash. " 'Tis not so bad as the last time," she said, not daring to look him in the face.

'Twas worse.

As gently as she could manage with trembling hands, she tore his blood-crusted tunic further to expose more of his chest. She prayed that this time she could hold herself away from the pain. It was a daily prayer for her, and it had yet to be answered.

"Lay very still." She rubbed her hands together, warming them, calming herself, calling forth the healing gift she held within her.

She placed her hands gently around the wound.

Pain leapt from Ian, burned up her fingers, scrabbled around her arms, and settled its claws in her ribs. The first flash was a shock, but Elena knew she mustn't let it stop her. Nothing must stop her from saving Ian's life.

With great effort she ignored the mirrored pain and willed the healing heat out through her hands and into the man beside her. After a dozen breaths the pain began to ease. Elena relaxed slightly, rolling her shoulders as she once again gathered the heat. After another dozen breaths the wound began to close. She concentrated, determined to heal this man.

Without Ian, their missing chief's arrogant, overbearing champion, Dougal of Dunmore, would surely take control of the dispirited clan and declare himself their leader. The result would only be more of what she struggled with this day. Blood and death, for Dougal cast destruction about him wherever he went, and all in the name of power.

Elena could not let that happen. Wise, caring Ian had always been her father's choice to follow him.

Without Ian's leadership all was lost for their clan.

Just as the blood flow ceased from Ian's wound and Elena fought to mend the flesh, Dougal roughly pulled her away from her cousin.

"Why do you waste your skill on this one? He will not survive." Elena glared at him, repulsed by the glint of glee in his eyes. "Save yourself for those who may rise to fight again."

Elena looked away, trying to calm the surge of anger and fear she felt whenever this man was near. Before she could take even one breath, Dougal shoved her toward another injured warrior.

"I need them all on their feet by first light."

Elena glanced back at her cousin. His breathing was even, though his skin still held the pallor of much blood loss. At least he would lose no more this night.

Candles sputtered and were replaced by silent clanswomen as Elena worked her way through the crowded room, healing each hurt, small and great. By the fifth man Elena could no longer focus on anything save stopping the pain assaulting her. By the tenth man she could barely stand, so great was her fatigue. By the twelfth man, and the last, Dougal had to cuff her repeatedly to keep her alert and focused on the task at hand.

When the last man was healed, Elena could not rise to her feet. If it weren't for the bloody gore that covered the rush-strewn floor she would have curled up right where she sat and slept for days.

But Dougal hauled her to her feet once more, turning her to face him. She had to look down at him, into mud-brown eyes that held no gentleness, only a lust for power, and some other even more ominous fire. She had never been able to name the fire she saw there, but she knew it did not bode well for those around him. It certainly had not so far.

"Get you to your chamber. Wash the blood from your hands and face and don the new gown that awaits you there." He released her arm abruptly. She staggered at the sudden loss of support. When she was sure she could walk without falling, she moved slowly toward the door, her exhausted mind slowly mulling over his words.

She made her way to her small, cell-like chamber. Protected, Dougal always said of it, though she knew only too well that wasn't why it had been given to her. She opened the door and stopped.

A tray of steaming stew, oatcakes, and a large mug of ale awaited her by a crackling fire. A gown was spread over her narrow bed, its color the same muddy brown as Dougal's eyes. She shuddered. She'd never wear that color, even if her own clothes were falling in rags from her body.

Despite her fatigue, she pushed the door wide open, then moved to the food, greedily gulping the ale and lifting the bowl to quickly consume the savory contents. When she had finished, she looked about again.

Why would Dougal have a new gown made for her?

She left the warmth of the fire and sat on the bed, not touching the clothing. Somehow she knew to accept the gift would seal her to a new fate, though she couldn't grasp how another fate could be worse than the one she endured now.

She would not have thought she could have soft feelings for her father, but in the face of Dougal, she found she wished him whole and back in this castle where he could rein in his champion. Her father had never treated her gently, but she knew he had protected her from many things, and many people. If he did not return soon or if Ian did not gain back his once robust health, Elena knew she would have to gather her courage and do something herself.

But what? As long as Ian lived, then Dougal would have no rightful claim. By custom *she* could claim the chief's position, but she had no wish to do so. Her father had long trained Ian to take his place. If her father's fate was not known soon, very soon, she or Ian would be forced to act. One thing was certain. Dougal would not bide his time long. He would declare the chief dead any day now, and her hand, or Ian's, would be forced.

She rose to return to Ian. The one thing she could do well was watch over him until he was able to take his place at the head of the clan.

As if to mock her decision, a chill draft entered her chamber, just ahead of Dougal.

"You are not welcome here," she said.

He shut the door behind him, and Elena forced herself not to react.

"You cannot keep me out much longer."

"When my father is found—"

"He has been."

Elena's breath caught in her throat. "Where is he? Is he well?"

Dougal moved toward her. "My gillies have found his body not far from here."

He waited, letting his words slice through the momentary hope that had blossomed within her. Elena groped for the bed, lowering herself to sit upon it once more. Shock and dread stole her breath.

"He is dead." She stared into the fire, searching for some glimmer of sorrow within herself for her sire.

"Aye, and I am chief here now."

Elena glanced at the man's face. There was no grief in his eyes, no remorse, not even a hint of sadness there. Nothing marked any sentiment over the passing of a man who had taken Dougal in and given him a home when he was but a wandering sword.

Nothing save greed—and ambition.

In time she would mourn the loss of a father, even one who never showed her any softness, but right now she could think only of the future.

"How did he die?" she whispered.

"A terrible accident. It seems his horse threw him. He fell and broke his neck." Dougal moved toward her. "*I* am chief now."

"Nay! Ian is chief." Fear wrapped about her heart, squeezing tight. "He has ever been my father's chosen one."

"Ian is in no condition to lead the clan. He has been so ill of late he can no longer wield a sword well enough to keep himself whole. He is no leader. I am chief. I now speak for the clan."

Elena rose, moving to the warmth of the fire, needing to put more distance between herself and this man. She took a deep breath, knowing what she must do, but wishing with all her might that someone else would come and do it for her. She turned to face him.

"I am the chief's daughter." She struggled to keep her voice firm. "By right and tradition I shall be chief if Ian cannot."

Dougal moved closer, a gleam in his eyes. "Aye." He reached forward and grabbed her thick flame-colored braid, pulling her closer to him with it. "You have that authority until such time as you marry. Then your husband will be the rightful chief."

"I will never marry. I will be chief until Ian is well enough to lead. 'Tis what the clan will want."

"I do not think it will come to that, my lassie."

She shuddered. The endearment felt like a threat.

Dougal wound the braid about his hand, forcing her to move closer to him until she was trapped, the braid held tautly, pulling her head toward him. With effort, she kept the merest hair's breadth of distance between their bodies.

"You see," he said, his hot, fetid breath singeing her cheek, "by daybreak, we will announce our betrothal. We will seal our union before the clan tomorrow evening. Then I will be chief—by right, and by tradition."

Wed Dougal? Her mind went dangerously blank, then a vivid, revolting image of him in her bed flashed before her, followed by another, of her kinsmen slaughtered, one by one, her strength failing to save them. Never could she accept him.

"I will never marry you!" She snatched her hair from

his grasp and tried to push past him, needing to escape his foul odor and chilling gaze.

Dougal caught her arm and smiled, smug and confident. Elena glared at him.

"You will, witch."

He pulled her to him and roughly pressed his lips to hers. Elena struggled, gagging, then slapped him. His release was abrupt. She stepped back quickly, stopping when she bumped the edge of the bed.

She struggled to keep from wiping the back of her hand over her mouth. She would not give him the satisfaction of knowing how he made her skin crawl. "I would be wife to the Devil before I would ever wed you!"

He reached for her, a leering grin spreading over his face as he yanked her close once more. "No one will touch you but me," he said, running a rough hand over her hip.

"Release me." She struggled to hide the panic quickly welling within her.

"I think not. I usually prefer well-rounded women, but there is something about you . . . perhaps it is your disgust . . . that draws me." He ran a dirty finger over her bottom lip, and Elena snapped at him, her teeth jarring together painfully as he avoided her bite. His face went hard, all expression removed save a dangerous fire that glowed from within. The fires of hell, no doubt.

"Here is your choice," he said through clenched teeth. "Marry me willingly, or marry me unwillingly. I care not which. But we will wed. You will make me the legitimate chief, and you will provide me with a legitimate son to follow after me."

Elena couldn't hide the shudder this time as he dragged her against him, one hand on her arm, the other firmly at the small of her back. She could feel his arousal. Frantically she searched about her for a weapon, an escape, a savior. But there was none.

"You see," Dougal continued, "we will have to be wed after we are found here together."

Elena's mind spun, grappling with the implications of Dougal's words—and actions. Even if he did not bed her, the appearance of the act would suffice to seal her fate, and the clan's. Before she could decide what to do, he pushed her backward onto her bed. Instinct took over as soon as she hit the mattress, and she rolled quickly out of his way.

She scrambled to her feet and lurched toward the door. Dougal dove. He caught her skirt, toppling her to the floor. Her hands and knees hit hard, startling a yelp from her. Then Dougal was on her, pushing her to the floor and turning her to her back in one vicious move that had her head crashing against the boards.

Elena struggled, shoving at him, thrashing, screaming. Somehow she twisted a hand free of his grasp but couldn't swing a fist. She went for his face, scratching, desperate to do some damage to him. Dougal backhanded her, and stars showered behind her eyes. She shook her head frantically as he pulled at her gown.

Blindly she reached around her, determined to find a weapon, any weapon. Her hand scraped the cold iron of the candle stand. She grabbed it, her fear lending her a strength she didn't know she was capable of. The candle stand toppled, pouring hot tallow over Dougal's bare backside, then pinning him to her with its weight. His bellow ripped through the chamber, and suddenly he was off of her, sending the iron stand crashing against the wall. He charged across the room and sluiced her wash water down his back.

Elena lay on the floor, dazed. A cold draft on her bared legs roused her. She had stopped him. For a moment. She shook her head once more to clear it, wincing at the pain. Her eyes focused, and her mind grasped the danger she was in. The consequences of her actions stole her breath but fueled her feet.

Before the water finished puddling in the rushes around Dougal, she fled. Whatever else happened, she would *never* wed a man so evil, so corrupt, so mad.

M adness clawed at Symon MacLachlan's soul. He battled it back with every breath his burning lungs could steal. The skirl of a wounded animal burst from his parched lips. His horse broke into a gallop. Pain pounded through Symon's skull in time with the beat of the animal's hooves. His stomach lurched and dipped, threatening to empty itself. Purging, purifying wind battered his disloyal body and desperate mind.

Symon slowed the horse as he tried to grasp where he was. He glanced about at the moonlit forest searching for some clue as to why he was here. All of a sudden the trees around him bowed, as if in deference to his passing. His stomach roiled. He closed his eyes and willed the grove to right itself, willed the madness away. He swayed in the saddle and a low, feral, growl escaped him.

He would not let this blasted madness win!

Symon concentrated on the things he could feel—the warm, sweat-covered hide of the tired beast beneath him, the familiar texture of his plaid, bunched at his shoulder and about his waist, the chill wash of an early spring breeze against his fevered skin. He gathered his senses and slowly opened his eyes.

Blessedly, the trees were upright, their leaves rustling above where they belonged, silhouetted against the moon-bright sky.

It was a bloody awful way to live, never knowing when the madness would crash over him.

The horse stopped suddenly, nearly unseating him. It moved neither forward nor back, but rather danced nervously in place, shifting from one foot to another as if unsure which way to go. Symon nudged it forward, but it halted once more after only a few unwilling steps. Standing directly in their path was the dark outline of an ancient stone circle. His mount shied, snorting and shaking its head, as if denying the sight.

Symon calmed the animal, sharing its dislike for the silent, pensive circle, hunkered here at the edge of the glen. He wished to deny the sight as well. But that was impossible. He knew this cursed place. He knew the madness had led him back here.

The stones stood silently in their primeval ring as if standing in judgment of him. All the ills that had befallen his clan these past six months, even his own hated reputation, had started here, in this circle, on that fateful day of his father's death. Symon clenched his shaking hands. The past could not be changed.

But it could be faced.

It was madness to enter the circle again, but madness was his near-constant companion. What more harm could come from this place than the death of his father and the torment his life had become these past months? Symon would not let his weakness get in his way. Something had brought him here, and he was determined to face his fate. Perhaps then he would find a way free of his curse. If he did not, he would lose all that he had ever worked for in life: his position, his honor. It had already stolen his self-respect.

Symon slid from the horse. As he tied it to a tree, a hound bayed in the distance and was quickly answered by another, adding to the horse's already nervous shifting. It pulled at its lead, eyes wide, breath coming hard and fast.

"Shh," Symon said, grateful that his voice obeyed him. He scratched the horse's cheek for a moment, quieting the animal and himself.

Finally Symon took a deep breath and moved toward the accursed rocks, drawn by the circle as a lodestone draws iron. The hounds bayed again, the sound echoing off the stones, warning him away. The hair at the base of his neck prickled in response.

"'Tis only a ring of mighty rocks." The sound of his own voice, though gravelly as always after the madness, calmed him.

Determined to meet his fate, he strode between two of the tall rocky sentries and into the circle.

A bare pace within, he stopped.

Gone was the clear air of spring, nor was the remembered blood-stink of battle present in the circle. It was like walking into warm, thick water. Sounds were muffled and the smells of a moment ago, damp, boggy earth and sharp, dusty rock, were muted here, more like the memory of a smell than the actual smell itself.

Mist began to rise about his feet, swirling up from the ground, reaching out and embracing the huge moss- and lichen-clad stones. Damp wisps of reflected moonlight filled the gaps between them with a transparent wall of white moonglow.

Hounds bayed once again, closer, accompanied now by a long wailing cry. The stallion stamped the ground.

Symon remembered to breathe.

It was only a trick of the wind, that wailing. It was only the remnants of madness that made that wail sound human.

Symon rolled his shoulders, noting the weight of his claymore high against his back, and the lesser weight of his dudgeon dagger tucked at his belt. At least his affliction did not extend to leaving himself weaponless.

A branch cracked. Symon whirled in the direction of the noise. Something hurtled from the mist and threw itself at him, hitting hard enough to force the breath from him. He staggered and his arms encircled the all-too-solid form of a woman.

Long-fingered hands gripped his tunic. Leaf-tangled hair caught in the stubble on his chin even as a peacefulness he no longer believed possible washed over him. Calm, like a healing salve on weather-raw skin, pushed the lingering confusion and pain from him. He felt clear-headed, balanced, and strong as he hadn't since the madness had first come over him in this very place.

Hounds bayed just beyond the mist, and the stallion snorted its misgivings. The unearthly wailing sounded again, this time from just under his chin. The woman pushed away from him, stumbling when he released her.

Peace deserted him.

He reached for her again, grabbing a bony wrist. Peace stole up his arm and briefly fluttered in his chest. She tried to stumble backward, her eyes fixed over his shoulder.

"Help me, I beg of you!" Desperation at odds with the peace he felt colored her low voice.

His decision was made in an instant. He drew his dagger and spun in one smooth, practiced motion to face the direction she had come from.

Huge, gray wolfhounds strained at the edge of the mist-shrouded circle, slavering like the hounds of hell, but they did not enter. Symon heard scrabbling as the woman moved to the far side of the circle. There she could easily slip into the mist and away from the hounds while Symon held their attention.

The easiest thing would be to let the hounds continue their hunt, but Symon had never been one to take the easy road.

So he would dispatch the dogs, and the keeper he was sure followed them. He would dispatch them by word or by blade, it mattered not, and retrieve the woman himself. Then he would regain that momentary peace. A peace he was suddenly determined to have.

He sheathed his dagger and drew forth his claymore, feeling calmer with the massive sword in his hands. Any reprieve from his own private hell was worth a fight. Even a fight in this circle. Especially a fight in this circle.

He planted his feet, balancing his stance, his claymore at the ready. A muttered curse came out of the mist, quieting the dogs, and sending them skirting the edge of the circle. A shaggy-haired man stepped between the stones, his dagger glinting in the moonlight, his heavily bearded face cast in shadows.

"Where is she?" the stranger demanded.

The voice was almost familiar, teasing his memory as if he should know it.

Symon said nothing as he moved slowly toward the man.

" 'Twas a lass ran this way. I will have her back."

Still Symon did not answer. Something about the rumble, the thick burr, not entirely of these parts, picked at him, but he couldn't call the memory forward.

"I saw her come this way." The other man's voice grew threatening. "The hounds tracked her. I'll have her back!"

Symon took in the man's stance, the way he shifted slightly foot to foot, his dagger hand swaying back and forth as if he was unsure which way Symon would come at him.

"Just point the way she went," the man said, "and I'll leave you be."

Symon took another step toward him. The stranger stepped back deeper into the shadows.

"I'm after the lass."

"You are on MacLachlan land. If you do not leave now, you will die on MacLachlan land."

"Where I die is between the devil and myself, you bloody bastard."

"As you wish," Symon said.

E lena filled her lungs, trying to take advantage of the moment to catch her breath. She peered around a great stone, watching Dougal challenge the huge, dark-haired warrior. She knew Dougal's injuries from the hot tallow and the heavy candle stand had been the only reason she had escaped the castle, and the only reason she had stayed ahead of him and his hounds until now. He must be desperate indeed, to follow her onto MacLachlan lands alone. But then, Dougal was not one to give up, and he would be even more determined—and dangerous—now that she had injured his pride, and his backside.

Her own skin felt flayed from the hours she had spent racing through the thick wood. She was cold, dirty, and scared. Dougal was as handy with a weapon as he was with those dogs, while the warrior who was defending her was not well. In that half-a-moment they had touched, her gift had asserted itself, sensing pain and soothing it.

And yet she had felt calmed, too, almost as if he held some power himself. Or perhaps it was his unquestioning defense of her that calmed her. But why would he do that when he was so clearly unwell? Did he know what she did? His eyes had held wonder in their black depths. She shivered at the intensity of the image. An angry Dougal was nothing compared to the barely contained need she had witnessed in that moment.

The two warriors exchanged threats, and Elena knew this was her chance. She could escape while they distracted each other. She stepped backward, her eyes fixed on the men, but a hound's low growl jolted her to stillness.

Dougal, his face cast downward just enough to keep the moonlight from illuminating the familiar rage she knew was there, edged around to the MacLachlan warrior's right, but the warrior engaged him, swinging his mighty claymore close enough to knock him off balance. Before he could parry, the MacLachlan was upon him, wrenching Dougal's knife arm up behind him, then resting the sharp edge of his own blade against Dougal's beard-covered throat.

It was over so fast, Elena did not even have time to react.

"Drop your dagger."

Dougal dropped it with a muttered oath.

"You see, lad, you were right," the warrior said.

"How's that?"

"You said this was between you and the Devil." The warrior paused, as if waiting for Dougal to understand his words. "I am the Devil of Kilmartin. Have you not heard of me?" The simple question belied the sharp concentration on the Devil's face, and the promise of violence in his posture.

Elena began to tremble. The hounds growled again, only an arm's length away. The Devil of Kilmartin.

She had run from one madman to another.

She watched as Dougal started to nod, just a bare movement else he would have slashed his own neck. He stopped, chin raised.

"Aye," he said instead, his voice unusually low.

"Do you wish to continue this, then?" the Devil asked.

"Nay."

" 'Tis as I thought. Give me your word you will leave the lass be and take yourself away from MacLachlan lands."

"You have it."

Shock coursed through Elena. She had never seen Dougal back down from anyone, or anything.

"Good." The Devil stepped back, but kept his claymore ready. A Highlander's word should be good enough, but apparently he didn't entirely trust Dougal. He was wiser than she would have guessed.

"Get you gone, and your hounds with you."

Dougal whistled, three sharp rising notes. The hounds whimpered but reluctantly abandoned their quarry. "You may have her now, Devil," Dougal said, his strangely altered voice carrying over the mist, "but you'll not keep her long." He raised his voice more. "You won't find anything easier with the Devil, Elena. You belong to me!"

Her skin prickled. The image of what she had fled scrambled through her mind. The knowledge of who had defended her terrified her. She'd be no safer with the Devil of Kilmartin than she would be with Dougal of Dunmore. She would never be safe.

A sob escaped her and she once more forced her tired legs to a run.

chapter 2

Symon sheathed his claymore. *The heady rush of battle* *fever* waned rapidly. He listened for the woman, Elena. A hazy pain filled his head again, but it did not increase to the earlier pounding. It had eased in that momentary contact with her. He looked around, ready to track her himself if necessary.

Anything would be worth even one more moment of that peace.

A scrabbling sound told him she was getting away. Symon cut across the circle in four long running strides, then passed through the barrier of the ancient stones. Instantly sounds brightened, shadows darkened, and the forest closed around him. He stopped, gaining his bearings, listening for the telltale crashing of someone running through the black wood.

There. He turned in the direction of the noise and tore through the bracken. In moments he had caught up to her. Another and he had her round the waist, picking her up off her feet, dodging her flying elbows, kicking feet, and scratching nails.

"Be still!" He struggled to contain the flailing woman. "Bloody hell, cease this now!" She did not so much as flinch at his bellow, though his own head threatened to leave his shoulders.

At last he pinned her to him, her stiff back to his chest, his arms wrapped about her middle, securing her own arms at her sides. Her chest heaved, and he thought he heard a muffled sob.

"I'll not hurt you, lass."

She said nothing. She was tall but over-thin. Her hair was a mass of tangles decorated with bits of pine straw and dead leaves, its color uncertain in the wash of moonlight. Her gown was ripped and mud-spattered. He sensed a fragility to her despite the pitched struggle they'd just been through. Why was she running? Why did that man want her back so badly as to track her with hounds?

And where was the peace he had felt before when they touched? He took stock, waiting for calm to wash over him. The lass remained rigid in his arms.

"What do you want of me?" she said at last, her voice rising and cracking as if she fought to control it.

Symon spun her in his arms so she faced him. She gasped and managed to wedge her hands between them. Warmth radiated from her palms. He waited for that fleeting clarity of mind to follow the heat, needing to prove to himself he had not imagined it.

But clarity did not follow. She balled her fists and shoved against him.

"Release me."

"Nay."

" 'Tis true? You are the Devil of Kilmartin?" She stood, her head held proudly, concentration etched on her face. For a moment he fancied her a priestess of the ancient builders of the stone circles.

"I am Symon, chief of Clan Lachlan." He pressed his fingers to his temple, physically forcing the returning stabs of pain back. "He called you Elena, but of what clan are you?"

She did not answer.

The surge of power he had experienced in the scuffle with the lass's hunter was gone and all the effects of his madness stormed back through him like a battle-crazed army bent on destruction. Symon's head was splitting asunder. His mouth was dry and his throat begged for water.

If he wanted to learn the truth of who this lass was, and what had caused that strange, wonderful moment, he would have to act quickly, before he once more lost his grasp on reason. He must secure the lass until he could question her. Most likely, she was a witch, but he did not care. Anything that would dampen his madness, give him even a few extra moments of clarity, would strengthen his position with the clan. It did not matter the source. Sweat broke out on his brow and between his shoulder blades. His stomach heaved and the trees threatened to bend and bow to him once more.

"Come." Symon dragged the girl by one thin wrist.

"Why should I go with you?"

Fear radiated from her, and he could feel her glare aimed at his back. Still he pulled her along. She could glare all she wished as long as she obeyed his command.

As they passed into the circle once more, she dug in her heals, forcing him to stop or risk snapping her wrist. "Where do you take me, *Devil?*"

He had to admire her courage, though her eyes showed the fear of a cornered animal. But he did not have time for pretty words to bend her to his wishes. The madness could crash around him again at any moment, and he must get her to safety before that happened. He could not guarantee she would live to see the next morn if he did not. And he desperately wished her to do so.

Symon released her arm and quickly scooped her over his shoulder.

T*he lass had fought him all the way to the horse but be-*came sullenly compliant when he told her she could flop like a sack of oats across his lap, or she could behave and ride behind him in relative comfort. She had chosen the latter, but just in case she changed her mind about co-operating, Symon kept a firm hand on her arm where it wrapped stiffly about his waist.

Every so often he would feel her relax, then jerk awake again. At last her arms fell slack about his waist as she finally succumbed to sleep. Her gentle weight settled against his back, her body heat mingling with his own. After a few moments he realized his head had begun to subtly ease and his unruly stomach had calmed.

Surprise roused him. He had not imagined the influence of her touch upon him. Though apparently she was strong enough to control this strange effect her body had upon his, at least some of the time. Anger mingled with grudging admiration. Few would deny him anything, yet she had denied him relief from his affliction, even when he had defended her.

And what was the source of her effect? Rumor held that the Lamont healer used aught but her touch to heal even the mightiest of wounds. Could this bedraggled lass be that healer? Nay. Since before he was born stories had filtered through the glen of the wondrous skills of the Lamont healer. And while he couldn't discern her true age, she was not as old as his score and five he was sure.

She could be daughter to the healer, or apprentice. But it made no sense that her clan would hunt her like a criminal if she possessed this skill.

He almost woke her, demanding she prove her abilities and work whatever magic she possessed to halt the next round of debilitating madness. But she had only eased the effects before, and then only briefly, while they touched. Could she do aught against the full force of his madness?

He took a deep breath, calming his seething emotions, trying to think through the possibilities the lass presented. If his suspicion was true, she owed him the use of her skills. He had saved her from her hunter; it was only right she would repay him in the way that would serve him best.

Of course, once before a healer had tried to help him, but she had quickly declared him beyond hope and hied off with a passing tinker. If this woman was the Lamont healer, would she do the same? Would she put an end to any hope for reprieve? Nay, if she did prove to be the fabled healer, she would heal him. He would make sure of it.

Symon rode on, lost in his thoughts, the lass sleeping

against his back. The full moon was sinking quickly behind the bens. The pale light would be gone soon, and they would have to stop until daylight.

All at once his companion jerked awake, nearly tumbling from the horse's back. Symon whipped his arm behind him, steadying her with his hand on her back, pressing her to him.

Symon stiffened, prepared for abuse from her lips at the forced contact. Instead she gripped him tightly about the waist and buried her face against his back, bringing the full force of peace and clarity with her.

"I will not. I cannot," she pleaded. "I cannot."

Awkwardly Symon took his hand from her back and rested it on her arm that was firmly clasped about him. His large, rough hand covered her smooth one. Quietly he reveled in the effect she had on him. "Shh, lass. 'Tis only a dream."

"A dream?" She snuggled against his back, sharing her warmth with him as if he were her lover there to comfort her. A tendril of her hair lifted on the breeze and tickled his cheek. Her scent, a curious spicy fragrance like rare cinnamon mixed with smoke, filled his senses. He felt comforted himself.

He waited for her withdrawal, but it did not come. He stroked her long fingers with his own, allowing himself a boon he had not known for too long—the simple comfort of another human's touch.

He did not want to stop the incredible flow of balm coming from her, but he also knew they must find a place to stop soon, before the moon set and they were left in complete darkness. They rode over a knoll, Elena still snuggled against his back. Symon knew a silly, satisfied smile adorned his face, but he didn't care. The lass had given him in sleep what she refused when awake. As they rounded a bend in the path they followed, the trees opened up onto a clearing.

Symon stopped the horse and swore.

He recognized the small thatched cottage that sat in the middle of the clearing just as the moon disappeared behind the bens.

E lena woke slowly, pleasantly aware of the firm back she rested against and the heat radiating from it. She burrowed closer, holding tight where her arms wrapped about his waist, enjoying the quiet sounds of the horse moving through the forest. She was just drifting back into a peaceful sleep when the horse abruptly stopped. She blinked, trying to clear the sleep from her eyes, but the moon was nearly gone, and all was dark about her.

"Damn!"

She felt as much as heard the deep rumble of his voice, and she had the curious feeling she should react, but she didn't want to.

"'Tis not what I would have chosen, but we have little choice."

"What?" she asked, trying to think who this was talking to her. Knowledge snapped into place and she quickly sat up. She had her arms around the Devil. She'd nestled against his back, shared his body heat, been lulled to sleep by the sound of his heartbeat.

Cold air replaced the comforting warmth of a moment ago, and she felt a curious loss. Those moments of sleepy contentment were so unusual, so out of her experience, that she desperately wished them back, despite the source of them, yet she could not give in to the need. She had let her guard down. She dared not do so again.

Symon swung down off the horse and strode across the small yard. Just as he reached the door, it swung open, but Elena could not see who stood in the door speaking to the Devil in a low gravely voice. After a moment he returned to her.

"There's a bed for you inside and a pot of porridge if you're hungry." His voice was sharp and Elena wondered what she'd done to anger him. "Come," he said, reaching up to help her down from the horse.

Elena had no choice but to allow his touch. The horse was very tall, but not so much that the Devil couldn't reach her waist with ease. His hands radiated heat through her tattered clothing, and he lifted her quickly from the horse. He released her as soon as her feet touched the ground, as if he were uncomfortable touching her.

Well, at least on that count, Dougal was correct. She was not a woman to attract the physical attention of men. But of course she did not wish the physical attention of this man, nor any other. She quickly shushed a little voice that reminded her how nice it had been moments ago, sleeping against the Devil's firmly muscled back.

Symon grabbed her hand and led her to the open door. "Auld Morag is within. She is a wee bit daft but harmless. Do not pay too much mind to what she says." With that he released her hand and disappeared into the deepening darkness. Elena heard rather than saw him lead the horse around the side of the cottage.

She shivered, uncertain whether to enter the cottage or not, when the gravely voice beckoned her. "Come in, lassie, come in and shut the door. 'Tis cold, 'tis, for my auld bones."

Elena realized just how cold she was and made her decision, entering the dark, smoke-filled cottage quickly.

S ymon led his horse to one corner of the byre, brushed him down with a handful of straw, and pulled a bit of oats from Auld Morag's stores.

'Twas more than he would get this night.

He pulled his plaid around him and headed back around the cottage. He had tasted salvation at the lass's touch. He would not chance her leaving him before he could test his theory. He couldn't help but remember the feel of her pressed against his back, her arms twined around his waist, the pleasant comfort of that simple act of trust.

He pushed that aside. He could not let soft thoughts, nor soft feelings, fog his purpose. She could serve him well, and thereby save his clan. And he would see it so even though it meant sleeping on the cold ground at Auld Morag's door. He dared not find a more comfortable bed lest she slip away while he slept. The doorway would suffice. And in the morn he would have his answer.

Symon sat, his back to the door. The scent of peat smoke and Auld Morag's burning herbs drifted to him, and he could hear the quiet murmur of women's voices from within. "Let her sleep," he muttered to himself. "I will need her rested on the morrow if she is to prove her abilities."

He loosened his belt, arranged his plaid to cover him, then laid his claymore by his side. He leaned his head against the hard door and was instantly asleep.

• • •

E lena coughed. *Her throat tickled from the strange bit-ter* smell that hung in the air mingling with the peat smoke as it rose to the low rafters.

Quietly she ate the porridge the old woman had offered her. She was tired, but a strange itchy feeling just under her skin told her she would not sleep soon.

The face of the warrior formed in her imagination. She pushed it away, but it persisted, floating before her, black hair wild about his angular face, his dark eyes filled with questions, his brow furrowed in pain, a pain she could ease if she wished to.

But she did not wish to. He was the Devil of Kilmartin, enemy to her clan, madman . . . and her rescuer.

She pushed the vision from her mind again. She would find some way to repay his kindness in the stone circle. But to reveal herself as the Lamont healer by easing his pains would be folly.

"Nay, lass. 'Twould not be folly." The old woman's creaky voice whispered near her shoulder.

Elena gasped, nearly dropping her bowl. The woman's lined face emerged from the darkness beside her. Quickly she scooted her stool to the side, putting not nearly enough room between them.

"Do not fash yourself, child. Auld Morag will not hurt you."

"How did you know my thoughts?"

"Ah, now, that is something I cannot tell. 'Tis simply one of my gifts, to know the thoughts of those I must advise." The old woman pulled the only other stool close and looked deep into Elena's eyes. "You understand the nature of such gifts."

Elena gasped, then ended up in a coughing fit from the acrid smoke that permeated the room.

"Breathe deeply, child. 'Twill clear your mind, open your heart. You are too fearful."

"'Tis wise to fear that which may harm you," Elena said quietly.

The old woman made a hissing sound, and Elena could not tell if it was laughter or derision.

If the old woman, Auld Morag she had called herself, knew all, then she could answer the question that plagued Elena the most.

"What is he going to do with me?"

"Symon? Ah, 'tis simple, lass. He wishes you to help him, make him whole and strong again. He will insist you use your gift to take the devil from his shoulders, heal his madness. Only he is too thick-headed to understand 'tis not healing he needs."

Fear leapt in Elena's belly, burning up through her until her breath threatened to cease altogether.

"Ease your mind, lass. He knows not what you are, though he has the thought in his mind. That one is stubborn, needing to see things with his own eyes before he believes."

"Why?" Her voice was quiet, unsteady, yet she needed an answer.

"Why is he stubborn? Och, that's a riddle I've yet to answer." The old woman moved to the fire, stirred it once, then threw another brick of peat on it.

Elena was sure the woman baited her. "Nay." Her voice was stronger now, and she struggled to keep the irritation she felt out of it. "Why did he defend me? Why would he help me, then bring me here against my will? Does he know who I am? Do you?"

Auld Morag drew closer, examining her face. She nodded, as if to herself, then settled on her stool again.

"I know you are Elena, daughter of Fergus, chief of Lamont."

Elena waited, trying to play out the old woman's game. When the silence stretched too tautly, she could hold her questions no longer.

"Why, since you know the thoughts of others, did he defend me?"

"I do not know what he would say, lass," she said, her eyes on the wisps of green-tinged smoke tangling about her, as if searching there for the answer. "Perhaps he does not hold with hunting women? Do not expect fine words from Symon explaining himself. He is a warrior, chief of his clan, aye, and some say madman. He does what he must, seldom what he wishes."

So they had that in common, then.

"Where are you bound, Elena, daughter of Lamont?"

Indecision clouded her eyes. Should she trust this woman? It was clear she had not done well on her own thus far. Perhaps the old woman could give her counsel, guide her on her way. Elena chewed on her bottom lip, deciding. Auld Morag seemed in no rush for an answer. Indeed she waited for Elena to make up her mind, as if she had nothing else in the world to occupy her.

"I don't know," she said. Her voice held only the smallest quaver.

"'Tis a long journey before you, then."

What she wanted was a safe place to live, at least until she could figure out what to do next. But what she wanted, more than anything, was someone she could trust, someone who would care for the woman, not the healer.

She could not chance falling back into Dougal's hands, for he had made it abundantly clear what her fate with him would be. So the question was, could she trust the Devil of Kilmartin? At the moment he seemed the lesser evil for she had sensed nothing in him except a desire to rid himself of the strange madness he carried. And since she could not cure madness, 'twould be a simple matter to keep her gift concealed. If he did not know she was the Lamont healer, if he continued to think her but a wayward lass, then she might be safe. For a while.

"Symon will offer you the hospitality of his clan," Auld Morag said quietly. "He'll take you to his home at Kilmartin. Bide awhile there. Decide with care what you must do, where you must go, and who you must trust."

Elena nodded slowly. "I have little choice."

"Choices come where you least expect them," Auld Morag said, "as does joy and sorrow. You have great strength, lass, but you do not see it yet. You have a great heart, if you but allow it to flourish."

The woman spoke in riddles and secrets, and Elena's mind was too tired to unravel the words. She thanked Auld Morag for the porridge and lay down upon her pallet by the fire. She had much to think on before the sun rose. She had much to consider before she faced the Devil of Kilmartin once more.

chapter 3

*S*ymon woke slowly to the sound of a steady rain dripping off thatch, the earthy smell of peat smoke, and the hard, cold stone beneath him.

His head throbbed, and every muscle complained of hard use. He opened his eyes slowly and looked about him. Memory rushed in, crowding his aching head with images of a bedraggled lass. A lass who was either daft or foolishly brave. Another memory presented itself, one of ease and balance and a clearing of the cloud afflicting his mind, relief for his suffering body. Aye, he remembered the lass who had stilled the ravages of the madness for a time.

Symon rose, cursing his unsteady legs. The need to touch her again, to feel the clarity and brightness she had caused, had him groping for the door latch. Cloud-softened light stabbed his eyes, increasing the hammer blows inside his skull. He paused, long enough to let his eyes adjust and his legs prove their ability to hold him upright.

At last he raised the latch just as the lass opened the door, brushing dirt from the skirt of her grimy gown. She looked up, saw him, and stopped.

"Good day to you," Symon said.

Elena nodded. Symon took the chance to really look at her here in the light of day. Her hair was flame colored. Not the color of a roaring fire, but the color of glowing embers, shifting and changing in the morning light from deep auburn to glossy brown to burnished gold.

The urge to drag her to him shook him in its intensity, nearly overwhelming his hold on reason. He fought it, disgusted with his own weakness. He was chief of Clan Lachlan, a warrior, born and trained to lead his people. He should be the one providing for others. He should not be some weak-kneed fool looking to this lass for help.

Yet he had little choice.

Purple-green marks marred her pale skin, telling of someone's hard use. Anger surged in him, tempered with an unusual softness. No one should treat a woman so.

"Did you sleep well?" he asked, needing to break the tension building in the silence. She nodded. Symon looked past the bruises. He was not so ill he did not appreciate her long limbs and narrow build. He could even appreciate the stubborn set of her chin, and the flash of determination that came and went in her eyes. He held his hand out for her to take, but she did not touch him.

She started to back into the dark confines of the cottage, then changed her direction and edged along the rough wall a few steps. Symon moved with her, until she bumped into a stump left there.

"Take my hand," he said, trying to keep the eagerness out of his voice. He needed her to touch him. He needed her to prove his suspicions; to feed his hopes.

The lass looked at him. "I don't wish to take your hand," she said, watching him, wariness etched round her eyes.

The pounding in Symon's head increased as he fought to keep his voice level and his manner mild. He fought to keep from grabbing her, testing her effect upon him, questioning her true purpose here. He stared into her eyes, commanding her with every thought to take his hand, prove him right. Save his life.

At last she put her hand in his, lightly, barely touching, as if she were afraid to press her skin to his.

Nothing—save the continued hammers inside his skull. No peace, no calm, no ease washing over him, not even the warmth he remembered, for her hands were icy. He had wanted so much more. A tiny hope-harboring part of him he'd thought long dead was disappointed. Abruptly he turned toward the byre, pulling her along behind him.

"Release me, Devil!"

Symon winced at the familiar epithet that sounded more harsh from her lips than from all the others who had named him so. She hauled back on his hand, nearly upsetting his tenuous balance.

"Where are you taking me? I'll not be dragged along like some animal." She tried to pull her hand free of his grip. "I don't belong to you."

Symon stared at her, then released her abruptly.

"Lass." Auld Morag stood in the doorway, a funny sort of look on her face. "Get your washing up done. I've a fine fat rabbit to help break your fast." She glanced at Symon and cackled, raising the hairs at the back of his neck. "Do not worry over Symon's scowling face. His head is pounding and his mouth's like sand. You know aught of headache cures, do you not?"

Elena's eyes were wide, and Symon could see the rapid rise and fall of her breathing. She was afraid. Auld Morag was a bit off-putting, but surely she had not frightened the lass so much last night.

"I have willow," Auld Morag continued as if Elena had answered her. "Make him a tea to ease his pain. 'Twill benefit us both if we cease the drumming in his head."

The lass said nothing, but shook free of his grasp and made to pass by him.

Symon spun about to follow her and immediately regretted the quick movement. He grabbed her arm to steady himself and closed his eyes for a moment. He could have sworn he felt her reach out and soothe his brow with cool fingers against his sweat-sheened skin, easing his head. But when he opened his eyes the sensation vanished. She had not moved.

Elena stepped back, away from Symon. She looked almost as puzzled as he felt. She wrapped her arms about her middle, whether in defense or because she was cold, Symon couldn't say, but hope sparked inside him once again.

"I know something of simples," she said, looking directly at Symon. "A tea of willow bark will ease your head. It will stop the light from hurting your eyes—"

"How did you know my eyes pained me?" he asked, sure he would catch her now.

But Elena said nothing, though her skin paled, causing

the sprinkling of freckles and her bruises to stand out in stark contrast.

He stared into her eyes, willing her to speak the truth. When she didn't speak at all, he pushed the issue. "You will heal me."

The lass stared at him a moment, her breathing growing more ragged. "I'll prepare you the willow," she finally said, "anyone can do such. But if you speak of the madness you are famous for, I cannot help you."

"But you can. I felt it. You are the Lamont healer, and I know what you did."

"Nay." She shook her head vehemently. "Nay, I did nothing. I am nothing." She edged away from him.

Symon grabbed her arm, pulling her close. "I know what I felt." He took her hand and placed it flat against his chest. "I know what you did."

Fear flashed in her eyes, yet she stood there, rigid, concentration etched across her face.

"See," she said, her voice low and strained, "nothing." She pulled her hand free and walked deliberately toward the wood.

Symon watched her go.

Nothing. Frustration raked across his skin, but he remembered the night before. While she remained awake, he had suffered, but when she finally succumbed to sleep, that curious calm had descended over him, soothing his mind and his body. Somehow he would have that peace again.

He would have to learn a bit more about her in order to discover a way to make her trust him. He could start by listening to the women's chatter he was sure would accompany the preparation of the meal and tea. His head would pound, but he just might learn what he needed. Symon waited until she returned then followed her into the cottage.

He'd never met two more silent women. *His bowl was nearly empty.* His head was much improved from the willow tea. And these two women had said less than a score of words between them in all the time their preparations and meal had taken.

"Who are your people?" he blurted out, needing at least that much confirmation of his suspicions.

Elena started. "Why do you wish to know?" She put her bowl down and clasped her hands in her lap.

"You are called Elena, aye?"

She looked from him to Auld Morag and back. At last she nodded.

"And your clan?" he persisted.

"'Tis not important. I am of no clan now."

"Be that as it may, I still desire to know who your people are." He took a large bite of rabbit and chewed it slowly, giving her time to answer. But she did not. Exasperated he dropped his bowl next to hers. "I think it fair to ask whom I've angered by defending you. Do I not deserve an answer?"

"Your reputation will serve to keep you safe from any anger, I'm sure." She rose, her meal unfinished. "I need some air," she said as she slipped out the door.

Symon started after her.

"Sit, Symon." The strength in Auld Morag's voice surprised him enough to stop him. "Sit! She will not run away. She has nowhere to go."

"Who is she, then?" he asked as he picked up his bowl and refilled it.

"I did not know you were blind as well as mad." The old woman watched him like a cat about to spring on a mouse. "Can you not see?"

"I see a lass in trouble. I see a lass who may be the answer to my prayers."

"But you do not see the obvious."

"Then tell me, what am I missing?"

"The prophecy."

Symon sat on his stool with a thud. The prophecy.

"Aye, now your eyes are opening, lad. Do you not remember?"

He cast back, trying to bring forth the exact words. It had been nearly ten years since Auld Morag had scared the wits out of him, going into a trance and spouting nonsense. At least he had always thought it nonsense.

" 'When flame and madness mingle . . .' " he said, the words coming to him slowly, " 'when cast-out thorns grow strong, then old wrongs will be righted, and MacLachlans prosper long.' "

"Aye, 'tis it, lad. Do you now see?"

"Elena is the flame," he said quietly, working it through. "Her hair is testament to that, and I, no doubt, am the madness." He glanced up to see a smile growing on Auld Morag's wrinkled face. "But the rest makes no more sense than it ever has." He shoved his fingers into his hair and tried to physically force back the pressure building in his skull.

Auld Morag shook her head. "You are still blind, but understanding will come."

"Why can you not tell me what it means?"

"'Tis not mine to reveal, lad. The prophecy was meant for you. 'Tis your destiny you must discover."

Symon stood. "Fine, then I will go and discover it." He strode to the door, then stopped and turned, unwilling to anger the seer. "I thank you for your hospitality."

The sound of cackling laughter followed him out of the cottage.

A short time later Elena was seated behind Symon on his huge black horse. He had offered her the hospitality of his castle and clan. She had had no choice but to accept it. Now it took every shred of concentration she possessed to hold herself away from him, though the movement of the horse made that difficult indeed. Part of her wished to touch him again, to curl against him where she could hear the beat of his heart and feel the heat of his hands upon her.

It had been worth enduring the pain in his head for those moments of contentment, for that feeling of being protected, cared for, for the heat of that contact.

But she would not indulge herself again.

Thrice she had seen the effect on his face, felt the healing in his body. Thrice his touch had sliced easily through her control, threatening to reveal her secret. He already suspected too much.

She should not be going with this man. But the memory of one day spent crashing through the rough wood of Scotland, chased by hounds, afraid for her life, was enough for now. Elena had never before been out of sight of Lamont Castle. The world was a much bigger, more frightening place than she had imagined. And she was finding herself ill-prepared for it.

Despite Auld Morag's cryptic words, she had little choice but to go with the Devil.

Symon stopped the horse abruptly, jostling her out of her thoughts and pushing her forward into his back. Quickly she pulled away. Why was it like fire on her skin whenever they touched?

"What—"

"Shh. Listen."

Elena listened carefully, but all she could hear was the cold breeze whistling through the trees and the sound of a burn near by. "I don't—"

"There."

The sound of a baby crying carried on the wind, and with it came the distinct smell of wood smoke.

Symon turned the horse in the direction of the crying.

"Where are we going?" she asked.

"'Tis too much smoke for a simple hearth fire. Something is amiss. Hold on!"

Elena had no choice but to wrap her arms tightly about him as he kicked the horse to a gallop. Branches whipped at them. Dirt and rocks flew behind them. She knew she should be frightened, but she wasn't.

They erupted out of the forest and into a clearing. Symon pulled up on the horse quickly, stopping him neatly at the edge of the dooryard. Elena peered over his shoulder. In the middle of the clearing stood the still-smoking remains of a cottage.

Heather thatch and wattle walls burned quickly and hot. Nothing was left save charred posts, ashes, and broken pottery. One blackened cauldron lay settled on its side in what was once the cook fire, its contents surely as burnt as the rest of the cottage.

"Who did this?" Her voice was hushed.

"I do not know. It could be Lamonts," Symon answered. "Or it could be the work of the *Sassunach,* the English. They think nothing of burning out a Scot."

Symon walked the horse around the ruin, never taking his eyes from it. Elena watched his profile as grief, guilt, anger all washed across his features in quick succession. Never had she seen Dougal, nor even her father, react to anyone's misfortune so.

"I should have been here," he said after a moment. "I should have stopped this." It was what she expected from a warrior, a chief, but the emotions that went with the responsibility were different in this man.

A quiet mewling sound caught her attention. She gave Symon a nudge, only now realizing she still gripped him about his waist. He slid off the horse and quickly helped her down. His hands lingered at her waist, threatening her control, though his touch was gentle and her gift unmoved. Elena closed her eyes and imagined a stone wall surrounding her, separating her from the warrior.

He stepped back, releasing her, and she opened her eyes, already missing his touch. The questions were back in his gaze, but the muffled squall of the infant kept him from speaking them.

Symon ran toward the sound with Elena close behind. She braced herself, just in case.

Beyond the far edge of the clearing, behind a huge boulder, the bairn fussed again along with the hushed sounds of a woman trying to calm it. Elena stopped.

"Molly?" Symon called, his voice loud enough to carry,

but gentle enough not to terrify the hidden pair. "Molly! 'Tis Symon. You know me, lass. Come out now," he coaxed. "They are gone."

The baby quieted further and after a long moment, a woman's face appeared. A gash on her forehead oozed bright red against her smoke-smudged skin.

"Get away, Devil." The woman's voice was gravelly, and tight with anger. "'Tis all your fault." She stumbled around the boulder now, a plaid-wrapped bairn in the crook of her arm. "You brought this curse upon the clan, and now you've brought it down upon me Callum. 'Tis the Devil's fault the Lamonts bedevil us." Her eyes lit on Elena, and recognition flashed there. The woman pointed directly at her. "They were searching for you!"

Elena gasped. Before Molly could say more, she swayed, her eyes rolling up in her head. Symon scooped the child from her arms and caught her about the waist just as she swooned. He laid her awkwardly on the ground, but Elena kept her distance. Symon watched her. She must not give in to the pull of her gift.

"So, 'twas Lamonts hunting you," Symon said.

She swallowed. "Is the bairn hurt?" she asked, desperate to turn his attention away from her.

"Nay, 'tis only worried that its ma is not coddling it." Symon gently bounced the tiny baby in his huge arm. It quieted, overcome with hiccups now. "Here, lass, take the bairn. Molly needs tending." He shifted the baby to her care.

Symon pushed the woman's hair away from her face, then wiped the blood from her forehead, examining her wound. He slanted a look at Elena. "Do you think 'twas relief that made her swoon? The cut is not so bad."

Molly's eyes fluttered opened, and she raised a hand to her head.

"Are you all right?" Elena asked, rocking the baby in her arms. She kept her feet firmly planted and fought the urge to help as Molly struggled to lean against an alder tree. Blood trickled from the gash, and Molly pushed it away with her hand, smearing it over her forehead and cheek.

"I do not want you holding me bairn," she said with a scowl. "I do not know what you did, but 'tis as much your doing, this burning, as 'tis the Devil's." She shifted her scowl to Symon. "You must be a good match to cause such trouble."

Shaken, Elena handed the bairn to her and quickly stepped back.

"Where's Callum?" Symon asked Molly.

"I do not know." She raised a hand to her mouth as if to stop the wailing sound that followed her words.

"Keep her calm, Elena. I'll have a look about."

Elena found herself examining the woman's injury from a short distance. She had helped the Devil with the willow tea; perhaps she could do something similar for Molly. The wound was typical of a head wound—more blood than was warranted from such a small gash. A bit of moss, tied with a strip of cloth, would quickly stop the flow.

"I'll be right back," she said quietly and headed for the burn they had crossed. She returned quickly with a piece of green moss. She handed it to Molly. "Press it to your forehead," she said as she ripped a strip of cloth from the bottom of her gown.

"Hold it just so. I'll tie this cloth about your head to hold it in place for a bit." She deftly tied the cloth as Molly sat stiffly, allowing it. "Sit quietly until the bleeding stops."

The woman's eyes drifted closed, but she held the bairn close to her heart.

Symon returned and shook his head at Elena's questioning look. "If I know Callum," he said to Molly, "he's running a merry chase through the glen, drawing the Lamonts away from you and his bairn. We'll take you to the castle. He's sure to come looking for you there."

He watched the woman cuddle her bairn close.

"Did the Lamonts say 'twas this lass they sought?" he asked quietly.

She opened her eyes and glared up at Symon. "Aye. They said our Devil had stolen a lass from them. Said 'twould be like this and worse until you returned her to them. 'Tis your blight upon this clan that causes such trouble, Devil. Why do you not leave us be?"

Elena couldn't help but notice the change in Symon at the woman's harsh words. All gentleness left his face. All concern left his eyes.

"Can you ride?" Symon asked.

Molly nodded without looking at him.

"We'll take you to Kilmartin. You and your bairn will be safe there."

Molly turned her icy gaze upon him then. "Aye, we'll come because we cannot stay here, but you cannot keep us safe from your curse. You spread it amongst us again and again, and now you've brought this lass to cause more trouble."

Symon's face was hard as a mask and just as unreadable. "We must haste to Kilmartin," he said. "The Lamonts may still be somewhere near. We need to return and see to the safety of the rest of the clan."

Molly rose slowly, accepting Symon's help stiffly when he lifted her and the bairn up onto his horse. Elena climbed on behind, afraid Molly would not be able to balance on the high horse by herself. She was grateful that the woman did not want to lean back against her, for that would mean sharing her aches and pains, and a struggle to keep her gift concealed. Though it distressed her not to help Molly, she would not give Symon any further cause to wonder. Auld Morag said he needed to see in order to believe.

He could keep his suspicions.

She'd not give him his proof.

chapter 4

E lena peered over her shoulder at the wide valley
stretching out below. A stubborn morning mist clung
to the hollows along the path of the burn where it cut its
way through the glen. Symon still led the horse with Molly
and the bairn perched in the saddle. Elena, however, had
taken to her feet a short while earlier, needing to put some
distance between herself and the angry, worried Molly.
They traveled a well-worn path up a small ben that com-
manded the head of the valley. Great gnarled trees over-
hung the path, their branches decorated with tiny pale
green leaves, newly sprouted, obscuring the view up the
steep slope.

The faint smell of smoke and the distant clang of a
blacksmith's hammer told Elena that the castle, Kilmartin,
was near. Symon led the horse around a bend where the

path doubled back on itself. The trees opened up, revealing an imposing gray structure crouched menacingly just below the summit.

Elena shuddered.

She was about to enter a strange castle. She had put herself into the hands of another warrior—a mad warrior.

A warrior who defended a lass he did not know.

Elena knew the stories she'd heard of the Devil of Kilmartin were evil, terrifying. Yet the man before her seemed . . . desperate. She had seen no evidence of evil. Indeed, he had handled Molly's wee bairn with gentle care and had shown great concern for both Molly and her missing husband. Of course, she also had not seen him mad. Could it be that was just a battle-lust distorted story? Nay, she had seen Dougal back down. He would not do so lightly.

Still, if she could lose herself in the castle, keep her distance from this man, this devil, she might yet be able to keep her gift to herself.

They passed through the castle's outer gate and up a short, dark tunnel lined with arrow slits and murder holes, and back into the bright mid-morning light in the bailey. Guards at the gate clearly knew Symon, though none said a single word of welcome to him. Elena could see people bustling about the bailey, but no one looked up to see who entered.

The hair on her arms and at the nape of her neck rose. Where was the shout of welcome for their returning chief? Where was the idle curiosity so common in castle life? At home there was rarely anything more interesting than the arrival of a stranger in the castle's midst. Yet here the people gathered about the bailey appeared to studiously ignore the travelers, purposely averting their eyes and keeping their backs turned, as if to keep from catching anyone's notice.

Perhaps the tales of the Devil were true. Perhaps he was lulling her into trusting him with his heroic rescues. Maybe she was more gullible than she thought. She would have to be careful. She would have to be wary.

The horse came to a halt. Symon handed the reins to a giant, golden-haired man, then went to help Molly down.

"Do not touch me, Devil."

Symon stepped away, his back stiff and a scowl on his face. Molly handed her bairn to the other man and dismounted.

"Take them to the Great Hall, Murdoch," Symon said to the giant. "I must speak with my brother." Symon strode across the open courtyard, people parting before him, seemingly without knowing he was there.

Until he passed.

Elena watched as person after person, young and old alike, turned after Symon passed and followed his progress with baleful glares. She had never seen such a reaction before, especially to a chief.

Murdoch nudged her forward, following in Symon's wake.

She had always assumed it was her own kinsmen who had dubbed him the Devil of Kilmartin. Now it seemed perhaps it was Symon's own clan who claimed that honor. But why did he remain as chief if he was so scorned? The clan could choose another chief at any time—unless. Perhaps they feared Symon too much to remove him.

Fear skittered down her spine, yet her own experience did not match the thought. This same man had protected her, shown her, if not exactly kindness, care. He'd fought for her, offered her hospitality without even knowing precisely who she was, nor what she was.

And she owed him her life.

Nay, she'd not let soft feelings dull her thinking. She owed him a debt which she would repay when she was able. But she'd not let that debt cloud her judgment. First she would keep herself safe, whatever it took to do so.

"Sit ye here, lass," Murdoch said, breaking into her thoughts. Elena sat on a rough-hewn bench, dimly aware of her surroundings and of the man's quiet departure with Molly and the baby.

S ymon banged open the heavy door separating a small private audience chamber from the Great Hall. The loud noise startled a serving girl out of his brother's lap. Rapidly covering her exposed breasts, she scurried past Symon, her eyes firmly downcast. The door slammed shut behind her.

Ranald MacLachlan, Symon's younger brother by a mere eleven months and nearly his twin in looks, rose quickly from the only chair in the confining room. A dying fire glowed behind him. He quickly covered his frustration at Symon's interruption.

"You have recovered?" Ranald carefully laced his trews and righted his tunic.

"Aye. I'm as recovered as is possible."

"There must be news, else you would not seek me out above your bed and bath."

"'Tis true, my brother." He bit down on the word, irritated that Ranald knew the nuances of his bouts with madness so well. "I do have news. The Lamonts have burned young Callum's cottage to the ground." He quickly recounted the tale.

"'Tis not unexpected," Ranald said, moving to the flagon of wine set on a small table near the fire. "They have been here again in your absence. Strange how you are always taken with your madness when they attack us."

His brother's jibe struck home, but he would not let him know how much. It was no secret that Ranald thought himself a better chief for the clan than mad Symon. But Symon could not agree, in spite of his troubles; he still believed his brother would not lead the clan well. Ranald's heart was in the right place, but his methods left much to be desired. For all the clan feared Symon, they did not trust Ranald.

Ranald turned back to him, handing him a cup of dark wine. "But I digress. There is more, aye?"

Symon winced inwardly at the callous dismissal of the Lamont attack, though he kept his face neutral. "Aye." He drank the slightly bitter wine. It did little for his dry throat. "I've brought Callum's wife and bairn here—"

Ranald nodded, his gaze riveted to Symon's face. "And?"

"I brought someone else."

Ranald quirked an eyebrow at him, though his eyes remained carefully attentive. "And who might that be? A lusty wench to quench your appetite? Or is it a fairy, come to mend the ill luck of the clan?"

"Nay. 'Tis a lass," Symon said, not rising to his brother's bait. "Auld Morag claims she is part of the prophecy."

Something flickered across Ranald's face, though it

passed so quickly Symon could not determine if it was interest or disapproval, or perhaps both.

"Auld Morag sent her?"

"Nay, but she believes Elena is the flame."

One corner of Ranald's mouth twitched. "Elena? What is her clan?" The gleam in his brother's eyes bothered Symon.

"I believe she belongs to Lamont."

Ranald's eyes glittered with interest in that piece of information. "Is she the healer?"

Symon noted his brother's heightened regard. "Aye," he said slowly. "I believe she is, or perhaps she is an apprentice."

"How many did you kill for her?"

"None."

The surprise on his brother's face sliced through Symon, hurting more than he would have thought possible. When would he be immune to these slighting insults?

"She was fleeing when I found her. I've not gotten the tale from her yet," Symon said.

"What makes you believe she is the healer?"

Symon thought back to that first moment she had crashed into him, and the feeling of calm and peace she had wrapped about him in that moment. But he kept that to himself for now. "She has some little skill at simples, for she has demonstrated such upon my own head."

"Then it could be she is not the healer, but only some lass with a bit of herb lore?"

"Aye, she could be, but I do not think so." He was reluctant to say more until he had proof.

"You clearly have made up your mind about the lass. Why then do you bring this news to me?"

Symon was surprised it had taken Ranald so long to ask this question.

"If she is who I believe her to be, 'twill not sit well with the clan. Yet I *will* keep her, Lamont or no." He had never been so sure of anything in his life. He would keep her and once more control his destiny. The prophecy made that clear.

"Do you really think she is the healer?" Ranald's pale green eyes sparkled as if he was pleased with the possibility, even as he twisted his words so they mocked the idea.

Doubt briefly flitted through Symon's thoughts. What if she wasn't what he thought her to be? There was still the problem of her apparent age, and the long-held rumors about the Lamont healer. And yet he felt certain she could settle that mystery, if she would. She held her identity close, but not close enough. At the very least she was a skilled apprentice healer. If he had to keep his hand on her for the rest of his life in order to fend off the madness, 'twas a small price to pay.

"Symon?"

He felt Ranald's eyes on him as he crossed the room again and again. He finally stopped at the window and looked out over the bailey crowded with people struggling to overcome a twist of fate, struggling to remain a clan. His loyalty and duty to that clan had kept him here, despite the growing mistrust and fear. Despite the loneliness. He was tired of being feared. Tired of feeling outside, even amongst his own people. Tired.

"You would keep this lass on a suspicion?" Ranald's voice came from just behind him.

Symon turned to face him. "I would, and I will."

Understanding dawned in the younger man's face. "You really do believe she is the—"

"Aye. But she is trying to keep it a secret. Her true nature betrays her, though."

"Then your madness is no more?" There was a strange note in Ranald's voice that Symon could not name. It wasn't hope, nor joy, nor even curiosity. It sounded more like desperation.

"I do not know yet if she can cure me. But I do know she can dampen the effects. 'Tis most amazing to have a completely clear head again—even though 'tis only for a brief moment so far."

Ranald reached for the wine flagon and refilled his brother's cup. "It must be welcome. But you say you do not know if she can cure it?"

"Nay. She is able to withhold her skill when she wishes. Force has not worked."

"Then what will?"

Symon looked at his brother carefully. "She runs from something—or someone. I wish to know who. I wish to know why." He drank from his cup. "Which is why I came to you."

Ranald nodded. "What exactly do you need me to do."

"I need you to find out what happened at Castle Lamont to send her fleeing into the forest, chased by hounds." He had his brother's complete attention now. "Or indeed, if anything happened. I know you have more . . . subtlety . . . than I do. Use that ability to find what I need to know, then bring it to me."

Ranald considered his brother for a moment. "And if I find this information, what then? Will it give you what you need to force her to aid you?"

"It will give me the leverage I'll need if she does not bend to my will on this matter. With this information I will know her weakness, her fear. Then she will have no choice but to help me, and that will help the clan."

Ranald paced the chamber for long moments, then turned to face his brother. "Very well. You are yet chief." Symon winced. "It may take some time, but I will discover this news."

Symon drained his cup then rose from his chair. "I'm counting on it. Now, I've a lass to woo."

"Woo?" Surprise stopped Ranald on his way to the door.

"Aye, there is more than one way to gain a lass's help. I would have it willingly, and if not that, then what you seek will insure her acquiescence."

Ranald nodded. "Perhaps you have learned something from me after all these years."

"Aye, perhaps I have." Symon wasn't sure he liked the implications of that. Quickly he left his brother where he'd found him, his mind already working on the problem of wooing a skittish lass.

Elena sat on a narrow bench in the nearly empty Great Hall where Symon's man had left her. A few people had entered the hall, only to glance at her and hastily retreat.

After a while she began to notice her surroundings. She looked up at the beautiful, timbered ceiling, then down the length of the huge hall. Empty trestle tables lined either side of the room, flanking a huge fire basket in the very center of the space. When lit, the smoke would rise to the high ceiling, and escape through a hole there where the sunlight now winked through.

The basket was empty, bare, as were the walls. There were no fine tapestries hanging, no rushes on the floor, no torch-filled sconces to light the space, nor candlesticks, as there were in her father's castle. The people she had passed in the bailey looked lean, hungry, hopeless, yet the dais at the far end held a finely carved table and included a chair so large it seemed a throne.

This clan was one contradiction after another. A chief who was distrusted, reviled. A substantial battlement so poor it could not be furnished properly.

Elena heard faint voices from behind a door at the far end of the long Hall. After a time Symon emerged. His plaid moved in time with his stride, drawing her attention. She found herself uncomfortably pleased with the well-muscled form of his legs, the broad expanse of his chest and shoulders, the intensity of his eyes—

Her breath hitched and her heart raced. He watched her as a starving man eyes a fat rabbit.

"There is a small chamber over the kitchen you may have," he said as he neared her, his eyes fixed on hers. " 'Tis not fine, but 'twill have to do . . . for now."

Elena nodded, unsure what to say to him, or how to calm the pounding of her heart. She followed him out of the far end of the Great Hall and into a dark vestibule. Heat radiated from the opposite wall where large openings in the wall showed a kitchen. Symon disappeared through a doorway on her left, leading her up a narrow, spiraling stair. Stopping at the first landing, he stepped into the hall-way and pushed open a heavy oak door.

Elena took care not to brush him as she ducked her head

and passed through the small doorway, into a room more spacious than any she had ever lived in. A simple box-bed was pushed up against the wall on her left. Directly across from her was a modest fireplace, though the lack of ashes told her it had been a long time since any fire had burned there. A small window with precious diamond-paned glass overlooked the glen they had climbed out of that morning. Sunlight streamed through it, creating diamond-patterned shadows on the wall. The floor was bare planks, the walls equally bare.

Symon cleared his throat. "Will it do?"

Will it do? No one had ever asked her opinion of her surroundings. She had always been told what she needed, never asked. Will it do? A tiny whisper of wanting passed through her. It would do well, after a bit of cleaning, a fire warming the hearth, some fragrant rushes strewn about the floor. Elena stopped herself. No, it would not do. She would not be plied with small comforts, lulled into revealing her secret.

" 'Tis fine."

Symon exhaled loudly. Elena turned to look at him. A hint of a smile hovered in his eyes, subtly changing the stern features she was quickly becoming accustomed to into those of a quieter, less battered soul.

"I'll see a fire is laid and some food brought up. Perhaps you would like a comb for your hair?"

She took the tangled mess that remained of her braid in her hand, picking small twigs and bits of bracken out of it. "I am rather heather-headed, aren't I?"

The smile hovering in his eyes deepened, gathering tiny lines at their corners, threatening to tip his lips into something other than the grim line they seemed to prefer. Something about him made her want to see those lips smile, those green eyes twinkle. She suddenly wanted to know what his laugh sounded like. It would be deep and rich, she was sure.

Forcing herself to abandon these thoughts, she looked down where she still gripped her braid in dirt- and soot-stained hands.

"I'd like a bit of water to wash the soot off me, as well," she said.

"What you want is a good dipping in the burn. That'll wash away the soot." One corner of his mouth twitched upward but was quickly controlled. He crossed his arms across his broad chest and leaned against the door, relaxing ever so slightly.

"And have you taken up the ways of the Saracens then?" Something about this new side of Symon made her tease. "Washing all the time?"

"Aye, that's it," he teased back, surprising her. "I'm secretly a Saracen come back with the Crusaders. Have you not heard of me—Black Symon the Saracen?"

A laugh escaped Elena, startling her so much she put a hand to her mouth to stop it. What was she thinking? She mustn't let this man too close. He already suspected something. She must keep him at a distance. She must remember that he was just like Dougal, a warrior intent on securing his position.

"You've a fine laugh, Elena-lass." His voice was low now, the teasing gone from it. "You should let it out more often."

"Nay," she said, equally as serious, "there's naught to laugh about." What was she thinking, laughing with this man. He truly was the Devil, distracting her from troubles, tempting her with a lovely bedchamber and teasing banter. His charm—when he let it out—was as heady as fine wine. She must put a stop to this now.

"What do you expect in return for your hospitality?" she asked.

Her words brought back the Devil of Kilmartin, banishing the softer Symon. He pushed away from the wall, once more the warrior.

"I bid you make yourself comfortable, then join me for the evening meal."

She nodded, though she did not trust his words. He was a warrior, and soon or late, he would make his demands again.

"I'll find Jenny and send her to you," Symon said, his face its usual scowl once more. Abruptly he left.

Elena sat on the bed and looked about. It was a beautiful room to her. Simple and spare, but the door was open, and she could walk about the castle if she wanted to. Symon had asked if it would do. Such a simple kindness warmed Elena, while another part remembered that he was the Devil of Kilmartin. Who knew what he was truly capable of when the devil was upon him?

A young fair-haired woman tapped on the open door, drawing Elena away from her thoughts.

"Mistress?" She bobbed her head in greeting, though she never took her eyes off Elena. "I be Jenny. I've brought you a tray of broth and bannocks. 'Tis ale, as well." She set the tray on a stool next to the cold hearth. "Niall is bringing some peat and a coal to start the fire. Meggie is finding some clothes for you. She's about your size. 'Twon't be anything fine, mind you, but it'll be better than the rags you've got—"

Jenny clapped her hands over her mouth and turned bright red. Elena nearly laughed for the second time this morning.

"So sorry, mistress, I did not mean—"

"'Tis all right, Jenny. This gown *is* rags. Anything Meggie can spare will be most welcome."

"The Devil"—she said the name furtively, as if she would be struck from above for uttering it out loud—"he said you wanted a bit of hot water for washing."

"Aye."

Elena watched the lass pour ale into an earthenware mug, then hand it to her.

"Is it true you will save the clan?" Jenny asked quickly.

Elena almost dropped the mug. "What?"

"Murdoch says 'tis so."

She should have know her arrival would be rich fodder amongst the castle's inhabitants, despite their seeming disinterest when she arrived. "Why would he say that?"

"Murdoch says you will lift the curse the Devil brought down upon us."

"Curse? Do you mean his madness?"

"Aye, mistress. Some say that one sold his soul to Lucifer, then tried to escape the bargain. Now Lucifer eats away at him, little by little, and the clan, too."

"And you believe this?"

Jenny pulled herself up to her full height, barely to Elena's shoulder. "You have not lived with the curse of the Devil these many months, mistress. Before the passing of the auld chief we were a strong, feared clan. Now we are little more than beggers and fools."

Elena realized she had insulted the girl who had told her more, and less, about Symon and this strange clan than she had guessed. She smiled. "I did not mean to question your words, lass. 'Tis only that—"

"Do you want the tub, or a basin?"

Elena stared blankly at the girl, unsure where this next turn of the conversation had taken her.

"To wash in," Jenny said, as if to a half-wit. "The Devil likes his tub. 'Tis more proof he is not right in the head. Bathing's not good for the humors, you ken."

An unusual urge to prod the girl leaped through Elena. Symon had been nothing but kind—if a bit surly—to her. She had felt his head ache, and his stomach roil, but there had been no sign of his mind being eaten away.

"Symon"—she said his name slowly, watching the chit's face—"likes his tub, does he?" A vivid image of Symon—water dripping from his midnight hair, head lolled back in utter relaxation, his broad chest naked and glistening with drops of water—surprised Elena, stirring something deep inside her. She pushed the errant daydream aside. She must be more fatigued than she had thought to be indulging in such flights of fancy.

Jenny gave her an odd look. "'Tis not a bother if that's what you want."

"What? Oh, the tub . . ." Elena did not share the girl's opinion of bathing, and despite the heat that gathered in her cheeks and the pit of her stomach at the thought of using the same bath she had imagined Symon in, a good soak would do much to ease the aches in her own body. She picked up a bannock and nibbled at its edge. "Aye, I'll have the tub."

A little food and a warm bath would do her good. She'd wash away the dirt and soot of the past two days. Then she'd have to figure out a way to stay clear of the chief of

MacLachlan. Symon was invading her thoughts and unsettling her. She could not let that happen. If she ever thought to have a normal, peaceful, life she could not let the Dev— Symon, she corrected herself—distract her. He was too dangerous to ever let that happen.

chapter 5

A candle mark later Elena was clean and dressed in the clothing Jenny had brought for her. The old battered tub had been a luxury, and it was pure pleasure to put on clean clothes. She belted a borrowed arisaid, a length of muted green and gold plaid, about her waist, then pulled one end up over her shoulders. She'd left her brooch behind when she fled, so she tied the corners together at her breast to hold it in place.

She sat, running her fingers through her thick hair, drying it with the fire's heat. While she had bathed, she had decided the first thing to do was to find a way out of this castle. Soon she would have to leave, before her gift was revealed, before Dougal came for her. It was up to her to protect herself now. There was no one else to depend on.

But first she must find her way about this castle, discover any exits, especially any more discreet than the front gate. Quickly she braided her hair and set about her quest.

She moved down the twisting stair. Noises from the busy kitchen and a comforting warmth drifted up to meet her. Elena stopped, inhaling the scent of roasting meat, pungent ale, and wood smoke. She gathered her courage and continued down, reminding herself that it was safe to wander this castle. No one knew what she was. Of course if Molly's tongue wagged as fast as that Murdoch's, they might not be happy to have a Lamont in their midst. She would have to take her chances, for she had to find a way out of the castle.

She moved down the stair slowly. When she got to the bottom, she peeked into the chamber. Seeing no one, she hurried around the corner and through an outer door. Late afternoon sunlight greeted her as she stepped from the dim interior.

From her vantage point above the bailey, she took in the dingy drabness of the MacLachlan stronghold. A sudden feeling of exposure flashed through her as faces turned up in her direction and a hush fell over those working there. She raised the arisaid over her head, shadowing her face with it. Fear skittered through her, but she forced it back, unwilling to give in to the urge to run back to her chamber and hide. She was in this predicament because she had not been willing to stand up to Dougal sooner. She could blame her father for leaving the clan in such a man's hands, but when she had not exercised her rightful claim to the chiefship of Lamont as soon as he disappeared, she had become just as responsible.

And now she was running again, or planning to. But where? And what would it gain her? Freedom? Peace? Or guilt, and continued fear? Nay, it would do no good for her to go back. Dougal was too strong, and she too weak. It would take more than a mere woman to oust Dougal of Dunmore now that he had the power he so coveted. It was best she keep out of his grasp. Without her to lend him the veil of legitimacy, Ian might yet have a chance to take his place as chief. She would not let Dougal wield her as a weapon again her kinsmen.

But she could not let the Devil of Kilmartin wield her, either. So then the question remained: Where would she go? That would take some thought, but for now, she could at least find a way to go, then she could decide where and when.

She remembered that the main gate was well guarded, though there was plenty of coming and going through it. Elena had lived in a castle long enough to know a postern gate would likely meet her needs better. She descended the stone stairs. When she reached the bottom, she turned away from the main gate and prepared to make a circuit of the walls.

A heavily bearded man erupted from a dark undercroft, knocking Elena aside in his haste. He brought the smell of moldy barley and ale with him out of the cool depths of the storage space. "Watch your step there, lass," he spat. "Else the would-be chief may say you're the one stealing the barley. Fah!"

Elena shrank back against the wall just as another man came out of the depths of the storage chamber. He stopped in the deep shadows of the vaulted opening. "I'll have those sacks of barley back this day"—his voice echoed in the man-made cave—"or I'll have the coin for it."

"'Tis a dark day in Kilmartin when you do not believe

the word of your kinsman!" the bearded man yelled back. "Aye, a dark day. I do not have your bloody barley, but I ken who does. You'll have it back by nightfall." He left quickly, his black hair flying and his plaid jerking back and forth in time with his stride. Elena turned back as the other man stepped out of the shadows and into the sunlight.

She blinked to clear her sight. It did not help. The man who stood before her, the would-be chief the bearded man had said, was nearly Symon's twin. Surely this was the brother he had spoken of. Looking at this man was like looking at a reflection of Symon. The same—but somehow backward.

Where Symon wore his dark hair loose about his shoulders, his brother wore his caught back in a strip of leather. They shared the same dark slash of eyebrows, but where Symon's eyes were the bright green of moss growing on a burn-side rock in early spring, his brother's were the paler green of frost-covered moss in midwinter. Symon carried himself ever ready to do battle. This man seemed folded in upon himself, less substantial. Perhaps it was a trick of the eyes, for the man before her wore trews with a long tunic that looked more English than any Highlander typically wore. The effect was decidedly diminishing.

And there was something about him that made her wary. His odd choice of clothing may have caused the crawling sensation at the base of her spine, but the look in his eye disturbed her most. She much preferred the grim determination she often saw in Symon's eyes to this look, for where Symon's gaze showed feeling, his brother's showed nothing at all.

Until they met her own.

Fire ignited in his eyes then, and a slippery smile flirted

over his lips. "Ah. You must be the lass Symon found in the wood." He moved toward her slowly. "I am Ranald, brother to the Devil. You would be Elena, daughter of . . ." He let the words slide out, teasing her that he might know who she really was.

"I am pleased to meet you, Ranald, brother of Symon," she said, emphasizing the chief's name.

Ranald appeared as surprised by her words as she was. He bobbed his head in acknowledgment of her point. "And I you, for it is not often Symon returns from his fights with the Devil with the salvation of our clan."

"'Tis the second time I have heard such daft words," she said. "Where did you get such an idea?"

Surprise sliced across Ranald's face. "Auld Morag . . . the pro—" He stopped, then started again. "The clan puts great store in the barmy witch's muttering."

"Auld Morag? She said nothing to me. I cannot save myself, much less an entire clan. I am no one's salvation."

Ranald nodded his agreement as he looked over her shoulder. She watched as his face subtly changed, taking on the hardness of one hiding within himself. Elena turned but saw nothing.

"If you will excuse me," he said, "there is business I must attend to before the evening meal. You will join us in the Great Hall, will you not?"

"I will."

"Good. Until then," he said, then moved quickly toward the main gate.

Elena pulled the arisaid closer about her face and wandered in the opposite direction. She had an odd feeling in the pit of her stomach, as if she'd eaten something that didn't agree with her. Something about Ranald didn't feel right. But then nothing had felt right the past few days. Perhaps she was looking for trouble where there wasn't any.

And yet, all was not right in Kilmartin Castle. Symon was despised for a madness she had heard of, but had not witnessed, yet he held the position of chief within his clan. His brother had been called the would-be chief, clearly not a sign of respect.

"Are you lost?"

She gasped. Her arisaid fell about her shoulder and her coppery braid slithered out. She had been so intent on Ranald she had not noticed Symon's arrival.

"Be calm, Elena. I'll not harm you," Symon said. He stood there, his eyes trained on her hair, his own dripping wet. The sweet smell of fresh air and cold burn water surrounded him, drawing her to him. He shook his head, breaking the moment and splattering her with tiny droplets, like diamonds in the sun.

"I was . . ." She was just searching for an escape route is what she wanted to say. "I was looking for the Hall."

Symon nodded his head. "I see." He watched her a moment, his gaze intense.

"You should have asked Ranald to direct you," he said.

Heat flooded Elena's cheeks, and she knew her pale skin gave away her embarrassment. "Were you spying on me?" She tipped her chin up, daring him to deny it.

"Aye. Did you have a nice talk with him?"

"He sees the world differently than you," she said.

"Ranald has always had a unique view of his surroundings. He is my only brother, and my most trusted adviser."

"Then you know he does not believe in the tale Murdoch is spreading?"

Symon tipped her chin up with his finger. "What tale?"

The momentary pleasure of his touch was overwhelmed by a swirling blackness that washed over her. Madness? It did not feel like madness. She stepped back, breaking the disconcerting contact.

"That I am to be the clan's salvation," she said.

Symon's mouth tipped into a slight smile. "He likes to spread tales. It endears him to the lassies."

He turned and motioned for her to walk with him. "I would acquaint you with my home," he said, "in exchange for a wee bit more of that willow tea you made me."

"I do not think the willow will do much good," she said to herself.

"Lass?"

"Aye. I have more of the willow. Auld Morag gave me her supply," she said. " 'Tis in my chamber."

Symon nodded, then led her not to her chamber, but along the way she had started. "We shall have someone fetch it." He stopped a boy and had Elena explain what was needed and where to find it. As they continued on, he pointed out the smith, the alewife, cousins, and other kin, keeping a constant stream of conversation going, as if he needed her to know everyone immediately.

But none of the people spoke to Symon. They acknowledged the pair's passing with only a grudging nod, or a short grunt and a quickly turned back. Elena couldn't help noticing the many furtive glances at her, though. Apparently Murdoch had spread his tale through the whole castle already. Symon stopped at what was clearly once a gate. " 'Tis all blocked up, the postern gate." His voice dropped. "Better than having to guard it."

Elena noted the bitterness in his voice. "You do not believe that."

It was his turn to be surprised. "I do not. 'Twas my father's doing. 'Tis still a point of debate between Ranald and myself."

"But you are chief, why do you not unblock it?"

"Aye, I am chief, but 'tis a near thing. I do not do that which they do not trust. 'Tis not so important, this gate, to test that trust."

"'Tis a strange place, this. The people sullen, rude to their own. The chief questioning his own decisions instead of commanding." She slanted a look at him. "Tales of Lucifer and lost souls. Why is it like this, Symon?"

He stopped, facing her. "Are you not afraid of the tales about me?"

She thought about his question. Did she fear the tales? Part of her did. She had clear evidence, in her clan's recent battles, of his cruelty. And yet she had seen none of that. Her own experience of the last few days showed him to be arrogant, brave, pushy, but never had he sought to harm her. The tales of the Devil of Kilmartin told of a monster, killing anyone in his way, ravaging women and causing destruction wherever he went. The truth was that she had not seen him in his madness, but the sane man before her did not cause her fear.

Symon waited, an expectant look on his face.

"The tales tell of a horrible monster, but I have only seen a man, afflicted by calamity, but strong enough to fight it." She thought of Dougal. "I do not think I have cause to fear you." She smiled at him shyly. "But I will be cautious."

A huge smile spread across his face, transforming it into

a dazzlingly handsome countenance. Elena's breath stuck
in her throat.

"You are an unusual person, Elena of Lamont." He
studied her face, as if he might find an answer to his pressing questions there. The smile faded. "Still, I must take
much of the blame for the ills that have befallen my people. I will do what's necessary to right things.

"Come," he said before she could reply, "I find that I
am hungry." He took her hand and led her toward the Hall.

Elena let him lead her, still dazzled by that flash of what
Symon must have been like, before his trials started. She
truly didn't fear him. With the likes of Dougal of Dunmore
about, she was certain she was safer with this mad warrior
than with the one in her own home.

Carefully she shielded herself from the headache she
could feel plaguing Symon. It took great concentration
not to give in to the call of her gift to heal him. But while
she was not afraid of the Devil of Kilmartin, neither would
she give him anything to hold over her.

*S*ymon heard the familiar, soothing sound of harp music
spilling down from the gallery overhead as they entered the Great Hall. The tables, so empty earlier, were
now crowded with people, talking, shouting, grabbing for
the meager contents of the platters. Symon stood, giving
Elena time to adjust to the throng. It seemed the castle
became more crowded by the day as more and more of his
kinsmen were run out of their homes by the English, or
the Lamonts. Day by day, as his madness gripped him, the
holdings of Clan Lachlan shrank, until one day all that

would be left was this fortress and a crowd of his starving kinsmen.

Unless the prophecy came to pass.

He felt a twinge of conscience. He had no idea if Elena would fulfill whatever her role was. He had no idea what "mingling" might entail. That she wasn't afraid of him pleased him greatly. Once he was rid of the madness for good . . .

As if the thought of madness was enough to call it down, the pain in his head tripled, his stomach clenched, and a foreboding sweat trickled down his chest.

For a moment he thought of dragging the lass back to his chamber to force her to heal him then and there, but he could not just yet. First he had to make sure she had no alternative, no way out. He had to bind her to his clan quickly, decisively, before she could slip away from them. She would fulfill her destiny, whatever it held. He would make sure of it.

He shook his head to clear the pain swirling through him and started forward.

Silence surged down the hall ahead of them like a wind-whipped wave racing ashore. Symon glanced at Elena as they made their way down the Hall. Her mouth was a tense line, and her gaze flitted over the crowd. Her hand was stiff in his.

Symon stopped her in front of the chief's table, turning her to face the assembled MacLachlans.

"You will make our guest welcome in Kilmartin Castle," he said formally, his voice strong and steady. "She is known as Elena." He turned then to her. "Please accept the hospitality of Clan Lachlan."

"With thanks," she said, a surprised look on her face.

Her safety assured by his words, Symon led her around the empty table. They sat and servers laid trays of food before them. Symon reached for his cup and rose to his feet. A hush fell over the Hall once more.

He looked out at the faces of his clan. Curiosity warred with apathy, and apathy seemed to be winning out.

"My kinsmen," he began, his voice booming through the hall. Symon raised his cup but leaned his weight against the table, praying he would not fall over before he could do what he must. "Many of you have heard Auld Morag's prophesy."

A muttering filled the hall and a voice yelled out, " 'Tis true?"

"Aye, 'twould seem so. Auld Morag said this woman"— he nodded slowly toward Elena—"is the flame. You know well what part I play. The rest has not yet been revealed, but clearly our time is at hand."

Elena gasped as a cheer erupted from the gathering. Symon allowed the crowd to trade speculations for a moment, then he banged his cup against the table until they quieted once more.

"Auld Morag foresaw her coming. The prophecy has come to pass. Elena's presence here assures our victory over our many troubles."

Elena surged to her feet, knocking over her wine goblet. "Nay!"

Symon grabbed her wrist, arresting her motion. He felt her sway, and she clutched at her stomach.

He turned to her and said under his breath, "Aye, 'tis your destiny—unless you wish to return to your clan?"

Elena shook her head.

He was pleased to see anger in her eyes, a flash of fight.

If she had wept, or collapsed in fear, he would not know what to do, but anger—that he was familiar with.

"She is our honored guest," he said once more to the crowd. He sat, releasing the lass. His stomach roiled, but he downed the spiced wine, praying it would dull the ache in his head. He would sit another moment or two, then escort Elena from the Hall and back to her chamber, where he would require her to heal him once and for all. Surely that was the way flame and madness were to mingle.

E lena sat, stunned, next to a madman, desperately quelling the stomach pain that had burst within her at his touch. She shook her head at his words. Her destiny? She could do naught for this clan but cause them trouble, for Dougal would not wait long to claim her. Soon or late he would come for her. There would be no victory in that.

Before she realized what was happening, Symon had risen, taken her hand, and was leading her out of the Hall through the small door behind the dais. He quickly closed the door and leaned against it, his eyes closed.

"I know who and what you are, Elena-lass."

"You cannot."

"I can. You are Elena of Lamont, and you are the Lamont healer."

Elena shook her head, though whether she denied his words or that she had been found out, she wasn't sure.

"I do not understand how one so young could be the healer of the auld tales, but it does not matter. You are the healer, and I am in need of your skills. In exchange, I have extended the protection of my clan to you. You in turn will heal me and thereby deliver my clan from the curse of madness we have fallen under."

"I cannot," she whispered.

He opened his eyes then, and their green depths were filled with hope and determination. "You can, and you will. Auld Morag foresaw it. You will heal the madness so I can lead the clan back to prosperity and power."

"I do not care what Auld Morag foresaw." Elena backed away from him, shaking her head. "I cannot heal you."

He crossed the room, wobbling slightly midway. She backed up as far as she could, but he continued until she was against the wall and he was a breath away from her. "You can and you will," he said, his voice low and tight.

"I cannot heal madness. I have tried before. 'Tis not possible."

"Then explain this." He grabbed her hands in his and pressed her palms to his chest.

Elena sucked in her breath as her vision blurred, her stomach threatened to empty itself, and her head felt as if someone had sliced into it with a heavy Claymore. She tried to escape, but the warrior was too strong. He held her to him as she struggled against her gift, for his affliction called out to it. Instinctively she built a wall of stone in her mind, imagining it wide and tall and very strong.

"Do not fight me, Elena," he said. "I have felt your touch upon me. I have felt you lift the devil from my shoulders! Do not deny you can heal me!" Desperation had him shaking her, reminding her all too clearly of her recent confrontation with Dougal. Fear overcame her concentration and her wall crumbled. Her gift surged through her hands and into the Devil.

"Naaay!" she yelled, wrenching herself free in that instant of healing. "I will not be used, forced. I will not!"

Symon supported himself against the wall with one arm, a stunned look on his face.

" 'Tis true," he said. "You truly are the healer. I felt it. 'Tis true."

Elena stared at him, fighting tears of despair. She was right back where she had been only a few days before. What was she to do now? She could not stay here, yet the attack on Molly's cottage told her that Dougal clearly knew she was amongst the MacLachlans. How far could she get with both Dougal and the Devil of Kilmartin determined to have her? She started to shake.

Symon pushed away from the wall. "Do not cry." He moved slowly toward her, as if he was afraid she would bolt. Elena tried to move away, but despair seemed to have nailed her shoes to the floor. Symon moved closer.

"Lass, I'm sorry. I did not mean to upset you so." He touched her cheek gently, wiping away a tear. The gesture was so gentle, so filled with the softness missing in her life, she found herself wishing to burrow into his arms again, as she had that first night. But she couldn't. He was just like Dougal, manipulating and using her for his own purposes. Just as Dougal had forced her healing gift from her, made her do his will.

He had forced her healing gift. . . .

She looked at him, examining his eyes, the color of his skin, the tense set of his jaw. She had not healed him, not entirely, though 'twould seem in that single moment she had done something. Yet before, when she had tried to heal madness, naught had come of it except a strange disoriented feeling in her own head. Nay, this time something had happened. She reached out a hand and laid it on his chest, curiosity overcoming her fear.

Pain pounded in his head and her own stomach echoed the turmoil of his. Those were things she could do something about. Sweat sheened her skin and her vision wavered. There was naught she could do for madness—but if by healing his head and gut he thought she had healed him . . .

Symon laid his own hand over hers. Swiftly her gaze met his curious stare. "What is it, Elena-lass?"

He knew she was the healer. There was naught she could do to change that. She slid her hand free and stepped back. She would no longer be held hostage to her skill. Indeed, she would use it as ruthlessly as these warriors would. She could heal his head and his gut, and she would.

For a price.

chapter 6

Symon sensed a change in the lass, a spark in her eye that hadn't been there a moment ago. "Elena?"

"What do you offer me for my help?"

Surprise whipped through him. "What do you wish?"

"My safety."

He watched her square her shoulders, as if she braced for a fight, and was startled to realize she was nearly as tall as he. "Did I not offer you hospitality?" he asked, circling around her.

"Aye, but 'tis not what I wish." She turned to face him. "If I help you, and I am not saying I will, you must ensure my safe passage to wherever I choose."

"Wherever?"

"In Scotland. I do not wish to venture beyond the Highlands." She looked away, twisting her hands nervously. "Just away from all who know me."

"Why does your clan hunt you?" He watched as she glanced back at him, and the determination in her eyes wavered, then burned even brighter than before.

"That has naught to do with this, Symon. Will you give me what I ask?"

He thought it over for a moment. How could he see the prophecy fulfilled and promise her what she asked? "Where do you plan to go?"

Confusion slipped into her eyes, and fear. "I have not decided as yet."

"You have nowhere to go," he said quietly, sensing an opportunity.

"I have not decided."

Symon nodded knowingly. Perhaps he could convince her that Kilmartin Castle was where she wished to be, in that way he could gain the time to unravel the rest of the prophecy. He needed time, but the only way he would get that was to accept her terms. "Very well. But you must stay until my affliction is gone."

"Nay. I told you. I cannot cure your affliction, but I think I can dampen its effects, at least for a while. I stay only until I deem it time to go. I will not be bound to you, no matter what Auld Morag's prophecy has to say."

Symon moved toward her slowly, indirectly, weighing her strengths and weaknesses as if he faced her in armed combat. "Yet the clan expects you to stay until all is well."

"That is due to your own folly. I care not what your clan expects of me. I will help you as I can, but you must assure me of safe passage when the time comes that I decide to go."

"Very well. But for now, we will allow the clan to believe you will stay." She started to interrupt, but Symon, close now, stopped her with a finger to her lips. The heat of her breath seared his skin. "My clan needs hope for the future."

"You'll not tell of my gift?" Her lips moved softly against the pad of his finger sending trails of fire up his arm. "Nor force me to use it on any other person?"

"Only Ranald knows of my suspicions." He was close enough now to feel her breath on his face, to measure its rapid pace. "I will instruct him to say nothing. You have my word."

"The word of a madman." Her voice was husky, a whisper. "The Devil of Kilmartin?"

"Nay." He moved closer now, the urge to place his lips upon hers overwhelming. "The word of Symon, chief of Clan Lachlan." He dipped his head to hers and sealed his promise with a chaste kiss. At least that's what he had meant to do.

Rapidly the simple kiss heated, and instead of Elena stepping back and slapping him soundly, as he had fully expected, she leaned into him. 'Twould be good for the clan if she found him attractive. 'Twould be good for the clan. Yet it wasn't the clan that wrapped his arms about the lass and deepened the kiss. Symon gave himself to the moment and the pleasure of this woman, allowing his hands to roam her back, pulling her closer. Heat swelled in him, along with a curious feeling of lightness. Elena moaned just as the door flew open, startling the lass out of his arms.

•   •   •

E lena felt her cheeks heat as Ranald entered, ushered in by the buzz of many voices still in the Great Hall.

"My apologies," he said to Symon as he glanced at her. "I did not mean to interrupt your . . . discussion."

Symon looked at her with a heat in his eyes she had not seen before. An answering heat flamed in her belly, but she would not let it show. Never had she felt what she had just shared with this man. Never had she felt so alive, yet consumed. He burned brightly, singeing her, muddling her thoughts, confusing her body.

Yearning pulled at her. This was so much more than the simple comfort he had given that first night. She wanted, what exactly she wasn't sure, but a need had sprung to life within her. A need she had not been aware of until this moment, yet she could not name it precisely. Nor did she want to, for naming it would give it power.

"There are many questions amongst our people," Ranald said to Symon. "They wish to know more of this woman. Will you return and answer those questions?"

Symon looked at Elena. She waited, sure he would trap her now with her confession. Sure of his victory when she succumbed so quickly to his assault on her senses. He crossed to her and lifted her hand to his lips. Fire burned up her arm and downward, fanning the flames that glowed in her belly. "I will answer no questions," he said, though she wasn't sure if he said the words to her or to Ranald. He turned to his brother. "And neither will you."

"Ah, you are bewitched by the lass already." There was no sneer upon Ranald's face, but Elena heard it clearly in his voice, and from the way Symon stiffened, he did, too.

"You will do as I asked before, nothing more. Take care of the task on your own. Do not involve any others."

Ranald inclined his head. "You are chief. I will do as you bid me."

"Let us return to our meal," Symon said, "and reassure the clan that all is well, both with our guest and their chief."

"Aye. But I do not think you will be keeping any secrets looking like that," Ranald said.

"What do you mean?"

"You look . . . better. 'Twill not take much for them"—he nodded in the direction of the Hall—"to see there is a change in you and guess she had some part to play in it." Ranald came closer to his brother, examining his face. "I would not say she has knocked the Devil from your shoulders, but she has surely given him a shove."

Elena knew she had healed him slightly in that moment when he had forced her skill from her, but now . . .

"Am I so frightful, lass?" Symon asked.

Ranald was correct. The tense lines about Symon's eyes had softened, and the sallow look to his skin was gone, a rosy healthy glow in its place. But how, she had not—

The kiss, the power in that simple kiss, and the haze it had drawn over her mind even as it illuminated every smell and sound and touch. Of course. Her gift manifested in touch. Somehow her gift must have done its work while her body was overwhelmed by her senses . . . and yet, even as those senses had been heightened, there had been no pain, only pleasure.

"Very well"—Symon smiled at her and the effect was dazzling—"perhaps you should return to the Hall with

Ranald." To Ranald he said, "Make my excuses. 'Twill
not be hard to do. I shall retire. You can tell them I was not
well. 'Tis a necessary deception for now." Symon turned
to Elena again. "Your secret is safe. Ranald will show you
back to your chamber after the meal." He moved to a
small door leading away from the Great Hall. "Then attend me in my chamber, brother, and bring food. I find I
am suddenly famished." He grinned and quietly slipped
out the door.

"Shall we return?" Ranald asked her.

She nodded, still stunned by all that had passed in this
tiny room.

S ymon broke into a tuneless whistle as he crossed the
bailey toward his chamber. He hadn't felt this good in
nearly a twelvemonth. He wasn't sure how the lass had
accomplished such a feat, but it didn't matter. The madness was pushed back, at least for now. He could feel it
still, at the edges of his mind, but the clarity and well
being he felt allowed his hope for the future to blossom.

Now he could be the leader the clan needed. The next
time the Lamonts attacked, he would be here, lucid and
ready to beat them back. But perhaps he would not wait
that long. Perhaps the time had come to take the battle to
them.

And yet, in a strange way, the Lamonts were responsible for his future. Guilt pricked at him. He had sensed the
girl's response to his touch and had pushed his advantage.
Perhaps this attraction between them was part of the
prophecy. If so, he could not say it wasn't welcome. Her
touch had healed him in more ways than one, and he

found himself hardening at the memory of her soft hungry lips.

Somehow he would convince her that this was where she wished to be. He had to. Only then could he keep his promise to her and see the prophecy fulfilled. The question was how to go about convincing her. He knew he could not command her, for that was what she seemed most adamant about. Nay, his usual method of attacking problems head-on would not work with Elena. This would call for the subtlety of one of Ranald's plans. Together the brothers would plot the rise of Clan MacLachlan by the wooing of a lass of Lamont.

S ymon sat, staring into the fire, when a knock sounded at the door. Ranald entered with a tray. The smell of venison made Symon's stomach rumble.

Ranald set the tray on a stool before the hearth and filled a wooden goblet with spiced wine.

"All is well?" Symon asked, waving away the wine in favor of the meat.

"Aye. There was much muttering when you did not return to the hall, but the lass's presence seemed enough of a diversion to keep them occupied."

"Good."

"You would really give this Lamont shelter?"

Symon turned his attention away from the flames to his brother. "Aye, Auld Mor—"

"I do not care what the auld witch said."

Symon scowled. "Then what is it you wish to know?"

"Why."

Symon rose from his chair and moved closer to the heat of the fire. "You know why."

"You would put the clan in deeper danger only to cure yourself?"

"I would never put the clan in danger if I did not believe it was for just cause. Ridding myself of this curse will let me lead this clan the way I intended; the way our father would have wished."

"Or it will bring the wrath of Lamont down upon us, and that of all their allies."

"Not if you find that information I need. If we know why Elena found it necessary to flee, we will have the bargaining chip we need to keep Lamonts from our borders and their allies in their own homes. There has to be some powerful reason they would hunt a healer such as Elena. Why is she not revered and honored by her clan? Surely this is the key to both keeping the Lamonts at bay and convincing Elena this is the place she must be."

"I have found nothing so far. Tomorrow I will ride out to see what information I can glean."

"You will go to Auld Morag, tell her what you seek. She will guide you."

"She will spout nonsense."

Symon considered his brother. "I do not like being in her presence any more than you do. However, I am still your chief, and, despite your mistrust, that auld woman has counseled this clan too long and too well not to ask her help in this matter. You will do as I say."

Ranald's face was carefully neutral. "Very well. I will go to her at first light. I will do as she deems necessary. But then I will follow my own counsel. We shall see who

is better suited to lead this clan, you and that auld witch—
or me."

With effort, Symon forced himself to calm. He un-
curled his fists, relaxed his shoulders, and purposely
drained his goblet.

Ranald glanced at Symon. "Her clan will want her
back."

"They'll not get her back. Morag saw her destiny. 'Tis
here amongst MacLachlans."

Ranald looked at him for a long time, then nodded his
head. "There is more to it than that, Symon. You ken it as
well as I do."

"I ken there is more, but I cannot say what it is."

Ranald nodded.

"'Tis like a buzzing in the gut," Symon continued.
"Something is wrong, and if we but knew what to look
for, I feel we would see it right before us."

"You promise the lass much. Will you honor me
equally as well?" Ranald stood at the fire, his back to
Symon.

"If it is within my power."

"Do not rush into this alliance. Give me time to discover the cause of her being here amongst us." He turned
to face his brother, his face set in grim lines. "I bid you
walk wary in this matter. I do not trust the Lamonts."

Symon considered Ranald's words. "'Tis reasonable. I
will endeavor to be patient." He grinned at his brother,
who only scowled in response. "Get you off to find this
information. I fear I have no great talent for patience."

"Aye. If there is need for me before I return," Ranald
said, "send Murdoch to find me. He seems able to find
anyone in these forests."

Symon agreed, though he did not like the intimation in his brother's words. Ranald would be needed if the Devil took Symon again. And that would only happen if Elena could not help him.

Ranald left and Symon paced the floor, trying to work out a plan to convince Elena to stay. He had promised not to rush into any alliance with the lass, but that did not mean he could not try to soften her to her fate. Indeed, if the kiss they had shared showed him anything, it was that softening her would be pleasant, at the least. But the lass was stubborn, and it was not Symon she wanted.

Safety, she said, and yet she did not seem to know exactly what she meant by that. Safety from what? Her own clan? Or simply from the man who chased her?

Frustration scratched at him. The answer was so close, yet held too tightly by the lass. Still, she had trusted him enough with one secret, perhaps he could win another from her. The question was, how?

E lena had been surprised when Ranald told her Symon's chamber was next to her own. Surprised, and worried. Now she heard Ranald's thumping gait pass back down the hall toward the stair, and she wondered what the two MacLachlans had decided about her fate. Had she sealed it by agreeing to help the beleaguered chief? She could not see any other way of gaining the safety she needed, though if he did not keep his word, she was doomed. Certainly he would think he held her in his grip after that kiss.

That kiss. Just the thought of it brought the experience back in full force. And the results as well. Yes, she had been consumed by the sensations swirling through her. And yes, he had gotten what he wanted from her. But how had he known what would happen? Perhaps he hadn't and he only thought to muddle her mind with his soft kiss, and his hard body—

She could not dwell on that.

Her gift seemed to reach out to this man despite her decision to withhold it. Again and again she fought to contain it, only to have him touch her. Lightly or otherwise and he seemed to pull it from her, or perhaps she gave it in spite of herself.

To fight it, she needed to understand it. To understand it, she needed to figure out how it happened. If she could sort through the myriad sensations of that kiss and find the moment when her gift asserted its power, she might be able to fight it. Elena took a deep breath and let herself relive those brief moments.

There was heat, and lightness, and a peculiar heaviness at the very same time. There was a prickling of the skin as when lightening struck nearby, and a liquid fire burning in the blood. She remembered the scent of leather and wool, the prickle of his whiskers, and the softness of his lips against hers. She remembered a curious fog that had come over her, blocking out time and place, who she was—and what. She could not remember another time in her entire life when she had been able to completely forget what she was.

And yet, despite the pleasure of that moment out of time, she was sure that was when her gift had taken over, overcoming years of practiced control, healing Symon. She did not remember it happening, but in that moment of abandon, she had forgotten.

It wouldn't happen again. It couldn't. If she was to have any power in this situation, she must be in total control of her gift at all times. Symon must not be able to use her gift whenever he chose. She must be able to withhold it in case he did not keep his word. And in order to do that there could be no more touching unless she did so to dampen his symptoms.

There could be no more kissing. She would keep her distance from him, though a tiny place inside of her yearned for that abandonment again, that moment of losing herself in the embrace of the Devil of Kilmartin.

chapter 7

*S*ymon searched the sparsely occupied tables of the Great Hall. Elena hadn't been in her chamber when he'd gone to escort her down to break her fast. She must be here eating, somewhere. The alternative was not something Symon wanted to dwell on. If she wasn't here . . .

But she was. He saw her, hunched over in a dark corner of the vast space, her back to the door. She clearly sought to escape everyone's notice, but from the furtive glances and blatant stares of his kinsmen, he knew she had not accomplished her goal. Of course that fiery hair, carefully tamed into a tight braid, would have stood out anywhere. He imagined its silky strands, sliding through his fingers. He shook off the image, focusing instead on what he needed from her. He tried to smile, hoping to appear less dangerous, and strode across the hall.

"There you are," he said as he straddled the bench, facing a startled Elena.

"I would show you about your new home when you have finished eating." Unable to resist, Symon reached out to smooth a small tendril of hair away from her cheek. It was just as silky as his imagination had told him, yet Elena winced at his touch and inched down the bench away from him.

"Do you not wish to acquaint yourself with this castle?"

"I do not need to," she said quietly. "I will not be staying here long."

The smile slipped from Symon's face. "Of course you will. You are safe here, and you have promised to aid me."

Elena looked at him as if he had sprouted an extra eye. "Have you already determined to forget *your* word?" she hissed.

"Nay. I will do as I promised."

"Then what do you want?"

"There is no reason you cannot learn a bit of my people. See the ways of the castle and its folk."

She leaned closer to him, and his heart momentarily sped up. "I will not . . ." She looked about her. "You agreed not to force . . ." If Symon believed such things, he would swear the fairy folk had stolen her tongue for she could not finish what she started to say.

"I gave you my word," he said quietly, getting irritated that he had to keep telling her this. "Why can you not believe me?"

Elena just stared at him, then rose quickly and left the hall before he realized she was going. A rising murmur followed her departure, as if conversation had been dampened in order to overhear what words were exchanged between the chief and his guest.

Symon followed Elena, finding her stopped at the top of the stone staircase leading down to the bailey. She stood, seemingly transfixed by the activity below. He followed her gaze, noting the beaten look of the people toiling there. Even the animals—horses, pigs, and sheep—looked forlorn, hopeless. He reached out and touched her arm, and she jumped, as if startled from a trance.

"What?" he asked, needing to know what she saw there.

She started to speak, then closed her eyes for a moment. He could almost feel her erecting a wall between them, pushing him away with her stubborn insistence that she would was not here to fulfill the prophecy. Her stubborn insistence that she had somewhere else to go, that Kilmartin could not be her home.

Temper flared in him. He must help his clan. He must overcome his curse. And she was the one that held the key, the key to his future, and that of Clan Lachlan. "Why can this not be your home?" he asked, his jaw tight, his fists clenched at his side to keep him from grabbing her and giving her a good shake. That's what he really wanted to do, shake her, and kiss her, and shake her some more. Stubborn, stubborn woman.

"Because"—she looked out over the bailey again—"because there is too great a need for me here." She glanced back at him. "There are too many reasons for you to change your mind. My ability corrupts those who would wield it, and I am not the only one to suffer for it."

"I am not like that."

"You are."

This time he gave into his impulses, grabbing her by her

shoulders and turning her to face him, turning her away from the bailey that promised only hopelessness. "When the time comes I will take you where you wish to go. I ask only that you use your gift to stop"—the look flashing in her eyes had him backtracking—"nay, not to stop, you say you cannot do that, to abate the symptoms of my affliction. I gave you my word, I will not break it, though I may try to change your mind."

"Aye, by words, or by threats"—her gaze shifted to his mouth, her eyes going soft and liquid, and he knew she had been as unsettled by their kiss as he was—"or seduction." She shook off his hands and stepped away. "Do not touch me again, Devil."

"But 'twill serve to convince the clan you are content to stay here," he said, his voice echoing the frustration growing within him.

She looked back at the bailey. "They are not so daft as to believe I will stay."

"They need only have the hope."

"There is no hope in this world. There are only those with power, and those who wish to gain it."

"And which are you, Elena?" His voice was hard, his temper held ruthlessly in check. "Would you gain your power by refusing to keep your word?"

Elena's hand whipped out. She slapped him soundly, the sound slicing through the noise of the bailey. "I have suffered enough at the hands of men like you. My own kinsmen have suffered as well. If I refused, 'twould make me just like . . ." She crossed her arms, erecting yet another barrier between them. "I will keep my part of our bargain, but it does not include you touching me, nor my learning aught of your people."

With those words she turned and descended the bailey stair. When she reached the bottom, she slipped along the base of the curtain wall, hastily disappearing from sight.

Symon paced the ramparts, watching Elena move slowly through the scattered people below, talking to no one, moving carefully away when anyone ventured near.

Murdoch appeared at his elbow and stood quietly, watching with him. "She's an odd lass, that one," he said after a few minutes, "but bonny."

Symon looked at his gillie. "What?"

Murdoch cocked a bushy eyebrow at him, his golden hair forming an odd sort of halo about his grinning face.

"What do you want?" Symon asked again.

"Is there some reason I cannot stand and gaze about, daftlike, if I wish?" Murdoch was smirking now.

"I am not daft, at least not today."

"Aye, you seem back to your auld self this day. Why is that?"

Symon saw the man look at him, but chose to continue watching Elena make her way about the bailey, avoiding answering the giant's query. He had promised the lass to keep her secret, though he wanted to sing out the truth to the world, or at least to Murdoch. True she said she could not heal him, but she certainly seemed to have. And he did not even know for sure how she had done it. Though the kiss seemed to have something to do with it.

The kiss. Touching her. That was what she had forbidden him to do, to touch her . . . and yet her touch was what he craved. Was it only because she was a comely lass, thin, but still rounded where a man wanted roundness? Or was this compulsion merely the effect of her healing art?

"She says I cannot touch her," he said out loud, forgetting Murdoch was standing there.

"Aye, lasses often say such things."

"You have much experience of this?"

Murdoch looked away, and Symon would have sworn the man blushed. "Enough. Usually it takes a slower pace, a gentler approach, when they say that. They want soft words, and promises, lots of promises. Of course, she could just be repulsed by you."

Symon started to defend himself, then realized Murdoch was grinning broadly at him again. "Aye, that must be it," he agreed. "I do not know how to soften her toward me. I have had little experience with gentle words."

The two men stood shoulder to shoulder, watching Elena wander below. She seemed to be searching for something, while still avoiding all who came near. Symon's attention was caught by a child skipping across the open space, singing tunelessly. She skirted the well, then broke into a strange almost dance, twirling and skipping and jumping and running, one after the other until she seemed unable to stop. She was heading straight for Elena, who seemed unaware of the child as she examined the bricked up remains of the old postern gate. As the child crashed into her, Elena grabbed her, steadying the wobbling wean.

Symon watched, amazed, as a smile broke out on Elena's face, her obvious amusement clear even this far away. He could not take his eyes off her, the transformation from grim determination to quiet pleasure shook him. That is what she should look like always, carefree, open, happy. She squatted down to look the child in the eye, and the two spoke for a moment, then the child's laughter pealed out, echoing off the cold castle walls. Elena rose and the little girl took her hand and led her away.

"Aye, she's a bonny lass," Murdoch said quietly. "If she does not want you, perhaps she'd be interested in me."

Symon rounded on the giant.

"Just teasin' you, Symon. Just teasin'. I would not interfere with one of Auld Morag's prophecies!"

Symon took a slow breath and nodded.

"But you may have witnessed the way to the lass's heart, there, lad," Murdoch said, turning his attention back to the scene below.

"I cannot give her a wean to bind her to me."

"Well, it has been done before"—Murdoch winked at him—"but I agree 'tis not the way of things this time."

Symon pondered the man's words a moment, then understanding dawned. Of course. "If she'll talk to the weans, then they can soften her to our need."

"Aye, lad. Why waste your time bashing your head against a stone wall if you can let someone else take it down bit by bit for you?"

'Twas not Symon's preferred way of doing things, but at the moment he did not have a better plan. "Do you ken the lassie that broke through?"

"Aye, 'tis wee Fia. Mairi's youngest. She's a fey thing, small and pale, and knowing beyond her years. She might just do your work for you."

Symon nodded. "Come on, then. We'll let wee Fia do her work. I'm sure we've something needs doing."

Murdoch nodded. "Aye, Ranald's returned."

"Why did you not say so?" Symon glared at the giant and headed toward the stair.

"I was enjoyin' the view." Murdoch snorted and followed his chief back into the castle.

E*lena examined the blocked-up gate, easing one way* or the other as MacLachlans moved around her. Blocking up a perfectly good gate was a bloody stupid thing to do. She looked about and a weight settled over her. The only way out appeared to be the main gate, well guarded, and obvious.

She did not trust Symon's word any more than she would trust Dougal's. She had learned that lesson too well. She could only depend upon herself to secure her future, which did not include living in this castle full of hopelessness and fear. She had enough of those on her own.

She eyed the old gate once more. Ducking out through a postern gate would have been a much less public way to make her exit than the main gate, but it wasn't a possibility now. Perhaps she could plan some sort of diversion, something to distract the guards. She'd have to ponder that problem for a while.

Just as she turned to continue her circuit of the curtain wall a child bounced against her, nearly falling until Elena caught her.

Looking down, she saw a slight girl of no more than four or five winters standing next to her. Shyly the child slid her small hand into Elena's and smiled. It was the first friendly face she had seen in days.

"Me da made me a doll. Would you like to see it?"

The timid smile on the child's face warmed Elena even

as the ache of partially healed scrapes and bruises surged through the small hand into her own. She squatted down so she was eye to eye with the child. 'Twas not a huge hurt. She could heal it easily with no one, not even the child the wiser. "That would be grand." She sought to distract her with some conversation. "How are you called, little one?"

Elena looked deep into the child's sky-blue eyes and concentrated on the healing heat, seeking out the bruises and a half-healed scrape on her knee, mending the hurts quickly, easily shielding herself from the child's pain.

"I'm called wee Fia. Your hands be warm, mistress."

"And yours are very cold, wee Fia." The child's hands were cold, but the color was ruddy in her elfin face. "Will you call me Elena?"

The child nodded. "Are you a fairy queen . . . Elena?"

Elena stood, one small hand still in hers. "Nay, lassie." Children were more perceptive than adults about some things. Had she noticed the healing? "Why would you think it?"

"You made the Devil smile. Everyone saw it. Me da says only a fairy queen could do that."

"Ah." Elena let out her breath and leaned close to the child. " 'Tis not so hard to make Symon smile, wee Fia. Ye need only speak the truth."

Fia's laughter pealed through the bailey, making people turn and stare. It seemed laughter was a rare thing in Kilmartin Castle.

The sound of it warmed Elena's hungry soul, and she could not keep herself from grinning foolishly back at the child.

"Where is this fine dolly of yours?"

"Follow me."

Elena nodded her assent, and the child tugged her toward a decrepit-looking shed next to the stable.

S ymon slammed open the door to his brother's chamber. "What did you discover?" he demanded before he'd even closed the door behind him.

Ranald continued chewing, forcing Symon to wait, bending him to his will at least in this small way. Ranald always took the advantage when he could. At last he swallowed, took a long swig from his mug, and wiped the ale froth from his mouth with the back of his hand.

"Not as much as you might wish."

Symon glared at him, his irritation growing by the moment.

"Fine." He rose from his chair and crossed to the window, where a flagon and mug stood ready on the ledge. "Here, have some wine. 'Twill calm you, brother," he said handing the drink to Symon. "Elena runs from a man called Dougal of Dunmore."

"The Lamonts' champion," Symon said.

"The chief of Lamont."

"What? Fergus One-Hand is chief of Lamont."

"Fergus was found dead near Castle Lamont . . . his neck broken . . . the day after you rescued Elena from this Dougal."

"But he is not Fergus's heir."

"Nay, that would be the lass you keep here."

"What is this man's connection to Lamont?" he asked, knowing he was not going to like the answer.

"'Tis complicated, that. He appeared five years past, selling his services to the Lamont. 'Twould seem he served well, for he quickly became champion and the La-mont's trusted adviser."

"Five years," Symon said to himself, sipping on the spiced wine. "'Twas not long after that our troubles with the Lamonts began."

"Aye, my thoughts as well," Ranald said.

"Where was he before that?"

"I could not find that out. It seems he appeared from the mist without a background, nor a clan to claim him."

Symon paced the room, stopping briefly to refill his goblet. "And his claim to the chiefship?"

It was Ranald's turn to pace, though it appeared he wished to place more distance between himself and his brother. "There is some . . . dissent . . . among those I spoke with. The very day Elena went missing, he claimed they were wed."

Symon's hand froze, his cup midway to his mouth. She was the chief's child, his only child, and by Highland custom she would be chief at her father's death, at least until she married. A strange dread spread like fire in dry tinder through him. "Wed?"

"Aye. So he says."

"You do not sound convinced."

"My sources say he has had his eye on becoming chief since he first appeared. They would not put it past him to force the lass into marriage to seal his position, but no witnesses have come forward, and neither has the lass. More than one person speculated that he has her held prisoner, or worse."

That would begin to explain some of the mystery surrounding their guest. The chief's daughter, fleeing a bridegroom she did not want, and who it seemed wanted her for the legitimacy she would bring to his claim of chief.

"Did they say naught of her gift?"

"That was most curious. When I suggested that Dunmore's interest might be in her gift, it was as if I spoke gibberish. Either her gift has been kept a close secret, or the entire countryside surrounding Castle Lamont is invested in the secret."

"I find that hard to believe."

"As do I," Ranald said. " 'Tis too good a secret to be held that closely by that many. Perhaps Fergus thought to protect her that way, keeping her apart, her gift hidden?"

"We have heard tales of the Lamont healer for . . . well, for longer than that lass has been alive. How is it possible her own people do not know of her?"

"I do not know, but no one could even describe the lass to me beyond her unusual height and bright hair, things that would be visible from a distance as easily as up close."

It seemed the lass was more of a mystery than Symon had first thought. She was the daughter of the auld chief, perhaps wife to the new. She was a gifted healer, yet her own clan barely knew her. She seemed determined to keep herself apart from everyone, yet a wee lass drew her out with a bit of a smile and a few words. She held herself stiff, apart, bristly, and cool, and yet, beneath his hands and his lips she warmed, melting like frost in the first rays of daylight.

"The Lamonts have been formidable enemies these past years, as if they know our thoughts and strategies before we do." He remembered the ambush that had led to his father's death. "We need to know where this Dougal of

Dunmore came from. I would know what sorts of allies he might have, who trained him, what drives him."

"And where he is."

"What do you mean?"

"He was last seen two days past. No one saw him leave the castle, and his own champion makes excuses, but 'tis believed he is no longer within."

"There is much still to be discovered about this Dougal of Dunmore."

Ranald nodded. "Auld Morag said as much."

Symon had forgotten he had sent his brother to consult the auld woman. "What did she say?"

"She said it would take more than I would find to solve this riddle." Ranald looked at him. "She also said the chief of MacLachlan must once more face his foe. The past would meet the future, and the circle would be complete. It was utter nonsense, as usual."

But Symon did not agree. Auld Morag was difficult to understand at the best of times, but she was nearly always right when you eventually deciphered her riddles.

"Go back. Find out where this Dunmore came from. I cannot say why, but I feel it in my bones that his origin is the key to this mystery. Find that for me, brother, as quickly as you can."

In the meantime, he meant to get what answers he could directly from the lass.

Wee Fia's mum was the castle's alewife. She was great with child, her ankles swollen, and her time near. Elena felt the woman's eyes upon her back as Fia showed her the doll made of straw twisted together and dressed with a few scraps of wool.

"'Tis a bonny doll," Elena said.

"Me da made it."

They played for a bit, Elena scratching the outline of a hut on the dirt floor and Fia arranging bits of bark and rocks for furniture. Elena could not remember ever having a doll, nor playing with another child. Her childhood had been filled with the pain of others, and the keeping of her secret from all who did not need to know of it.

After a while Fia's mum—Mairi she had said when they entered—rose from her stool and moved to stir a cauldron standing over a fire in the middle of the hut.

Elena could see the heaviness in the woman's body, the child within carried low in her belly. A tea of nettle would ease the swelling in her feet. But 'twas not her responsibility, Elena reminded herself. She rose to leave, and as she passed, Mairi grabbed her arm.

"Is it true, mistress?" she asked quietly. "Have you come to save the clan?"

Elena looked into the woman's pale eyes and saw a flicker of hope kindle there. She had not seen its like in any of the adults she had met in Kilmartin so far, and it made her pause.

"Why does Clan Lachlan need saving, Mairi?" Elena searched the woman's tired face for any sign of collusion. Openness met her. Honesty. Hope.

"'Tis hard times for this clan, mistress." She shook her head and returned to her boiling cauldron, stirring a frothy gruel.

"Aye. A body can see there's been hard times. But why?"

"Why? We be cursed, of course. You argued yourself with the blight of Kilmartin. The devil walks our halls in the guise of a chief." She spat, as if ridding herself of a vile taste. " 'Tis the Devil of Kilmartin that causes all our ills. Death and destruction follow him, bringing the end of Clan Lachlan. Ranald is not much better, denying the auld ways." She grimaced. "At least he is not cursed. Little good it does us, though."

Elena looked carefully at the woman as she stirred the huge black pot. She sensed no falseness in her, no evil. Fear. That was the feeling emanating from her. Fear overlaid by a fragile layer of hope. Elena sighed. She did not want this woman's hope, when she had so little of her own.

"Perhaps he will change."

"For the worse, not for the better. I fear for me bairns, mistress. What will become of them when the Lamonts, or the English, or the Campbells, or anyone else who finds us weak, drives us off our land?"

" 'Tis the bairn that makes you worry so. I'll bring you a tea tomorrow that will ease the swelling in your feet, make you more comfortable until the bairn arrives. 'Twill not be long now, I think. A few days at most."

Mairi nodded twice, surprise clear in her eyes. "Fia"— she turned to her daughter—"Mistress Elena is tired. Take her back to her chamber like a good lass." She turned back to her cauldron as Fia dropped the doll and grabbed Elena's hand.

"Do not mind Mum. She's vexed by the bairn. Me da says she'll be fine once it's come."

Elena squeezed the child's hand and let her introduce her to a boy with a badly cut hand, a woman with a twisted and swollen ankle, a man with an odd rash. The parade of injuries and ills continued as they made their way slowly around the bailey. Elena began to think the child knew of her healing ability—impossible—or everyone in Clan Lachlan was in need of a healer's skill. The child stopped only when Elena asked about an old weathered byre off in a corner, flanked on one side by the curtain wall and on the other by a swine pen.

She had watched several children disappear inside as she and Fia walked, until she thought the walls would burst outward from the crowd.

"What's in there?" she finally asked.

A twinkle flashed across Fia's face and a grin spread wide. " 'Tis the auld bolt-hole, mistress."

"A bolt-hole out here?" If a castle had such a thing it was usually well hidden in some unnoticed spot in the bowels of the castle. If this was a true bolt-hole, it was in a very unlikely place.

"Aye, though 'tis a dark tunnel. It is not big enough for a great person like Murdoch, though you might be able to wiggle through. Do you want to try? It comes out by the banks of the burn near a bonny waterfall."

Elena tried to remain calm as the child answered all her questions without her having to voice them. Inside she was giddy and tempted to test the door to her freedom, but she knew she did not need it yet. If Symon followed through on his promise, that would be the safest way for her to go. But if he did not, she would have another plan. She would control her own destiny, find her own safety.

"Nay, Fia, perhaps another time. I would like to return to my chamber now. Can you show me the way?"

The girl bobbed her head, grabbed Elena's arm, and

dragged her toward the kitchen tower, stopping here and there to introduce her to yet another ailing clansman.

As they passed one of the dank undercrofts, Elena heard a voice that stopped her breath.

"'Tis Ranald's wine, the spiced wine he wants." The voice was low, odd, as if its owner sought to change it from its normal range, yet Elena knew that voice, heard it in her nightmares. She grabbed Fia's hand and pulled her away from the doorway, around a corner, and crouched in the shadows.

"What is it, mistress?" the little girl asked, her eyes wide with worry.

Elena realized she was frightening the lass and tried to make her voice light. "A game, wee Fia. 'Tis a game, hide-and-seek. Have you not played it before?"

Fia shook her head, her gaze still fixed on Elena's face.

"We must be very quiet, and if we are not found, we win!" She was sure she would die if the owner of that voice found her. After a moment she heard the voice bid farewell to whoever was in the undercroft, and footsteps moved toward the gate tower where Ranald's chamber was.

"We were not found!" Elena said brightly. "The kitchen stair is just over there, is it not?" she asked the girl.

"Aye."

"And my chamber is above the warm kitchen?"

"Aye."

"I want you to return to your mother now, Fia. Tell her I will visit again tomorrow with a tea for her. I will see you then, sprite."

"But—"

"I can find my way now, sweetling. I thank you for your company." She kissed the girl's forehead and gave her a gentle push in the direction of her mother. When the child had looked back one last time, then scurried into the shed, Elena breathed a sigh of relief and turned her attention to her problem.

How had Dougal entered this castle? She was sure it was his voice she had heard. No matter how he changed its tone, it held that unmistakable oily quality to it, slick and sickening. What was he doing here?

But she knew the answer.

He had come for her. It was surprising that he was being subtle in his tactics. She had been sure any attempts to regain her would have been by an assault on the castle.

Her hands were icy and her breath was difficult to catch, coming in fits and wisps. What to do? Her mind was blank for a moment, filled with blackness. She fought her way through it, knew she had to think, and think clearly if she was to remain free of Dougal.

She was not safe here after all. Odd, that only now did she realize she had felt safe here, at least most of the time. Symon had that effect on her, making her feel protected and safe, even as she questioned his motives. He had protected her once before unasked; would he do less now, especially when the trouble was within his own walls?

She must tell Symon. He would find Dunmore, and then what? It did not matter, as long as he did not give her back to the black-hearted man. And he would not as long as he believed her gift would help him. He needed her gift. Perhaps at long last it would be the means of her protection instead of her pain.

But where was he? Last she had seen him he was pacing the ramparts like a caged beast. She looked about and noticed Fia peeking out the door, watching her. Quickly Elena raised a hand and waved. The small girl grinned and pointed at the kitchen stair. Elena nodded her understanding and headed in that direction. Once inside she could search without the lass thinking she was lost. The last thing she wanted to do was put Fia or any of the other MacLachlans in danger from Dougal.

chapter 8

Symon watched Elena climb up the stone stair from the bailey, lost in thought. He held sanity tightly to him, fighting the first signs of madness through sheer effort.

His thoughts circled Ranald's news over and over again. If Elena was wed to this Dougal of Dunmore, it would be hard to bind her to his clan—or to him. The thought surprised him, but he knew it to be the truth. He would bind her to himself if she would only let him.

But she was wed already.

Here was a lass who did not shun him, did not seem to fear his reputation, though that would change very soon, he knew. He had allowed himself to hope for a better future with this lass. A future that this Dunmore threatened. Despair warred with the fury.

He still had the bargain with her, though. And she would fulfill her part of it now.

Elena stepped out of the sunlight and into the dark space where he awaited her. She gasped as he grabbed her arm and hauled her up the twisting stair leading to his chamber. Pain throbbed in his head and pierced his eyes. Distantly he heard her protest, but the pain was too strong and he needed her to stop it. Now.

At the top of the stair she wrenched her arm free, grabbed her head, and crouched low, as if she expected blows from him.

"I will not harm you," he said, each word costing him in pain and effort.

After a moment she rose. "I'll make you some more willow tea," she said and moved past him to her door.

"Nay, 'twill not be enough this time." He followed her into her chamber. "'Tis time to keep your part of the bargain. Then—" He paused, waiting for the stabbing wave of pain to pass. At last he was able to say, "I have questions for you." A light burst in his head, his stomach clenched, and he nearly pitched to the floor.

He caught his balance and leaned against the damp, cold stone wall, forcing the knifelike pain in his left eye back, away. Sweat dampened his linen tunic, and his muscles shook as if he'd fought fiercely for hours.

Holding on to the wall for support, he groped his way to the bed and lowered himself to sit at its edge. He knew Elena watched, but she did not offer to help.

"'Tis time for you to live up to your part of the bargain," he said when he could, holding his head in his hands lest it explode.

She moved to him slowly, reluctantly, and gently placed

her fingers upon the crown of his head. He felt her flinch at the touch, and he sighed. The damned madness had destroyed the small victory he had gained. She backed away, and he instantly regretted the loss of her touch.

"This is not madness," she said quietly.

"Aye. 'Tis. It will not be long now before the devil shakes me in his fist again."

He opened his eyes slightly, the dim light in the chamber stabbing into his head. She stood, near the door, a puzzled look upon her face.

"I will make the willow tea for you. Jenny will bring it up—"

"Nay. You will bring it, then perform your magic upon me."

"I have no magic, and this is not madness. 'Tis a headache. Perhaps the start of the ague. I promised only to do what I could to dampen the effects of the madness. I am not bound to help you in this."

"I tell you this is the madness, the first stage. It only gets worse from here on. I may not know you when you return. Bring Murdoch with you. He will keep you safe. I cannot say the same for me." He collapsed back on the bed, exhausted with the effort of so many words.

Elena moved to his side again, looking into his eyes. "I sense no madness in you." Her words were calm, but her voice shook. "A tea of willow will be enough."

Symon groaned as another wave of pain arced through his skull. "Tea, then. But do not return without Murdoch."

He heard Elena close the door behind her, and he lay back on the bed, waiting, knowing, fearing what would happen in the next hours. Disappointment twisted in his gut. She had promised to help him, only to deny him when faced with the truth. She was unwilling to even touch him, despite her promise.

E*lena raced down the stair to the kitchen, her horde of* willow gripped in her hand. Never had she experienced such a pain, nor seen anyone work so hard to overcome it. Quickly she enlisted the help of a young boy she'd seen lurking about the kitchens before, fetching a small kettle, and water, setting it to boil over the ever-present fire.

Symon was right. The tea would not be enough, but this was not madness, and she was not bound to aid him.

This was not madness.

She was not bound to aid him.

She repeated that to herself over and over as she waited for the water to boil and the tea to brew. She had nearly convinced herself that she was right when she had the lad carry the kettle up to her chamber.

Moans and cries like that of an injured animal escaped her chamber. The lad froze, and Elena had a sudden need to keep the chief's affliction from the gaping stare of the lad. She took the kettle firmly from him and sent him back to the kitchen, telling him to send Murdoch. Slowly she opened the door, unsure what she would find inside.

Symon paced rapidly, covering the length of the room in four or five strides. His fingers were threaded through his hair, his hands bracketing his head as if it might fall off if he didn't hold it there . . . or maybe he wished to rip it from his shoulders. Elena could feel the pain from where she stood, not sharp and clear the way she could when a warrior was badly injured, but dimly, as if he held it to himself, struggled to keep it from touching anyone around him.

He turned and saw her. "Murdoch?" His voice was barely above a whisper. He squinted at her, the flicker of firelight clearly difficult for him to bear. "Not safe."

Elena moved into the room slowly. "You do not look dangerous to me, or at least no more so than anyone hurting as much." She set the kettle on a hook over the fire and dipped a wooden cup into it, filling it with the tea.

"Drink this." She walked carefully toward him, slowly, not wishing to startle him. Not entirely sure she was safe. But not entirely sure she wasn't, either.

Symon grabbed the cup and downed the liquid. " 'Twill not work," he said as if this was her fault. "Madness . . ." He flinched, dropping the empty cup to the floor and pressing the heels of his hands to his eyes. "Heal me," he demanded.

Elena shook her head, though he was not looking at her. It took all her concentration to hold his pain at bay, to shield herself from it. Even in this strange, dim form she was affected by his physical torment. She stepped back.

Symon grabbed her before she could take a second step and pulled her close. "Heal." He pulled her into a tight embrace, held her tightly to him, her hands spread flat against his chest.

Elena fought for breath. The barely controlled pain burst through her shaky defenses until she felt she would faint from the onslaught. Sweat popped out on her brow. She struggled to break free, to build her wall to protect herself, but she couldn't. He'd broken through as Dougal had never been able to do, and now her only thought was that she might die if she could not gain her release.

"I. Cannot." She pushed against him, but he was too strong.

"Help me!"

The pain was so great she did not understand how he could stand, how he could hold her so tightly against him, how he could demand her help. She could not heal madness, but she had pushed his pain away before. It would be so much easier if he just let her go. But he didn't. She would have to case the pain. Ridding him of it would save her, too.

She worked her hands up from his chest to his face, one hand on either lean cheek. He held her close still, but he closed his eyes and rested his forehead against hers. Elena imagined the heat pouring from her hands into his pain, pushing it back, breaking it apart. Again and again she imagined herself tearing it apart, burning up each piece of torment until there was nothing left. Nothing but a curious blackness, a taint in his blood, but she did not care. She had released herself from the pain.

She removed her hands, but he did not let her go.

"Release me," she said, surprised at the hollow sound of her own voice.

He lifted his head and opened his eyes. Fatigue had drawn lines about them, etching them deeply below and at the corners. His skin held a faint green tinge, and his mouth was a grim line. He let go of her and took a stumbling step backward.

Elena's knees buckled just as Symon's did.

E lena sat where she had fallen for a few minutes, trying to gain her bearings. She'd thought he was different, was beginning to think so, at least. He had treated her with respect, bargaining with her for her gift—not forcing—until it met his needs. Madness? 'Twas not like any madness she had seen or heard of—or felt.

Symon stirred and Elena jumped to her feet, her knees wobbly but holding. She must leave now, before he roused, before he could stop her. Before he could hurt her again.

Determined not to fly into the wood completely unprepared this time, she grabbed the blanket from the end of her bed, wrapping it about her for a cloak. Her sack of willow bark was already tied at her waist. She looked about for anything else that might be of use, but saw nothing. She should take Symon's dagger, long enough to be a good weapon, light enough for her to handle it, but her struggle with Dougal came back at her. He had been hard enough to fight off. Symon was much bigger, much stronger. She did not dare get within grasping distance of him.

Quickly she left the room and hurried down the twisting stair. The servery was busy with the evening meal, and she was able to slip through the harried workers and out the door without drawing attention. The meal must have been in full swing as the deeply shadowed bailey was nearly empty. Elena steadied her breath and headed down the stair, skirting the open area. At last she reached the byre where she had seen the children disappearing this morn. As she slipped inside, she said a quick prayer that wee Fia was correct in her estimation that Elena could fit down the narrow passage.

In the dim light from the bailey Elena could just make out a black hole, low in the wall at the back corner of the hut. She crossed to it, wishing she had a lantern, or a candle, or even a sliver of moonlight to see by. She faced the black maw of the tunnel. She would do this. It was the only way. She would slip away from the MacLachlans and go as far away from her own clan as possible. Somewhere she'd find a clan willing to take her in; a clan who knew nothing of her.

She stared into the lightless space gathering her courage. A rustling made her start. "Who's there?" Her voice filled the byre, reminding her of another voice, one she had heard earlier—Dougal was somewhere in the castle. It was one more reason why she should leave now. The rustling came again, a squeak accompanying it, and she relaxed slightly. Mice were no threat.

She took a deep breath of earthy-damp air. A faint coolness wafted over her cheek, sending tendrils of her hair dancing. 'Twas only a tunnel. Wee Fia said 'twas short. Weans came and went this path daily. 'Twas only a tunnel.

Elena's breath came rapid and shallow. She swallowed. Her ears buzzed, but she bent over slightly and forced herself forward, one foot, then another, into the mouth of the tunnel. Panic grabbed her by the stomach, squeezing her, crushing the breath from her, stopping her feet. Sweat trickled between her breasts. Her hand shook where she braced it against the moist stone wall just inches from her shoulder. Voices sounded behind her, distant, calling. She thought she heard a horse pounding out of the castle. Panic twisted its fist in her gut.

The voices were louder. She heard her own name shouted. Symon must have regained his senses, known she would use this opportunity to run.

She had no choice. No choice. She must run. It was her only hope. But she could not force her feet to move.

The voices came closer. Suddenly the door of the byre

flew open. Elena looked over her shoulder, and into the eyes of a MacLachlan.

"She's here!" he shouted, and Elena's feet took over, racing her down into the mouth of the earth. She ran, down, down, her arms outstretched, her hands scraped raw where they stopped her from running headlong into the walls where the tunnel twisted and turned. Something tripped her, and she landed on her knees. Fear and darkness had her back on her feet immediately, running as fast as she dared in the utter darkness.

After an eternity Elena burst from the ground into a grove of rowan trees, rustling in the gentle night air. The burn burbled nearby, the sound of falling water danced in the distance. Elena braced herself against a tree, gasping in the cool air, desperately trying to calm her mind enough to think clearly.

Slowly she gained control. Her mind quieted into coherent thought. No one had burst out of the tunnel behind her. Fia had been right, she realized. The tunnel, just barely large enough for Elena to scurry down, was too tight for a heavily muscled man to traverse, even if they did know that's where she went.

The moon was rising, casting pale light into the grove, glinting softly off the burn. Elena picked her way through the ferns and bushes to the side of the water, where she kneeled and slaked her thirst, then washed away the grit that had gathered in the scrapes on her hands and knees. She was free—of Symon and Dougal.

A hound bayed. Panic and fear flooded back in, shoving the momentary calm away. A horse pounded through the forest, sending Elena's heart into double time. A whimper escaped her even as she gained her feet and pelted through the thick forest. She had done this once before. She did not have enough luck left to escape again. The horse gained on her and her mind screamed, forcing her feet faster and faster. The horse was beside her, and she heard her name. Still she ran, swerving around trees, crashing through bracken.

Suddenly the horse was beside her again. The rider seemed to throw himself from the saddle directly at her, tackling her. They landed on the ground, and the breath left Elena's lungs in a whoosh. Her sight wavered for an instant as she desperately drew in air.

S ymon heard another horse pounding through the bracken ahead of him. Irritation coursed through him. Damn her anyway, fighting him, then doing what she said she could not, ceasing the madness, thank the heavens. If she had not stopped the pain, he would be haring off against the wind instead of searching for a daft healer too stupid to stay inside the castle walls where she was safe.

Anyone could be lurking about in this wood. From the sound of it, someone was and he prayed it was not Dougal of Dunmore. He would not lose the woman back to him, no matter if they were well and truly wed or not. The lass had no love for the blackheart, and Symon had finally found a way to control the madness.

Nay, he'd not lose her to anyone, not even herself. She was his now, and that was all that mattered. His affliction demanded it. He would do whatever he must to keep her.

But first he had to find the damn lass.

A muffled scream sounded ahead of him. Quickly he

stopped the horse, dropped the reins, and drew his dagger. He ran as quietly as possible in the direction of her voice.

Not far ahead he could hear a struggle, branches breaking, harsh breathing, the sharp sound of flesh hitting flesh, and a quick cry of rage. He turned toward the sound and burst upon a small clearing. The man had her backed against a tree, his hand poised to backhand her. Elena saw Symon, but her assailant, who had his back to him, did not.

"Harlot!" The man spat the word, then swung at her. Elena ducked. His hand scraped the tree trunk, raising a howl from him. "Bitch!" He spun, grabbing Elena as she tried to run past him.

"Let her go," Symon said, his eyes on the other man. Something about him was familiar.

"Do as he says, Dougal," Elena said.

Symon cursed his luck under his breath.

Dougal looked from one of them to the other, though he kept his face in the shadows. He did seem oddly familiar. Symon supposed it was from the last time they had faced each other over this woman.

"I'll not take orders from the likes of you, wife," Dougal said to Elena, though he kept his eyes on Symon now. Elena gasped.

"Then take them from me," Symon said. "Release her. You are on MacLachlan land, and she is under my protection."

"You cannot protect her from her own husband."

Symon glanced at Elena.

She stood as far as away from Dougal as her captured arm would allow. She shook her head, fury flashing in her eyes. "He is not my husband, Symon. He merely wishes it to be so. 'Tis the only way he can rightfully claim to be chief of my clan."

Symon nodded his head, assessing the two before him. These were the very questions he had needed to have answered. But who was speaking the truth? Something about the lass's defiant glare at her captor and Dougal's smug look of satisfaction tipped the balance. He did not like this man, and the nagging sensation that there was more to his dislike than his treatment of Elena would not go away.

"She does not appear to be a cooperative wife," he said, slowly circling the pair, trying to distract Dougal's attention long enough for Elena to get free. He wanted to rip Dougal apart, but he did not want Elena hurt in the fray.

"She is most uncooperative." Dougal pulled her closer, placing her between him and Symon, his arms wrapped possessively about her waist, her arms penned beneath his. His leer made Symon want to clench his fists, but he did not give in to the telltale sign of his anger. "She is a feisty lass."

"'Tis one word for her."

Symon continued to circle, forcing Dougal to turn to keep Elena between them. She had her jaw firmly clenched, and her eyes bored into his, confusion eating away at her courage. He wished he could reassure her, but that would give too much away.

"I found her quite willing, actually."

Dougal started to grin, then must have realized what Symon had said. Elena gasped as he tightened his hold on her. "You did not touch her," he said.

"Nay, she touched me," Symon said with what he hoped was a knowing smile on his lips. "She was a bit clumsy, but a few lessons have smoothed that out." He reached out as if to caress her cheek.

Dougal spun her behind him, releasing her as he pulled his dagger from his belt.

"Run, Elena!" Symon yelled to her and was pleased to see she did just that.

Dougal looked from Symon to the place where Elena had disappeared into the dark forest, then back at Symon. Symon recognized the look of pure hatred, and the face, but he could not place it. In the split second he was distracted, Dougal charged at him, catching him in the right shoulder with his blade, stabbing deeply.

Symon smacked Dougal away, surprise dulling any pain as the knife pulled out of his flesh. The two circled each other.

"You've taken enough that belongs to me," Dougal said through clenched teeth.

"I've taken naught that belongs to you." Symon saw a movement behind the other man.

Dougal spun, ducking the branch Elena tried to hit him with, and hooking an arm around her waist. "You'll not have her, too!" he cried over his shoulder as he dragged her into the surrounding forest.

Symon pelted after them, catching them up quickly. He grabbed Dougal by the hair, stopping him with a vicious jerk. Off balance, the man lost his grip on Elena, who quickly moved out of his reach as he fell to his knees, Symon's dagger at his throat.

Rage filled Symon. More than anything he wished to slit the man's throat, both for his assault on himself and for his attempted abduction of Elena. But the idiot's words wouldn't go away. "You've taken enough that belongs to me," he'd said.

"What have I taken of yours?" Symon said, irritated with himself for wanting the answer.

Dougal said nothing, so Symon jerked the man's head backward until he glared up at him.

"What have I taken?" Symon demanded.

"You always were a blind one."

"Why were you within the castle today?" Elena's question cut through the darkness.

Symon glanced quickly at her. In the castle? Impossible!

"I was not in the castle, you daft bitch. I've been in these woods for two days now, but I had not figured out how to gain entrance yet when you came running into my waiting arms."

"I never—"

"She's a bit off in the head."

Symon jerked the other man's head again, causing him to gasp. "Then you'll not be wanting her back."

"Nay, I'll have her back, if I have to kill every last MacLachlan to have her."

Something in Symon snapped. He jerked the man to his feet and shoved him away. "Then start here. Start now, for you'll have to come through me first."

Dougal took one look, then turned, and sprinted away. Symon started after him.

"Nay, Symon, don't leave me here!" Elena cried out.

Symon stopped, torn between hunting down the dog and killing him or staying with the frightened woman. He listened as the crashing of Dougal's passage faded and the night closed in around him.

"Come. We need to get you back to safety before your Dougal finds his courage again."

She looked at him strangely, her eyes glistening as if she might cry, but she didn't. "He is not my Dougal, nor will he ever be," she said quietly, pushing past him in the direction of the clearing.

"Then you'd best not run to him again," Symon said, unable to stop the frustration he felt from slipping out.

She rounded on him, anger snapping in her eyes. "If you had not forced my gift—"

" 'Twas necessary—"

" 'Twas not madness!"

He closed the distance between them, and she took a half step backward. He wanted to shake her, to make her understand, but he forced his hands to remain at his side.

"I do not know what experience you have of madness, but what you saw earlier—what you stopped—was the beginnings of my curse. You pushed back the devil. You say you cannot, but you did, at least the worst of it."

Elena shook her head, confusion masking her face. "I have tried to heal madness before. 'Twas nothing like what you endure. Never has pain been part of it."

"I do not know of others' madness, but mine, mine has many parts, beginning and ending with pain."

She nodded. "Then I was wrong to fight you. 'Twill not happen again."

"I thank you for that. And I am sorry to have scared you so much you felt you must escape."

"Escape, aye, but I did not run to Dougal. I did not know he was out here."

"I know that, lass. I have seen how you feel about the

man. I shall hope you never come after me with such a weapon."

Elena looked at the ground. "I could not let him hurt you."

Symon reached out to raise her chin when a deep pain reminded him of Dougal's single victory. He lowered his arm again. The wound was not so great as to impair his movement. He looked at the tired lass, remembered seeing her collapse, even as he had. Saw the evidence, once more, of Dougal's harsh treatment of her. She had been through much this day, and he would not call upon her to tend him now.

"Besides, I thought he was within Kilmartin Castle." She quickly recounted what she had overheard this afternoon.

"We need to get back to Kilmartin," he said, his mind spinning with the news. "If Dougal of Dunmore really was able to enter the castle, we need to find out how he did it before he tries again." He helped her up onto the horse, then climbed up behind her and urged the horse homeward.

chapter 9

❧

Elena paced the confines of her chamber, her prison. True, there was no lock upon the door, but with Dougal somewhere out beyond the castle walls, leaving on her own was no longer a possibility. Her safety might not even be assured within the castle. She knew she had heard Dougal within the undercroft. Positive. Yet his denial had sounded so . . . honest? Symon acted as if he believed her, but she knew she must not let down her guard.

And what of Symon? It wasn't until they were back inside the castle and he had helped her down from the horse that she had even realized he had been hurt. It was uncanny how he was able to shield his pain from her at times, almost as if he sensed it could hurt her. But that was impossible. He didn't know. And yet, he hadn't mentioned his wound to her. Hadn't asked her even to bind it for him, much less to heal it.

And what did that mean? Was he sticking to his part of the bargain, even though he claimed she had not done her part? More likely, he simply did not trust her.

She took a deep breath, stopping it half-drawn as her ribs throbbed and burned. Distracted by her injuries, she turned her attention inward. Focusing on the place the pain beat strongest, she gathered her strength and concentrated. Healing herself was far more difficult than healing others.

As she struggled to ease the bruising, she remembered how it had come to be that way. The scene flooded back to her in all its vivid detail. When had Symon gotten hurt? It must have been when she ran into the wood to find a weapon. And yet he had been circling Dougal when she'd returned. Heat rose up her cheeks as she realized her return had given Dougal yet another chance to take her. She should have done as Symon said. Even hurt, he had been more than capable of defending himself against Dougal.

Shame washed through her, cold and bitter. She was the reason Symon had been out there. She had run off, put him in danger, indeed gotten him hurt, then pulled the wrath of Dougal onto this entire clan. Of course he did not wish her tending him.

Exhausted, she ceased her pacing and sat down. She hadn't allowed herself to consider it, had been too busy trying to find a way to escape Kilmartin, but she realized tonight, as they neared the castle gate, that in a few short days this place was more a home to her than Castle Lamont had ever been. The people had been kind to her, happy to see her, sure she would help them, though they didn't realize exactly how. There was something for her to do here, without her gift. But it could never be her home.

Her gift wasn't a secret. The Devil of Kilmartin would forever hold her in his grip, hostage to the knowledge he shared with her. And yet, she had a hard time envisioning the Symon she was coming to know with the image his by-name conjured. Of course he was mad. He claimed she had pushed back his madness, though that was impossible. But there was nothing evil about him, nothing demonic, unless you counted the effect his kiss had had upon her senses, or the way he drew her gaze whenever he was near.

The way he made her think of a future she couldn't have. A future she could not have because of her gift.

Yet even as he forced her gift from her, Symon had been concerned for her safety, and left no bruises in his wake, as her father and then Dougal always had.

The thought of Dougal and his vow to kill as many MacLachlans as it took to take her back sickened her. She remembered the burnt-out cottage, with Molly and the wee bairn, her husband missing . . . or worse. Wee Fia's elfin grin flashed through her mind, and she knew she could not let Dougal do anything to harm these people who had taken her in, trusted her with their hope.

She could not let him hurt these people any more than he already had. Which meant she had to leave, but not to return to him. She must leave in such a way that Dougal knew she had gone, even drawing his attention to her flight. But she would not allow herself to fall back into his clutches.

She must ask Symon to help her. He would by necessity know her whereabouts when she left, which was not to her liking. It would be better if no one who knew of her gift knew where she went, but it could not be helped. It was the only way to escape Dougal and keep him from harming these people further.

Before she could change her mind she rose from her bed, straightened her gown, and ran her fingers through the tangles in her hair.

She opened her door and peered out into the dark hallway. No sound came from below, and the castle had the feeling of very late night about it. Quietly she knocked at Symon's door, which swung open almost immediately.

Murdoch scowled down at her, and she resisted the urge to flee.

"Come in, lass," he said quickly. "Perhaps he'll let you tend to him. He's angry as a cornered cat-a-mountain and won't let me near enough to see to it." He stepped back and revealed Symon, his plaid hanging about his hips, his upper body bare and gleaming in the flicker of candlelight. Blood oozed from the outer part of his right shoulder.

Elena entered slowly. "I will see to him, Murdoch." She looked at the giant. "Will you leave us?"

His eyebrows rose and he looked from her to Symon, who nodded his assent. Murdoch shrugged. "You know where to find me if I'm needed."

Symon grunted and the other man left, pulling the door closed behind him.

"Sit. I will bind your shoulder," she said, turning to the clean strips of linen Murdoch had obviously brought for that purpose. A bowl of steaming water and a bloody rag sat next to them.

"I do not want your care."

Elena wasn't surprised at the sharp note in his voice. She picked up the rag and the bandages and moved to where he had sat upon the edge of his bed. Slowly she began to wash away the blood, revealing an angry-looking wound. She went to lay her hand upon his arm, seeking the extent of the wound, but he jerked away from her touch.

"You do not need to heal me. 'Twill heal fine on its own."

She looked directly into his pale green eyes, snapping with anger. "Aye, no doubt. But 'twill heal faster if you let me tend it, or at the very least let me bind it so the blood will stop flowing."

He glowered at her a moment, like a child, told to do something he did not want to do. He drained the goblet he held, tossed it on the bed, and stuck his arm out for her to see to.

Elena looked at him a moment, deciding. She could bind it only and that would do, or she could show her good faith by restoring his sword arm to full health. She needed his help, and 'twas not a terrible wound; indeed she could barely sense any pain. She had healed much worse than this and survived easily. If she showed him she was willing to help him, perhaps he would be more willing to help her. It was in the best interest of his clan, and her own.

She knew he watched her, could feel the heat of his gaze on her skin, but she did not look at him again. Instead, she lowered his arm to his side, then closed her eyes, slowed her breathing and rubbed her hands together. Heat gathered in them. She opened her eyes and placed her hands on either side of the puncture. Dimly she felt pain there, as if she was a great distance from it. She pushed the heat from her hands into his skin, moving her hands around the wound, willing it in her unique way to close itself, heal, heat, warmth, fire.

She took another breath and placed her hands over the wound, imagining the breath of a fiery red dragon swirling around and around, closing the muscle and skin.

Symon's large callused hand closed over hers, startling her out of her trance. "'Tis enough," he said, pulling her hands from his arm and holding them in his own.

Elena looked down at her handiwork. The wound was healed completely, leaving behind only a pink line, marking where the damage had been. And yet there was more, she could see it in his eyes, and now that he had loosened his control over the pain, she could feel it in his blood, the strange blackness that ran there. She closed her eyes and felt his hands grip hers more firmly.

"Lass—"

"Shush," she whispered. "Let me finish."

He didn't say another word, and she let herself sink into the taint. It was unlike anything she had experienced before, black and vile, snaking through his body. She followed it, pushing it ahead of her, burning it with her gift. Slowly she overcame it, purging whatever it was from him.

Gradually she became aware of her name being spoken, quietly, just by her ear. She opened her eyes and found her hands spread over Symon's chest, his own gripping her upper arms, holding her close. Dazed, she let him guide her to sit next to him. Never had she experienced such a healing. There had been no hurt nor pain after the first moments, and yet she knew she had healed him. Euphoria spread through her, mixed with the exhaustion she expected.

"Was that the madness?" she asked.

He had one arm around her shoulder, and he pulled her

tight against him. "Aye. The madness you did not think you could conquer."

But it did not feel like madness. If felt like . . .

Lifting her hand to his lips, he kissed her knuckles lightly, pulling her attention to his mouth, distracting her.

"Sleep now, lass."

Sleep would be good, but there was something else she needed to do, to say, first.

Symon nudged her back onto the thick mattress, then spread a deliciously heavy covering over her.

What had she come to tell him? She started to speak, then gave in to the weight of his finger against her lips.

"We have all the time we need now."

Fatigue overwhelmed her, dragging her eyes closed. She'd sleep, then she would remember what she had come to say.

*H*ounds snapped at her hems as she stumbled through the dark forest, searching for something. Teeth scraped her heels, sending streaks of terror through her, yet she raced forward. At any moment one of the huge dogs would take her down. She dashed through the last of the trees, thunder rumbling around her, and into the arms of a man.

The hounds set up a howl as if they had lost something dear to them. The man held her tightly against him, the dark of the night obscuring his face. Oddly, she didn't panic in his arms. There was no misery, no twisting fear striking through her.

Safe.

She reached for him, but her hand came away bloodied.

He crumpled at her feet, and she bent, desperate to use her gift, to heal him, but it wouldn't come. She struggled against it, forcing it to heal him, but the heat wasn't there. Dougal stood before her, laughing, his bloodied claymore raised high over his head. Thunder clapped over them and rain sheeted down. Wind dragged at her, pulling her away as Dougal's claymore slashed down—not over Symon, but over her mother's head. . . .

E lena sat straight up in the bed, her breath coming in gasps, tears coursing down her cheeks. She rubbed them away with the backs of her hands as she tried to remember what had awakened her. Thunder rumbled outside and she grasped at the wisps of the dream, a heavy sense of foreboding telling her she needed to remember. Symon had been in danger. . . .

"Symon!" When he didn't answer she felt the hounds of her dreams close in on her. "Symon!"

A soft snoring stopped mid-breath, and before she could fully focus on the form lying near the fire, he was beside her, his weight dipping the mattress.

"Do not be afraid." His hands were warm on her shoulders. She shuddered, remembering the scene with Dougal, and the wound she'd healed in Symon. He pulled her close, cradling her against his broad chest, his arms circled about her.

"Shh. You are safe, lass."

He stroked her hair, calming her and warming her at the same time. His hands roamed over her back, easing the tense muscles there.

Sighing, she rested her cheek against his chest, the curly

hair tickling her where the lacing on his tunic was open. She breathed in deeply. The scent of smoky peat fires and the dark, earthy smell of moss-carpeted forests mingled with another scent that was distinctly Symon, surrounding her, wrapping around her as securely and comfortingly as his arms did.

She inhaled again and rubbed her cheek against his chest, enjoying the sensuous feel of his warm skin against her own. She let herself sink into the sensation.

Symon's hands traveled over her, trailing heat and a strange tingling. She looked up and was caught by the expression in his eyes. The flickering light of a lone candle revealed none of the clear-green eyes she'd come to know. They were black, the pupils wide. And they were fixed upon her mouth. His breathing came rapid and shallow. He looked as if a battle raged within him.

She touched his face, disturbed and intrigued by his concentration. "Symon?"

He moistened his lips.

Elena's fingers moved to his mouth, tracing the path his tongue had taken. She couldn't help it. The sight of his mouth shook her, causing thoughts and sensations she'd never experienced before to swirl through her.

She wanted to taste his mouth.

She should have been shocked at her thoughts, but she wasn't. Heat rose in her belly, coiling there, sending curling tendrils of longing out through her limbs. Her breasts tingled, aching with need. The heat sank deeper.

Her fingers still traced his mouth. She moved her hands to his face and drew him toward her.

"Elena," he managed to whisper, his lips so close to hers she felt the caress of his breath there. He threaded his fingers through her hair, though she couldn't tell if it was to keep her away, or draw her closer. His eyes, dark and serious, searched hers. He hesitated, then closed the distance between them.

Elena had recognized the beginnings of desire in herself a moment before. Now she felt its full blinding force. His lips were warm and surprisingly soft against her own. Slowly he deepened the kiss, causing a shattering storm of sensation as his tongue swirled over hers. She abandoned herself to the experience, savoring the rasp of his whiskers on her face, the heat and wet of his mouth, the circle of his arms as he pulled her to him.

She took as much as she could, then gave it all back to him, her instincts guiding her where experience could not. She was on her knees now, though she didn't remember how she got there. His hands were on her, caressing, kneading, demanding. He slid one hand from her back, skimming it over her ribs and up to lift the weight of her breast.

Never had she felt the heat racing through her now. She had never felt desire—her own or a man's—before. It was a dangerous, drugging thing that pulled at her senses, overwhelming her until she could barely think, barely remember why this could not be.

Thunder rumbled outside, triggering the memory of her dream, and suddenly she understood exactly why she could not let this happen. She pushed away and sat back on her heels.

"What is it, lass?" Symon reached for her again, his eyes clouded with passion.

She swam up from the flood of her own desire burning through her veins. She wanted nothing more than to throw herself back into this man's arms, but the image of Dougal's claymore slashing downward over first Symon's head, then her mother's frightened her more than Dougal ever had. The dream's warning was clear. She must not allow herself to care for this man, or she would suffer the same—or worse—as when her mother died.

"I . . . we can't do this." Wanting would only bind her to him, and she could not let that happen. She moved off the bed, putting as much distance as possible between them.

Symon raked a hand through his hair, and Elena could have sworn she saw it shake. "You are not wed to Dougal, are you?"

She shook her head vehemently.

"You wish my protection?"

She nodded, reluctantly.

"Then let us wed. We can say our vows to each other now, here. Then you will be safe and this will be proper"—he left the bed and crossed to her, taking her hands in his—"and right."

Elena's heartbeat tripled, and she had to force herself not to react to his touch. Wed him! She carefully removed her hands from his and crossed her arms in front of her. What would it mean to wed the Devil?

"I will keep you safe," he said quietly, "and you will keep me well."

Disappointment choked her before she could deny it. This seduction was just another way to make her stay. She found she had hoped it was for different, more personal reasons even as she used her disappointment to shore up her resolve.

"I will not stay here. 'Tis too dangerous."

"But you are safe as long as you remain within the castle."

"Nay." She was in as much danger now as she had been when Dougal held his knife to her throat. She grasped for reasons she could tell him. "Dougal has been within these walls. I could not mistake his voice. But even had he not breached these walls, I would not stay."

Symon just looked at her, his face stormy.

"You heard his threat." Her voice dropped nearly to a whisper. "He does not threaten lightly."

"You think leaving will nullify his threat?"

"As long as he knows I am gone."

"And if Dougal were not out there?" He moved closer, distracting her with the effect his body had upon hers. "Could you not make this your home? My people seem to have accepted you. Could you not help them as any simple healer would? You could offer them that small comfort, that aid."

Elena remembered her promise to Fia, and her mum, and all the others who would benefit from her herb knowledge.

"Aye, perhaps, if Dougal were not out there. But he is. I will not give him cause to bring further harm to you"— she looked at him quickly—"or your people."

A smile played at the edges of Symon's mouth, reminding her of the havoc those lips could lay upon her senses.

"'Twill not solve the problem of my people. They need your help as much as I do."

Elena's heart skipped, the dream once more flashing through her mind—Dougal's claymore slashing down.

Destroying everything. There had to be a way to save something.

"Perhaps if I trained someone," she said. "Jenny? At least she could learn a little."

"There is a stillroom, though like as not 'tis in need of stocking. I do not think anyone has used it since my own mum died."

She looked at him, wishing there were some way to solve both of their problems at once. But there wasn't. "Will you take me away from here, find me a place to live free of Dougal and all who know of my gift?"

Symon brushed his knuckles across her cheek. "Your destiny is here, lass. Why do you fight it?"

"I need to be away. Dougal, once he sets his mind to something, does not release it easily." 'Twas the truth, though not the entire truth. She would not tell him she feared if she stayed she would fall in love with him, then die with him. "He will do as he said, kill as many MacLachlans as it takes to get me back." She looked at him defiantly. "I will not let him harm this clan, and I will never go back to him."

At last Symon nodded. "Very well. I will not keep you here against your will, but it will take some time to find somewhere safe for you to go." He thought a moment. "Perhaps my mother's people, the Munros. They live in the far northern Highlands. Yes. It will take some time to make the arrangements, a fortnight, perhaps more. During that time, will you give young Jenny what knowledge you can of herbs and such?"

"What of Dougal?"

"I will take care of Dougal. He will not get inside Kilmartin again."

Elena reached up and kissed him on the cheek. "Thank you. I will find Jenny and start right away." She turned, desperate to get away from him now, lest the wanting that filled her, making her heart pound and her breath come too rapidly, overcame her good sense once more. At the door she looked back. The expression of sadness on Symon's face stopped her.

"What of you, Symon? Will you be all right—the madness—when I'm gone?"

"I do not know," he said quietly. "I know you have cleared my mind and my body of the affliction, but I do not know how long 'twill last."

It was strange, the way this madness reacted to her gift. What little experience she had with the unbalanced was that the affliction was in the mind, not in the blood—

She felt the blood drain from her own face, and she quickly crossed the room back to Symon.

"What is it, lass?"

Silently Elena placed both palms against his chest. She tried to ignore the skitter of excitement the feel of his warm skin beneath hers caused and instead forced herself to focus on the internal. She closed her eyes, concentrating, searching, but there was nothing. No madness, no evidence of anything wrong with his mind. She tried to remember exactly what she had done to overcome the blackness in his veins. She had burned the blackness from his blood . . . and she could never do that with madness.

Her eyes flew open and she found herself staring into his brilliant green gaze.

"What?"

"Symon, 'tis . . ." The ramifications of what she was about to say hit her, throwing all that she had thought of this man, and his clan, into turmoil. "'Tis not madness you suffer under."

"Aye, 'tis—"

"Nay," she said quickly, "I can do naught for the devil-ridden. 'Tis not madness. 'Tis poison."

chapter 10

❦

"Poison? Impossible." Symon pushed her away and strode across to the window, where the first rosy tinges of dawn were washing the sky. "Poison would not cause madness. I'd be dead."

"That depends on what poison was used, and what the poisoner wished to accomplish."

"Who would poison me?" He turned to face her, and found her before the fire, warming her hands. "And why?" He reached for her, spinning her to face him. "Why steal my sanity? It would be so much simpler just to do away with me."

"I do not know. I should have seen the truth much sooner, but you were so sure 'twas madness, I did not question what I felt."

"And what did you feel?" he asked, unable to keep the disbelief from his voice.

She shook her head. "You do not believe me."

"You ask me to deny my own experience, trust in a *Lamont*"—the name was like a curse—"believe that one of my own kinsmen, one of Clan Lachlan, would stoop so low as to poison his chief?"

"You are the one who bade me heal you, Devil."

Her words smacked him as hard as any hand could. "Aye. And you did. For that I am grateful. But this . . ." He could not even begin to imagine the consequences of such a thing.

"You should be relieved," she said, as if trying to soften the blow.

He glared at her. Relieved? When someone he had trusted, served, was poisoning him?

"Think, Symon. If 'tis poison, then all you need do is find the source and you will solve your problem. You do not even need me."

Something in her words caused his stomach to clench, but he could not focus on feelings right now; he had to think, and think clearly.

"Is there no one here who wishes you harm?"

Symon shook his head once. "Nay."

"You are universally loved by everyone?" Her voice held a note of derision.

He glared at her and began to pace the length of the room. " 'Twould have to be someone who wished me ill before the madness—before my afflict—" He cast about for a new way of describing what had happened to him. "Before all this happened. There are plenty who would see me gone from these walls now, but not when this first came upon me."

Elena moved to the stool and sat, facing him, the light of the fire behind her turning her already vivid hair fiery-colored. The prophecy came back to him. *When flame and madness mingle . . .* Is this how they would mingle, in common cause to find his poisoner? Would she leave him—them—if they did solve this mystery? Of course he had already promised to find a new home for her within a fortnight. But that was only to get her to agree to stay, give him longer to convince her that Kilmartin was where she belonged.

"When did the feigned madness start?"

"I do not speak of that time."

"Then how can I help you?" She rose to leave.

Symon noted the determined look on her face, and realized he was pushing away the one person whom he was sure had a good reason to wish him well and whole again. He swallowed, considering the best way to begin, the best way to tell the lass of his greatest humiliation. "Sit. I will tell you."

She nodded and arranged herself on the stool again, the fire once more glowing in her hair. She folded her hands in her lap and assumed a pose of patience, though the snap in her eyes belied her outward calm. Clearly, she had a great deal to gain by him being poisoned instead of mad. He should be skeptical because she had such a huge stake in it, yet he had felt her healing him, seen the concentration it took, and the toll it took upon her. He knew how her body responded to his and was sure that was not feigned. He had to trust someone, and she appeared to be the one destined to share his burden.

"You remember the circle where first we met?"

"Aye."

" 'Twas in that very circle that the madness visited itself upon me the first time."

She did not say a word, so he continued, turning away from her, unwilling to see the irritation in her face turn to pity, or hate. He had seen enough of that and he wanted no more of it. He would tell her what happened only because it might help sort out this trouble.

"My father, Ranald, Murdoch, a few others, and I were hunting, early last spring. The food stores in the castle were low, and we thought to bring in some fresh game, perhaps a roebuck or two, or a boar. We'd planned a feast of sorts, for no particular reason, other than we were all sorely tired of porridge and salted meat. We rode out, happy to be out of the castle after so many weeks of cold and darkness. As we neared Auld Morag's cottage, we were set upon by your kinsmen. 'Twasn't the first time Lamonts had attacked us on our own land, and 'twas usually more by way of reiving than true harm, but this time 'twas different. They ambushed us, chasing us down the glen until we took a stand within the circle of stones. There weren't many of them, but the mist came up and 'twas difficult to tell who was who and where an attacker might come from." He looked over at her, not knowing exactly what he was hoping for from her. She sat, her face full of concern, but she did not try to stop him, nor defend her kinsmen.

"What happened then, Symon?" she asked, her voice quiet and gentle.

"I do not know."

"What do you mean?"

"I mean I do not know. The world went fuzzy and tilted beneath my feet. I don't know what happened because I did not stay. Ranald says I howled and he thought I'd been hurt, then he saw me run off into the mist, out of the circle, leaving my da and all the other lads to fend off the Lamonts on their own."

"Were you hurt before the madness came over you?"

"Nay."

"Did you have aught to eat or drink before you left these walls?"

Symon tried to remember, but it had been over a year before. He shrugged. "I cannot say for sure. 'Tis likely I had porridge and perhaps some ale, since 'twas mostly what we were eating at that point."

Elena was lost in thought. "When was the next time it happened?"

Symon had to think a moment. "'Twas a fortnight, more or less. Then another fortnight after that. It seemed to fall into that pattern for a few months, coming on once a fortnight, lasting a day or two, then all would be well."

"Did anyone try to help you?"

"Aye, Ranald, and Murdoch, but no one else wanted aught to do with me, even though I was their chief."

"What?" she rose to her feet, coming toward him.

He pulled himself from the painful memories and looked at her. "Ranald—"

"Nay, what do you mean, you were the chief then? You said your da was alive."

Symon grimaced. "He died that first time, in the circle, after I ran away. I was not there to guard his back as I should have been. 'Tis my fault he died there. No one who was there that day has ever accused me of such, but I feel it in their eyes. I know I am chief only so long as they choose to keep their own counsel. 'Twill not be long now before one of them decides I cannot lead this clan any longer."

"Could it have been one of them who poisoned you?"

"I do not see how. I don't know over much about poisons, but I do not think I ate or drank anything the others did not also consume that day. I was not injured before the battle. I do not see how it could be. Perhaps you're wrong, lass. It could not be poison. 'Tis some form of madness you have not seen before."

She nodded, then pressed her palm to his chest once more, closing her eyes, concentration etched over her beautiful features. Symon itched to trace her mouth with his thumb as she had done to him, but something in her posture told him not to move.

"There is no trace of anything coursing through you now," she said, then looked up at him, only tilting her chin up a bit to stare into his eyes. "Beware what you eat or drink, and note carefully who serves you. 'Tis clear we cannot solve this mystery right away, but with careful observation, we can find the culprit." She lifted her hand from his chest and pushed his hair behind his ear, her palm whispering past his cheek. "I know you do not wish to believe that someone could poison you, but I truly believe it to be so."

He grabbed her wrist and brought her palm to his mouth. He kissed her lightly in the center of her hand, then released her. "I must discuss this with Ranald—"

"Nay, you must not!"

Her vehemence stopped him. "Why not?"

"You must not discuss this with anyone until we know more. Anyone could be the culprit."

"Not Ranald. He is my brother."

"Does Ranald have anything to gain if you are no longer chief?"

"Nay . . ." But that wasn't entirely true. Such a thought smacked of disloyalty. Ranald was his brother; he would never cause such misfortune to befall his own family and clan. "Nay."

Elena watched him carefully for a moment. "Fine. Still, 'twould be best if this was just between you and me for now. When we know more, have some proof, then will be the time to discuss it with Ranald."

He did not like what the lass implied, but he had to agree that right now, 'twas only her theory that this was poison. Ranald did not care overmuch for the lass, anyway; Symon would not give his brother reason to deride her.

"Very well. We will keep it between us, but not for long, Elena."

A knock came at the door and Symon opened it. Murdoch stood, a grin on his face and a tray full of food in his hands. "Ah, the lass talked sense into . . ."

Symon grabbed the tray as it wobbled in the man's hands.

"Your shoulder . . . 'tis healed . . . how?"

Symon spun away and handed the heavy tray to Elena, then scooped a clean tunic from a peg on the wall and quickly slid it over his head. "Twasn't as bad as it appeared. Really barely a scratch."

"But I saw—"

"Forget what you saw, lad. 'Twas barely a scratch, you ken?"

He knew Elena held her breath, could feel her fear, though she stood paces away from him and he wasn't facing her. It was almost as if in healing him she had created some connection between them, joining them . . .

Joining them.

Murdoch finally seemed to work through what Symon had said to him, shook his head as if a fly buzzed him, then quickly smiled and took the tray back from Elena. "Right. Well, I thought the two of you might be hungry." He balanced the tray on the stool Elena had sat upon. "Wee Fia's been asking for you, lass. I told her you'd be down in a while."

"Thank you, Murdoch," she said, and Symon could feel her start to breathe again.

"Is there anything ye'll be needing, then?" the man asked, looking from Elena to Symon. "Somat to drink? A priest?" The twinkle in his eye spurred Symon to action.

"Nay, lad, out! Tell young Fia that Elena will see her very soon."

The giant winked at Symon and tipped his head in question toward Elena.

"Out!" Symon said, a grin at the man's audacity lightening his thoughts for a moment.

Murdoch left, chuckling.

"You'll have to excuse the daft bastard. He means well."

Elena nodded and picked up an oat cake. She nibbled it, staring into the fire. She picked up the porridge, spooning a bite into her mouth, then staring again, into the fire. At last she picked up the mug of milk, tasted it, and repeated the staring. At last she looked at him over her shoulder. "I think 'tis safe to eat this. I get no feeling of poison from any of it."

Understanding burst through him. "You don't have to play the king's taster, Elena. I'm sure Murdoch is above reproach. He has naught to gain by my downfall."

Elena leveled him with a glare. "Do you like the madness you've experienced these many months?"

Her question required no answer. She knew the answer as well as he did.

"I will go find Fia," she said. "May I have her take me to the stillroom? There are many here who would benefit from a few simples."

Symon nodded, tired of arguing with her. He needed time to consider all the ramifications of her theory. She grabbed two oat cakes and quickly left. He moved to the fireside, taking up Elena's vigil there.

E*lena found wee Fia waiting in the bailey, her straw* dolly tucked under one arm. She was shifting from one foot to another. Her face lit up when she spied Elena and she skipped and hopped her way across the crowded yard stopping just in front of her.

"Good morn, sprite, how are you?"

"I have a loose tooth!" She wiggled it with a grubby finger. "Mum says 'tis a good thing. Means I'm a big girl now, so I'll be able to help with the bairn when it comes."

"Aye. 'Tis an important job, that. You'll be the big sister and have to teach the bairn all kinds of important things."

"Do you have a sister, Elena?"

Elena got to her feet and took the child's hand. "Nay, 'twas only me."

"You did not have anyone to teach you important things, then?"

Elena shook her head, thinking the child was more correct than she could ever know.

"I can be your sister," Fia said shyly.

Elena grinned down at her and squeezed her hand. "I'd like that, sprite. Can you start by showing me the stillroom?"

Fia wrinkled her tiny brow and wrenched her mouth about as if she were deep in thought. Elena stifled a giggle. "I do not know what a stillroom is," Fia finally said, very solemnly. "But if 'tis here, me mum will know. She's auld as ever and knows everything about the castle."

"Let's go ask your mum, then," Elena said, hiding her smile from the child.

Wee Fia pulled her hand, and before Elena realized where the child was taking her, they were in the tunnel leading out to the gate. Elena stopped and Fia looked up at her with big eyes.

"Where is your mum today?" Elena asked.

"She's out gathering wood for the kettle fire."

Elena felt a moment of panic at the thought of anyone being out where Dougal could get at them. She pulled the child back into the courtyard, away from the yawning gate.

"We'll ask someone else—"

"But me mum knows—"

"You will not leave" came Symon's rumbling voice behind them.

Fia squeaked and jumped behind Elena, hiding her face in her skirts.

"We were not," Elena insisted. Quietly she said to him, "Do you think 'tis safe for women to be out there alone?"

"They are not alone."

Elena nodded, understanding that though he was not completely convinced Dougal had been in the castle, he knew all too well that he was somewhere outside it. And he was taking steps to protect his people.

"It seems wee Fia doesn't know the whereabouts of the stillroom." She reached behind her and urged the child to her side. "Perhaps you could tell us where 'tis?"

Elena watched as Symon looked at the wean, snuggled up against her side, fists clutched in her gown. His face softened and he crouched down so that he was no closer to the little one, but at the same level.

"Aye, you know it, lassie," he said, his voice a bit lighter than usual, a bit less rough. "'Tis the herb room, behind the wine cellar, just over there." He pointed at the undercroft where she had heard Dougal's voice, but his eyes were on Fia.

The child nodded, then took Elena's hand and skirted around Symon, in the direction of the dark storage room. Elena felt her heart speed up and her breath hitch. What if Dougal was in the castle? What if he was lying in wait for her? Sweat popped out on her brow, and she glanced back at Symon, who stood now, watching them go. She did not wish to frighten wee Fia, but she could not bring herself to enter the dark cellar. She balked at the doorway, and Fia looked up at her.

"I almost forgot." Symon's voice came from behind her, more jovial than she had ever heard it. "I need to select a bottle of wine. May I accompany you?" he asked as he caught up to them.

Elena tried to thank him with her eyes, but he just nodded slightly at her and preceded them into the cool storage room.

They all stopped just inside, allowing their eyes to adjust to the dim light. Sunshine filtered through the arched opening but did not penetrate the back of the large space. She heard a clink and saw an oil lamp flare to life. Symon lifted it and proceeded to the rear of the space. There, illuminated by the flickering lamplight, was a substantial door with a large iron latch on it. For a moment the latch seemed frozen in place, then suddenly Symon forced it free with a metallic scrape.

Elena moved nearer the door as he disappeared inside. The cold, musty smell of long disuse oozed out of the doorway and wrapped around her. She stood, sure that Symon had been swallowed by the eerie darkness, when his voice echoed out at her.

"'Tis not much to look at, lass, but you should come in."

Elena eased over the threshold and watched Symon move about the small cave-like chamber. A second lamp flared, then another. "I do not see anyone here but you and me, and that imp peeking in the doorway." He winked at Elena. "I'm sure wee Fia can help you from here." He gave the child time to scurry in the door and around the far edge of the space before he took his leave.

Elena and Fia spent the rest of the morning sorting through the scant herbs and old containers of unknown salves, decoctions and syrups. Most were so old they were long past their usefulness, even if Elena had known what they were. She sent Fia to have someone fetch a tub of hot water so she could wash out the small jars and precious glass bottles.

While the child was gone, she opened a cupboard in the farthest corner. Surprisingly, this cupboard was nearly empty, but the lamplight revealed the recent imprint of someone's hand in the thick dust. A pottery jar sat in a dark corner of the bottom shelf. She nearly didn't see it, tucked under the shelf as it was. She reached for it. Footsteps sounded in the outer chamber. She turned, expecting Fia to skip into the room. The footsteps stopped just beyond the pool of light her lamps shed through the open door.

"Who's there?" she called. "Come into the light."

No one answered, but she was sure she heard the sound of breathing.

"Who's there," she called again, suddenly glad Fia was gone, but at the same time wishing someone had stayed with her. She searched around for anything she could use as a weapon. Her hand landed on the cold stone of the mortar. She hefted it, praying she could throw it straight if it came to that.

"I know someone is there. Why do you not step into the light?" She sidled around the edge of the chamber, wishing the door opened in, so she could slam it shut, putting as much of the chamber between her and whoever lurked without.

All of a sudden the door did slam. Elena jumped, a small shriek escaping her. Momentary relief raced through her, until she heard the unmistakable scrape of the metal latch being closed. She raced to the door, only to discover there was no latch handle on the inside.

"Let me out!" she yelled, banging her fist against the door. "Let me out!"

"Nay, Elena. I will not."

Her hands went still and she fought for breath. Dougal. "Symon knows where I am," she said at last, suddenly fearful if wee Fia should return to find Dougal holding her captive.

"Aye, and I know where he is. 'Twon't be long now before he rides the devil's shoulders again." Dougal's voice came low and menacing through the thick door. "Then we'll see how long Clan Lachlan can withstand Clan Lamont."

"Nay!"

"You would side with the Devil over your own clan?"

"What do you want?"

"Only what is due me."

"You do not need to harm the MacLachlans."

"Aye. I do. Make yourself ready for your punishment. No one thwarts me. Never again. A day or two here should convince you of my truth."

Her fingernails bit into the heels of her hands, but she did not reply.

"Fine. I will return to release you—after I have killed the Devil and after you have learned your lesson." His greasy laugh beat against the door, then quickly faded away to silence.

Elena forced herself to wait until she was sure he was gone, though the panic coursing through her nearly overwhelmed her. When she had not heard anything for a long time, she let the panic free and began to beat on the door and shout for help. She had to get out. She had to warn Symon. Somehow Dougal had gotten in again.

•   •   •

S ymon had paced the wall walk thrice around the castle in one direction, then thrice again in the other. Still he could not make sense of Elena's pronouncement. It made no sense. Who would poison him and why? If someone hated him that much, why did they not just kill him outright. Clearly they had the means to do so without being exposed as the killer. And that made Symon even more nervous. If she was right, then there was a sneaky bastard amongst them. But she couldn't be right.

There had to be another answer. And somehow she was the one who would see it. Symon descended the stairs to the bailey. He had not seen her come out of the undercroft that housed the stillroom. Wee Fia had danced her way out and across to the kitchen tower, clearly on some errand, then a short time later a man exited, a wine cask balanced on his shoulder.

But Elena remained inside. He rounded the corner and entered the darkened storage chamber. A muffled pounding met his ears long before his eyes adjusted to the dim interior.

He raced to the back of the chamber and jerked at the closed door. The latch scraped free and he swung the door open. Elena fell into his arms, tears running down her face and her fingers bloodied.

"Shh, lass." He held her trembling form, awkwardly patting her back. "Elena, I'm here."

She looked up at him, her eyes dark and full of fear. "He was here again."

Symon looked at her, and understanding hit him. "Dougal was here?"

She nodded, hiccupping quietly and wiping tears from

her cheeks, leaving bloody smears like some pagan princess. "He locked me in. He's waiting for you to go mad again before he attacks."

Symon turned and headed for the bailey. Elena squeaked and quickly followed. "Do not leave me here."

"I've got to warn the guards."

Elena trotted along, trying to keep up with his long strides. "What will you do?" she asked.

"Double the guards," he said as they reached the gate tunnel. He looked back at her. "And keep you in my reach at all times." He bellowed for the man in charge and explained the situation. "I want every chamber and stair searched. The gate is to be kept closed at all times and only those known by you personally are to be allowed in." The man nodded. "Report to me when the search is complete."

"Aye," the man said, then turned and started barking out orders, sending kilted men running to all corners of the castle.

Symon turned back to Elena and took her hands, holding them up before him. "Did he do this to you?"

"Nay, I . . . I . . ." She looked at her feet and tried to curl her bloodied fingers away from his view.

He reached out and lifted her chin, forcing her to look at him. "What happened to your hands?"

She swallowed, then raised her chin a bit higher. "I cannot stand to be locked in. I would rather claw my way through the door than endure that."

"Can you endure it if you are the one with the key?"

"What do you mean?"

"I mean to keep you safe, but it seems, despite my doubts, that the bastard can enter this castle at will. Until I can determine how he does that—or capture him—I need to make sure you are safe. If you are locked in a chamber, but you hold the key, can you bear it?"

"You would lock me up?"

"Only when I cannot be with you. I have duties. You have to sleep."

She shook her head vehemently. "I cannot bear a locked door."

"Very well." He dropped his voice. "Can you heal yourself?"

Elena nodded. "When I have to, though 'tis more difficult than . . . than the other."

"Come, we'll clean away the blood and see how bad they are." He took her hand and led her toward their chambers.

"And will you lock me in then?" she asked. Her voice trembled slightly.

He stopped, took both her hands once more in his, and looked her straight in the eye. "Nay, lass. I will not."

"Then how—" Understanding dawned and her eyes widened.

"If you weren't sure of our marriage before, 'tis assured now. Whether we call the banns and summon a priest or keep to the auld ways, we will be wed in the eyes of the clan."

"Is there no other way?" She swallowed and fought tears that gathered in her eyes.

Gently Symon reached out and ran his fingertips over the smudges of blood on her cheek. "Would it be such a terrible fate?"

Indecision settled over her like a heavy cloak. Symon sighed and led her to his chamber.

chapter 11

I t was a very long afternoon. *Elena and Symon took turns pacing the confines of his chamber.* At first they had been occupied with cleaning up Elena's hands, but after that it had gotten quiet. Symon would not leave her unless she agreed to lock the door. Elena could not bear the thought of a locked door. Symon stopped his pacing and looked at her.

"Why can you not abide a locked door?"

It was more demand than question, and it surprised her that he had not asked sooner. She shrugged.

"You do not know?" he asked, disbelief laced through his words.

"It does not matter. I will not be locked in."

He crossed to where she sat on the stool before the fire, grabbed her by the shoulders, and pulled her roughly to her feet. Elena flinched, ducking her head and closing her eyes. She waited for the blow, but it did not come. When she dared peek through her lashes, she found Symon staring at her, waiting.

"'Tis clear you were not treated well by your own," he said quietly. "I have not hurt you yet. I will not hurt you ever." He let go of her shoulders and stepped back. "What did they do to you?" he asked, almost more to himself than to her.

She shook her head. "'Tis best left in the past," she said.

"Nay, 'tisn't left in the past. It is here with you, and it is putting you in danger. If it has aught to do with this man who threatens you, I need to know. I need to understand what he is capable of so that I may know his strengths . . . and his weaknesses."

Elena considered the warrior in front of her. He certainly had strengths, and weaknesses. He needed her, and, she realized with a start, she needed him. If she was ever to escape Dougal completely, she needed this man to help her. She needed him to overcome Dougal, and if opening herself up to the past would help him, then she would have to do that. He had trusted her with as much.

She turned away from him. "Dougal is capable of anything."

"Anything?"

"Aye. I do not think he would kill me because he would not waste my gift, but he has"—she stopped and steadied her voice—"he has killed others who came between him and getting his way."

"What did he do to make you so afraid of a locked door?"

Elena hugged herself and closed her eyes, forcing herself to remember. When she could speak she began. "Dougal came to my clan five winters past. He was ill, hungry, and he had a festering wound that should have cost him his sword arm. I do not know what passed between him and my father, but I was called to heal his hurts. I did not want to touch the man. I cannot say why. 'Twas not unusual for my father to call upon my gift for warriors; indeed, that was the only way in which I was allowed to use my strength. But I did not wish to heal this man."

She moved closer to the fire, holding her hands out to its warmth, though she doubted anything could remove the ice from her veins. "My father was not a man of soft feelings, and I knew to defy him in this would only cause me more pain, so I did as he bade me, healing Dougal with my gift. Even so, it was some weeks before he was strong enough to be up and about. Once he was, he still was not able to wield a claymore for many months longer. But he and my father would closet themselves for long periods of time. Before I knew it, Lamont clansmen were raiding all the surrounding clans, often returning sorely wounded. My gift was required more and more often, and for more and more men.

"There was a time several years ago when my father rode to Stirling and instead of leaving the clan to my cousin Ian, as he had done so often before, he left Dougal to the task. In the course of a seven day Dougal had led three different attacks against neighboring clans. The more tired our lads became, the worse the wounds became until I could not bear it any longer.

"I made the mistake of confronting him in front of the clan, in the midst of the injured and dying. I remember seeing his fist hit my stomach as if it happened to someone else. I do not remember aught else from that day, nor for many thereafter. I do not know how long I was unconscious. When I did awaken I had been—" Her voice hitched and she fought to control it. "I was locked in a small room. There was no light, except for an occasional flicker from under the door. Nine times Dougal brought water. Never did he bring any food.

"At first I screamed and fought against the door. Then, when he came with the water, I would beg to be let free. After a while, I only begged for food." Tears ran down Elena's face, humiliation flamed her cheeks, but pride kept her talking. Pride and the hope that Symon would learn something that would help him overcome Dougal.

"Enough, lass. 'Tis enough."

"Nay." She turned to face him. "You wanted to know what he was capable of. I am nearly finished."

He nodded, and waited. She was grateful he stayed apart from her. If he had shown her any softness, any tenderness, she would have been lost, unable to say what she must.

"The tenth time he came he told me his terms for releasing me. I had to swear never to defy him again, neither in public, nor even in private. I had to swear to support him as chief when the time came for my father to step down. I had to swear only to use my gift at his bidding, and never to speak of what had happened to me, not even to my father. He promised worse if I did and . . . and began to tell me, in great detail.

"I was so afraid of him, so weak, so tired. I could barely speak, yet I would have sworn to take my own father's life to make him stop, to escape that prison. Finally he took me from the room and back to my own chamber. There he had me gather my things and move them to a small chamber near his own. A chamber with a door and a strong lock.

"For a long time he kept me locked in, though I was brought food and drink. I was only allowed out to mend the horrors he wrought upon my kinsmen. When my father returned several months later, Dougal stopped locking me in during the day, though still at night the door would be barred. And he never left me alone with anyone except when he was away raiding other clans.

"He recently took to acting the smitten suitor, almost as if he dared me to break my promise not to defy him. When my father's body was found, Dougal . . . he sought to make me his bride in the very way he had described to me. That's when I ran."

Symon waited while she gathered her emotions. When she had calmed and wiped her tears away once again, he said, "I will not lock you in. This I promise."

The words were simple, spare, and she trusted them completely. She nodded, not trusting her voice. Symon stood, watching her, as if deciding whether he dared approach her or not. At last he moved slowly toward her. He reached out, lightly touching her shoulder, inviting, offering. She turned into his chest and relished the strength of his arms closing about her. He rested his cheek against her hair and murmured soothing nonsense, as if she were a fussy bairn.

"He will not hurt you again, Elena-mine," he said quietly.

She nodded, comforted by the reined-in anger she heard there; comforted by the way he turned her name into an endearment. Just as she had instinctively distrusted Dougal, she instinctively trusted this man, this so-called Devil. A more virtuous man she had never met.

"We will figure out this mystery—these *mysteries* for they seem to multiply by the day."

She felt as if a huge weight had been lifted from her shoulders. Not only did he believe her, but he joined his cause to hers. Together they would sort out her problem of Dougal, and his of the poison.

Absently Symon stroked a large hand up and down her back. "We need only figure out where to start. If Ranald were here, he would know. He is a master of subterfuge and secrets."

A skitter of dread scrambled over her. Was that not exactly what would be required of the poisoner? But she did not voice her worry. Their bond was too new, too fragile yet for her to doubt the loyalty of his brother. But she would have to consider it.

N ot long later Murdoch knocked at the door. "No one was found, Symon," he reported. "The guard's been doubled, and no one enters the castle unless they get passed by Coll or me."

"We need to know how the bastard's getting in and out without being seen."

"Aye. Do we know where he's been seen in the castle?"

Symon looked to Elena, where she sat staring into the fire, as she had for the last hour. "Elena?"

She startled, as if awakened, and looked to him.

"Where did you hear Dougal the first time?"

It seemed to take a moment for the question to sink in, then she got a thoughtful look about her. "In the wine cellar." She rose to her feet. "The same place I heard him today."

Symon nodded and Murdoch left without another word. "Are you hungry?"

"A little."

"Let's go down to the kitchen and see what we can find there."

She followed him out the door, saying nothing. Symon hated the lost look she carried about her. He wanted to tell her everything would be fine, but he wasn't sure that was true. They had an enemy entering the castle apparently at will, and a poisoner to boot. One thing at a time. They'd eat, then see if Murdoch found anything. After that, well, they'd figure that part out when they got there.

S*ymon sat next to Elena in the Great Hall, facing the* door. She picked at a bowl of stew, eating little, mushing it around a lot. He picked up a mug of ale, not his favorite, but his supply of spiced wine had dwindled to nothing. 'Twas Ranald's special recipe, one he'd share with no one. Symon would have to wait until Ranald's return before his supply could be replenished.

Murdoch found them there. He sat next to Symon and waited.

"Well?" Symon demanded. "Did you find anything?"

Murdoch looked at the lass, then back at Symon.

"Elena can hear whatever you have to say, lad." He glanced at her and she nodded. They both leaned forward, anxious to hear what Murdoch had to say.

The giant cleared his throat. "There is another bolt-hole."

Symon couldn't move. How was this possible? Another bolt-hole, one that no one, not the weans, not the older warriors, no one knew about? "Where?" he finally ground out.

Murdoch tilted his head at Elena. "Right where she said. In the wine cellar. Mind you, we had to move near every cask and bottle in there, but 'twas there, cleverly hid behind a pile of casks. Even looking for it, I do not think we would have noticed it except for the footprints in the dirt, leading right into the wall, or so it seemed. 'Tis a clever fit door, made to look like the very wall itself."

"How is it we didn't know of this?"

Murdoch shrugged. "That part of the castle is very auld. Perhaps it was merely forgotten."

Symon looked at his gillie for a moment. "And?"

"And we have not figured out how to open it yet."

Symon stood abruptly and headed toward the door. Just before he got there, he stopped, turned, and pinned Murdoch with an angry glare. "Do not sit there, man. We've got to get that door open, find out where it leads."

Murdoch rose slowly. "Aye," he said as he followed his chief. "In the meantime, there are several braw lads working on the problem, and another four ready to stand guard whether they get it open or not. 'Tis sure the next time the daft bastard tries to gain entrance, he'll have a surprise or four waiting for him."

Symon nodded. The man had a point. When he looked at Elena, still sitting at the table, her stew gone cold in front of her and her eyes big, he knew he could not drag her back down into the undercroft where she had been terrorized. And he could not go without her. He had promised to keep her safe.

"Get you back down there," he said to Murdoch. "Send word if it opens, I'll"—he looked back at Elena—"we'll be in my chamber."

Murdoch strode past him and Symon reached out, stopping him with a hand on his arm. "When Ranald returns, send him to me immediately."

"Aye, Symon." The man turned and looked at Elena. "Keep the lassie safe. I'll see to the rest."

Symon gave silent thanks that Murdoch had never forsaken him, then returned to sit across from Elena.

"Do you think he's left the castle?" she asked.

"Aye. Else he would have been found."

She stirred her stew, lost in thought. "Something is not right."

"Aye. There are many things that are not right just now."

"Nay, I mean with Dougal." He waited for her to say what was bothering her. "Why would he know a secret way into this castle? I didn't know I would be coming here. How is it that he can secretly enter a castle he has had no reason to enter before now?"

"I do not know, but 'tis a very perplexing problem. Perhaps there is someone here who knew of the secret bolthole. Someone he bribed for the information?"

" 'Twould not be above him to do just that, but then why when he found me alone did he lock me in? It would have made more sense for him to take advantage of the opportunity and take me away with him."

The lass made a fine point, if only he had the answers to her questions. "It does not make sense." He turned to her. "I sent Ranald off to find out where Dougal came from before he joined the Lamonts. I don't know what he will find, but I cannot help but think 'twill answer many questions."

"I have often wondered as much," she said quietly. "I asked my father once. He said it did not concern me." She looked away, her eyes darting around the empty Hall. "I didn't dare ask Dougal, not after . . ."

"Do not fash yerself, Elena-mine." He smoothed a stray tendril of her hair from her cheek. She whirled around at the touch. "We will figure this out. In the meantime," he said, wishing to distract her from her past, "there is this other mystery, this poison. Have you thought further on it?"

"Nay," she whispered, "I'm sorry, I—"

"You were distracted," he finished for her and was rewarded with a shy smile.

"Aye, that's it."

"'Tis late. I think you need a good night's sleep. We'll tackle my problem in the morning. Perhaps this other trouble will be resolved by then."

She agreed and quickly followed him up to their hallway. Outside their chambers she hesitated. Symon guided her silently into his chamber. Once inside she stopped.

"You can have the bed, lass. I'll be sleeping in front of the door." He turned his back and stoked the fire while she slipped off her gown and climbed into the big feather bed.

When he was sure she was settled, he stripped off his plaid, then rolled himself in it and settled his back against the door. 'Twas a fortunate thing that he could not see her lying in his bed from his vantage point upon the floor. His thoughts wandered far too easily in that direction without the visual stimulus to go with them. Strange how quickly things could change. Just yesterday it was he, looking to her for his safety and salvation. Today she looked to him. If he was honest with himself, he was well pleased that she had finally decided to trust him. 'Twas a pity Dougal of Dunmore had to be the cause.

Symon shifted to a more comfortable hard spot on the wood floor. At least it was not stone. One had to be thankful for small favors.

E lena woke slowly the next morning and for a moment didn't know where she was. The bed was so big, and so soft, she thought she must still be dreaming. A soft snore from the direction of the door reminded her of where she was. And why. Quietly she sat up and looked over at the sleeping Symon, still sitting up against the door, as he had been last night.

A curious softness washed over her as she watched him sleeping. She indulged herself, finally allowing herself to admire this warrior who had done so much for her in such a short time. Never before in her entire life had anyone cared enough to allay her fears, protect her, even as she slept. She remembered the heated kisses they had shared and felt her core heat. The desire she had so newly discovered spread through her, heating her, giving her wild ideas. If only . . .

If only there was no Dougal, and no gift. She might be happy here. She could be useful, and Symon might, just might come to feel something for her other than pity. She did not want his pity. What she wanted was the fire that had flared to life between them wiping out all other thoughts, all other feelings. When she had been in his arms she had known complete abandon, at least for a moment.

She would give anything to feel that again, to be so lost in the wonderful sensations his lips and tongue and hands brought to her as to forget all else in this world. She rose quietly from the bed and padded across the cold floor. She crouched in front of him, her shift puddling about her feet. He looked so peaceful in sleep, so content. Did he feel the same way she did when they touched? She thought he must. He had seemed bemused when she had pulled away, as if overwhelmed by his senses. Without thinking, she reached out and touched his lips with her fingertips.

Symon's eyes snapped open and his hand gripped her wrist. Elena's breath stopped. Confusion passed swiftly over Symon's face, then he released her wrist, watching her. Gingerly she let her fingers move over his lips and was pleased to see heat in his eyes and feel his breath quicken at her touch. He did feel it. She smiled to herself, then explored his face with her fingers, running them over his strong jaw, his thick dark slashes of eyebrows, his high, sharp cheekbones. Slowly she leaned forward and pressed her lips to his.

Symon groaned and she started to pull away just as he snaked an arm about her waist and pulled her into his lap, deepening the kiss.

"What do you see, Elena-mine?" His breath whispered over her skin.

Elena thought about his question. What did she see? "A warrior. A chief. A man."

"Not a devil?"

"Nay, no devil. A man who takes in strange lasses and offers them his hospitality, his protection . . . even his bed."

His pupils widened and he took her hand, still resting

on his cheek, bringing it to his mouth. He planted a gentle kiss in the center of her palm, then held her hand in his. "I would give you more, if you would but let me."

Elena wasn't sure what he meant. "You don't need to give me more, Symon."

"I would protect you always, could protect you always if . . ." He let the words hang between them.

"If?"

"If you would marry me."

Elena stood, breaking the contact with his warm hand. She returned to the bed and pulled her woolen gown over her head, then arranged the sleeves of her shift underneath.

She felt Symon's eyes on her, then he rose and arranged his plaid, wrapping it about him with a wide leather belt. "You still will not consider it?" he said at last.

Elena felt torn between what she wanted and what she knew had to be. She could never stay there, become the wife of the chief of MacLachlan, and keep her secret safe. And then there was Dougal. As long as she remained, he would take his anger out upon the MacLachlans. But most of all, if she allowed herself to feel what he stirred in her, she would suffer as she had when her mother had died. She shook her head, unable to voice all the reasons why she could not hope for the happiness she had always craved.

Symon was next to her before she even realized he had moved. He grabbed her, kissed her with all the pent-up frustration they both had felt for days. She struggled free of him and tried to ignore the arousing effect his mouth had upon her body.

"We have a bargain, do we not?" She tried to make her voice cold, hard, but a slight wobble threatened to expose the turmoil she was feeling. "You will find me a new home, somewhere far away from the likes of Dougal of Dunmore? And I will help you find the source of the poison."

"Aye. I will not go back on my word."

"Fine. If you think 'tis safe enough, I would like to return to the stillroom. I had not finished examining the contents yet. There may be something there that will be of use in neutralizing your poison. At the very least I promised wee Fia's mum I'd bring her a tea of nettle to ease her swollen ankles. There was some there, though I don't know if 'tis fresh enough to do much good. I need to find some wood-rasp to ease her way when the bairn comes, too." Elena rattled off this list, more to distract herself from the large man looming over her than because she needed to tell him.

He huffed out a breath, then turned and opened the door, waiting there for her to accompany him. She did, leading the way down the stairs and out into the pale early morning light. A few people watched their progress across the bailey to the undercroft that kept the wine.

At the dark entrance to the chamber Symon stopped Elena and stepped in front of her. "Wait here a moment."

He did not have to tell her twice. Her heart was hammering, and the last place she wished to go was into the dark maw of this chamber. Yet she did not know what else to do. The auld stillroom was not well stocked, but then, she had no stores at all. Given a little time she could determine what was most needed, then perhaps Murdoch would go in search of the herbs for her. For she could not set foot outside the gates. It did not matter if Symon accompanied her or not. She could not take the chance of falling into Dougal's hands again.

"Come," she heard from the depths of the darkness. She stepped out of the sun and let her eyes adjust. Symon stood at the back of the chamber, a lamp in his hand. Elena jumped when she realized he was flanked by four Highlanders, two on either side. "We will be well guarded here. Come."

Elena moved deeper into the dank space. With each step she trembled more, until Symon held out his hand to her and she lightly placed hers upon it. His large hand curled around hers, and she felt much safer for the contact. "We have much to do," he said to her, ushering her into the still-room.

Elena stood perfectly still as Symon moved about the room, lighting the oil lamps as he had done yesterday. When they were burning brightly, she moved past the shelves and cupboards she had searched already, stopping at the corner cupboard she had opened just as Dougal arrived. The cannister at the back bothered her, though she couldn't figure out why. She lifted a lamp, lighting the space, and noticed a lack of dust. Everything else was covered with a thick coat of dust, even inside the cupboards. Yet this one looked as if someone had dusted it yesterday. She ran a finger over the clean wood. Someone had cleaned this recently, but only this cupboard, stuck in a dark corner of a room no one used anymore.

She reached for the pottery jar, lifting it gingerly, the hair on the back of her neck standing up.

"What have you found?" Symon asked as he helped her lift the heavy jar to the worktable in the middle of the room.

"I do not know for sure, but I think maybe one of the answers you are looking for."

Symon lifted the lid for her, and they both peered inside. A woodsy, moldy aroma drifted out of the jar. Elena motioned for Symon to draw a lamp closer. Carefully she tipped the jar, spilling a little onto the table. A small puddle of brown liquid rested there, spreading out slowly.

Elena leaned down until her nose was almost in it, then took a long sniff, inhaling the aroma, trying to match the scents she discerned to her experience with herbs. When she could not, she dabbed her pinky in the puddle and tapped a drop of the mixture on her tongue. She waited. No burning, no numbing. She drew her tongue in and breathed through her open mouth, intensifying the flavors and scents by the flow of air over her tongue.

"Cinnamon," she said at last, "cloves." She considered the flavor another moment. "Thyme . . ."

Symon leaned down to sniff the open jar again. He began to chuckle. " 'Tisn't poison there, lass."

She looked at him, waiting for an explanation.

"I think you've found Ranald's hiding place for his secret recipe."

"Secret recipe?"

"Aye. He makes the finest spiced wine this side of Loch Awe, but he will not share the recipe. He makes his mixture up, then hides it, mixing it only with the proper wines and in precise amounts, or so he says. We could hide the jar somewhere else."

"Why would we do that?" she asked, interested in the amusement flashing in his eyes, crinkling around his eyes.

"Ah, you've never had a brother, have you, lass?" She shook her head. "Well, you see, brothers take great delight in tormenting one another, playing tricks, getting them in trouble and the like. Ranald and I may be grown men, but that doesn't mean we do not still enjoy a bit of horseplay."

"You and Ranald are close," she observed.

"We once were; there is more between us now."

"Are you the only two?" She placed the top on the jar and put it back where she found it, looking quickly through the rest of the empty cupboard, just in case she'd missed something.

She realized he had not answered her, and she glanced over her shoulder. He leaned against the worktable, a brooding look upon his face now, his shoulders squared and tense.

"Symon?"

"What? Oh, aye, we are the only two, though for a time there was another who claimed to be our brother."

"Is he dead?"

"I don't know. He was banished from here when I was but seventeen summers."

"Banished?"

"Aye. He had been amongst us since I was seven and Ranald was six. He was eight."

"Who was he?"

"He called himself Donal. He appeared at the gate one winter's day, eight years old, but ordering men about as if he were chief himself. He said his mum had told him he was the son of my father. When she died he made his way here to Kilmartin, demanding to see the chief, demanding to be claimed as the rightful heir."

"He was eight?"

"Aye. His mother had schooled him well in arrogance and swagger."

"Was he your brother?"

"My father said no, though whether 'twas to appease my mum or 'twas the truth I never knew. He did let the lad stay, but the fact that he would not claim him as his first-born son only rankled Donal more as he grew older. When he was eighteen he tried to kill my da. Ranald and I stopped him. We nearly killed him, beating him until he could not stand."

"But he didn't die?"

"Nay. Da stopped us, banishing Donal as soon as he was able to drag himself from his bed. Da told him he would learn humility at the hands of the world and sent him out. We never heard of him again."

"Ten years is a long time to consider someone family, then send them away."

"Aye, though to be honest I do not think either Ranald nor I ever missed him for a moment. Da spent a long time drunk that summer, but he finally accepted it and we moved forward."

"How did your mum feel about Donal?"

"She never liked the lad, though I think she tried to hide it, at least at first. She did not have to try for long." He looked up at Elena. "She died when I was ten."

"How?"

"I don't know for sure. 'Twas a stomach complaint. Auld Morag tried to help, but Mum wasted away over a few months. 'Twas a blessing when she died. At the end the pain alone was enough to kill her."

"Do you miss her?"

"Aye, though I have not thought of her in a long time." He pushed away from the table and scanned the room. "There are more cupboards over here," he said, obviously unwilling to dwell on this any longer. He opened another cupboard and began pulling jars and bottles and cloth sacks out, shoving them willy-nilly on the worktable.

Elena sighed at the jumble, but did not stop him. Sometimes keeping your hands busy was best. She reached for the first bottle and began her investigations.

chapter 12

Elena worked her way through the pile of things Symon pulled out of the cupboards, sorting by type of container, then carefully opening each jar, bottle, and sack and identifying the contents. The dried herbs were not difficult, though most of them were so old as to be useless. The ointments were a little more difficult, though only two or three presented a real challenge to her. The glass bottles were the most difficult and had to be approached with the greatest caution. Elena knew that many such things did great good in small quantities, but could cause equally great harm when misused. Those things she could not identify were relegated to the growing pile of refuse. She would carefully pour out the contents, then clean the precious glass vials for other uses.

As she put those few useful items back in one of the

cupboards, organizing them carefully, as she would if this were her own stillroom, she noticed a small cloth bundle. She pulled it forth and noticed immediately that the cloth seemed newer than the other sacks they had found so far, its colors brighter. Very little dust had settled on it. Perhaps this was more of Ranald's secret recipe, since clearly he was the one using this space.

Carefully she unwrapped the leather cord and spread the cloth out so she could see the contents.

"What is that, Elena-mine?" Symon peered over her shoulder at the small bundle spread open before her.

Slowly she lifted a dried mushroom from the cloth, raising it to see it more clearly. She sniffed it, then put it down and poked through the other mushrooms there. "I don't know," she said quietly while she racked her memory for the use of such things. Mushrooms were dangerous, causing illness and danger and bad luck. These looked like the red-capped ones that grew in fairy rings, fly-bane some called it, for it seemed to kill any fly who flew about it. But why would someone store them here? True, they should not be near the kitchen, but perhaps scattered about the privy pits. She turned one over, grasping for understanding.

"Are they poisonous?" Symon said, right in her ear, his warm breath fluttering over her neck.

She picked one up and meant to touch it to her tongue when Symon stopped her hand. "What are you doing?" he demanded. She turned her head and found herself eye to eye with him. Concern etched his features, and she found her heart melting.

"'Tis only a test, as I've done so many times already this morn."

"But if 'tis poison?"

She shrugged, slowly slipping her wrist from his grasp. "I will be careful." She stuck out her tongue again and ever so slightly touched the mushroom to it. She waited, her eyes closed, her attention turned inward, assessing, testing. Was that a tingling she felt on her tongue? Aye, and it seemed her mouth watered overmuch. She searched deeper, alert to even the tiniest warning signal. She had nearly decided that it was benign when a surge of blackness pressed into her. She dropped the mushroom and quickly turned her gift upon herself, stopping the blackness even as she had stopped it in Symon.

" 'Tis the poison," she said before she opened her eyes.

Symon spun her toward him. "Are you all right? Are you, lass?"

She nodded, concentrating on the last of the tingling in her tongue and lips. "Aye. But this is what you have been poisoned with, though I think it must be in a weaker form than this."

Symon wrapped the mushrooms up quickly and stuffed the small bundle into a fold of his plaid. "At least now we have the source."

"We have but one source. Those mushrooms grow throughout the wood. 'Twon't be hard for whoever put it here to come by more. We need to find out how you are getting it. Then you will be safe. Only then."

Symon was thoughtful. "If we leave the lads outside guarding Dougal's bolt-hole, whoever left this here will not be able to retrieve it without being seen."

"Aye, but it's bound to be someone who has business in the wine cellar, else he would not have stored it here in the first place. Your own brother uses this room. I do not think you will easily learn the culprit's identity that way."

"You may be right, but at least 'tis another bit of information."

She agreed, and that was more than they had known before. Her stomach growled and Symon chuckled. "Let us finish up in here and get you something warm to fill your empty belly." He reached for the remaining jars and placed them in the cupboard, closing the doors with a bit more of a bang than was necessary. "I'll have Murdoch ask who has been in and out since the lads took up their vigil. They would not tell me, but they'll tell him easily enough."

They blew out the oil lamps, and Symon led the way out the way they had entered. Before they had reached the sun-filled arch that separated the wine cellar from the bailey, they smelled smoke and heard the shouts.

Fire leapt from the thatch roof of the stable. Horses whinnied their fear, and men ran to release them from the burning building. Symon sprinted across to the well and began pulling up the bucket. Elena watched, not knowing how to help, as a line of men and women formed, passing buckets of water as fast as Symon and another man could pull them up from the well. Another group took long hooks and pulled the burning thatch off the building onto the ground, where others beat at the flames with wet cloths.

Almost as fast as it had begun, the fire was tamed and then the last ember was extinguished. Elena watched as Symon entered the now roofless building, then was astonished when he quickly returned carrying a young lad. She could see from clear across the bailey that he had been badly burned. One sleeve of his tunic hung in blackened shreds and the arm hung just as limply, the skin an angry red. His head lolled back, and she found herself rushing forward, needing to know if it was too late for him.

• • •

Symon grunted as he laid the lad on Elena's narrow bed. Elena stood near the door, her arm around wee Fia, who had followed them, clinging to Elena's skirts. Symon looked expectantly at the healer. She had looked so concerned when he had brought the boy out, but now she hesitated to cross to the room.

Of course. She did not want an audience.

He crouched down and motioned for Fia to come to him. She hesitated, glancing from Elena to Symon and back.

" 'Tis all right, Fia. Symon will not harm you." Elena waved her hand in his direction, as if shooing the wean to him. Fia looked at him again and finally approached, blue eyes wide, her little face serious.

He whispered in her ear, "I have an important job for you, wee Fia." She nodded and leaned toward him. "Mistress Elena will need some bindings for the lad's burns. Can you find Mistress Jenny and ask her to give them to you?" The little head bobbed rapidly. " 'Tis very important, this job, but you're a fine wee lass, so I think you can do it. Aye?" The small head continued to bob. Symon took her hand and led her to the door.

Fia looked over her shoulder at Elena, then smiled timidly at him. "She's a fairy queen, you ken?"

A smile escaped before he could stop it, and Fia's eyes widened further. "A fairy queen?"

Fia's face was very serious. "Och, aye. Me da says so. Will you wed her?"

Even the weans had hopes. Symon sighed, ignoring the tightening in his stomach. "I do not know. Go now. Find Jenny quickly." The girl disappeared down the stair, and

Symon shut the door firmly. He stood with his back to it and nodded to Elena. "I'll make sure no one enters while you heal him."

"I cannot—"

"Of course you can." He almost yelled at her, his emotions too raw where she was concerned. All his softness had been spent getting the child away. He lowered his voice with effort.

"Nay, you don't understand," she said, her chin trembling slightly.

"You are right, I don't understand how you can stand there and let this lad suffer when you know you can help him."

"Do not judge what you do not ken. You promised you would not hurt me, aye?"

"And I will not, I appeal to your conscience, not with violence against you."

She stood, staring at the lad, her arms wrapped protectively around her middle.

"Why would God have given you such a gift if it wasn't to help the weans and the bairns?" he asked quietly, standing behind her. "Why? Is this not what you would choose to use your gift for?"

He watched the battle rage through her. It was obvious she did not want to heal, but he was sure the need to ease the suffering of the lad was equally strong. She may refuse to heal a warrior, but she was soft-hearted where the weans were concerned.

"I can see it in your eyes, Elena. Go on, now, before that little one returns. I'll keep guard at the door so no one will discover what you do here."

She lost the battle as he hoped she would and sat beside the moaning lad, on the edge of the bed.

Gently she placed his injured arm in her lap and pushed the tattered sleeve clear of the oozing blisters.

Symon found himself mesmerized as she began the healing. He watched her rub her slender, long-fingered hands together, her eyes closed in concentration. A slight hesitation, then she let her hands hover just above the worst of the blisters. She gasped, though he doubted she was aware of it. Tension gripped her shoulders, and she let her head lean to one side, stretching her pale neck, as if in pain herself, almost as if, in the healing process, she took the pain into herself. He had thought perhaps a glimmer of the pain reflected from her patient onto her, but this was something deeper, more dangerous. Guilt ate at him. He had caused her pain, had hurt her, by convincing her to do this.

He could see her struggling to breathe, and a dull sheen of sweat rose on her skin. He had to stop her. He crossed the room and placed a hand on her shoulder.

A shock of agony lanced through him, and his left arm burned as he jerked his hand free. He searched his arm, but there was nothing there except a hollow echo of pain. Hesitantly he placed his hand on her shoulder again. Again the pain lanced through him, sharp as the slice of a well-honed dagger, but this time he forced himself to leave his hand there.

How did she stand it? A warrior knew he must withstand such pain. His life taught him how to bear it. But not a woman. Not this kind of pain. Yet here was a woman who, despite knowledge of what she would feel, chose, however hesitantly, to heal this boy.

Symon's respect for her rose.

Sweat gathered at her temples and trickled down the side of her face as she worked. Symon gathered his courage, sat behind her, and placed his other hand upon her shoulder. He used his warrior's training to let the pain flow through him, focusing his mind away from it and onto the battle at hand. He did not know how he could help her, but perhaps if he could feel the pain through her, he could help her push it away. He poured all his formidable battle-trained concentration into easing Elena's burden.

Immediately Elena's shoulders began to relax. Her back seemed less rigidly held. Her head straightened and her breathing eased. She continued her healing. Slowly the blisters disappeared. The skin sank from angry red, to healing pink, and the boy seemed to drop into a deep sleep. Symon did not know how long he sat, hands on her shoulders, attention focused on shielding her from the pain. Finally she removed her hands from the now healed injury. Carefully she placed them in her lap and took a deep shuddering breath.

Symon kept his hands on her shoulders, searching for any more pain, but he could feel nothing more than the heat of her skin beneath his palms. She trembled and he pulled her back against his chest.

"Ah, Elena-mine, can you forgive my ignorance?"

She said nothing, just leaned into him, her arms wrapped tightly over his about her middle. After a moment she turned, still keeping his arms about her. "What did you do?"

He looked deep into her eyes and tried to find the words to describe the experience. "I do not know. I touched you as you healed the lad, and I . . ." The enormity of what he had just experienced humbled him. He understood the pain she felt was real, vivid. That she chose to help in the face of that told him more of her spirit than anything he knew about her so far. Her courage was formidable.

"You understand now." It was a statement, not a question.

"I am sorry to have pushed you to it, Elena-mine. I would not have done it if I knew how much you suffered."

" 'Tis true. I do suffer, but when you touched me . . . 'twas as if someone had thrown a wet blanket on a fire."

"What do you mean?"

"I don't know what you did, but somehow you took the pain and held it away from me. Never before has such a thing happened. Such a joining . . ." She looked up at him, her eyes awash with wonder.

Her words shook him. They had joined, and yet they were separate. He had to bind her to him. He could not give her up. Not after what had just passed between them. What would pass between them. And he wanted so much more to pass between them. Reason had little to do with it. That she could heal him was wonderful, but what he was feeling for her, with her, went so much deeper than his need of her gift.

A small knock came at the door, and Jenny pushed it open, wee Fia at her side.

Elena pulled herself from Symon's comforting embrace and beckoned the girls into the chamber. She took the bandages from Fia.

"Can you spread some fat on his skin to keep it soft," she said to Jenny, "then bind it well with the linen?"

Jenny nodded.

"Do not try to move him. He has much mending left to do. Does he have a mum?"

"Aye, she fainted dead away when she saw Jamie carried out. She hit her head," Fia piped up.

Concern twisted in Elena's stomach. "Is she recovered?"

"Aye. Me mum's with her."

"Sprite, will you go to her, tell her young Jamie will be fine in a few days time?"

Fia nodded.

"Off with you, then." Elena kissed the child's forehead and pointed her toward the door. "Stay with him, Jenny," she said to the other girl. "When he wakes, he will be thirsty. Let him drink as much water as he will. A broth would be good for him, too, though he may not want that right away."

Jenny moved to the lad's side as Elena and Symon moved toward the door.

"Let me know if he does not wake by morning."

Elena wavered on her feet, and Symon caught her around the waist, then scooped her into his arms. "She will be in my chamber," he said.

Jenny nodded mutely as Symon carried Elena out of the room.

A strange kind of euphoria filled Elena. Never had she experienced anything like she had just shared with Symon. Never had she felt so at peace with her gift. She had saved the boy's arm. Symon had helped her.

She rested her head on his shoulder and savored the feel

of his arms holding her. If she could stop time, now would be the moment she would choose. Somehow his simple assurance that this was what she was meant to do, his belief that helping that boy was the right thing to do, not because of any strategic advantage, or political alliance, simply that it was the right thing to do and she was the one who must do it, gave her the courage and the strength to face the pain she knew would come. And it had.

But then something miraculous had happened. At Symon's touch she had felt his strength join hers, had felt him pull the pain away until it was but a distant buzz, annoying, but easily ignored. His strength had joined with hers and together they had healed the boy.

Suddenly she had found a purpose for her gift, and a way to practice it without all the pain. If only she could stay here and practice it. Dougal would not go away simply because she had found a place she wanted to be, a clan she could help. Nay, as long as she was here, he would seek harm to these people, and her.

But that was the future.

For now, if they were discrete, she and Symon could help his clan. Her fear had been transformed in an instant, making her feel calm, and sure, and strong. And the man who had ignited those feelings held her safe in his arms, ready to protect her, willing to stay with her. For now she would revel in that.

Symon came to a stop and Elena opened her eyes. They were in his chamber, beside his bed. Slowly he lowered her feet to the floor, letting her body slide down the length of him. He seemed as moved by what they had shared as she was.

He took her face in his hands and kissed her, gently,

sweetly. "Is it not clear, Elena-mine? Can you not see what even the weans know to be true?"

Elena didn't want to talk, just now. Didn't want to break the magical web that spun about them, separating them from time and place, giving them this moment.

"Will you be my wife?"

Elena's heart lurched. In this moment she wanted nothing more than to stay here, where she had purpose and friends, and a man who valued her gift beyond his own immediate needs. But she couldn't. Dougal wouldn't give up the strategic advantage of her gift even if she was married to Symon. He wouldn't leave Symon and his clan alone as long as she remained with them.

And there was the message of her dream. If she dared love this man, she would suffer as she had when her mother died—but only if she remained here in Kilmartin Castle.

A sense of freedom floated down over her. She could not stay because of Dougal's threat, but since she could not stay, she could indulge her feelings, if only for one night.

For this single night she could pretend that this was her home, Symon was her husband, and that she was wanted and loved as any simple woman might be. Morning would come soon enough. She would not tempt fate by wishing for more.

She rose on her tiptoes and kissed him, trying to let him know all that she felt, though she dared not put it in words.

S ymon leaned down and met her lips with his own, kissing her gently, nibbling at the corners of her mouth, tasting her lips. He pulled her against him, deepening the kiss, coaxing her lips open, dancing his tongue over and around her willing one. She tilted her head, greedily feasting on his mouth as he did on hers. He groaned as she inexpertly, but oh, so enthusiastically participated in the kiss. Triumph filled him at her response. He would have Elena by his side.

He felt his body harden quickly, but held himself in check, slowing the kiss. He explored her lips, then moved to the sensitive place behind her ear, and the exquisitely delicate length of her neck. He allowed his hands free roam of her back, enjoying the way her body had subtly softened since coming to Kilmartin. Gradually his hands swooped lower until he cupped her round bottom in his palms, pulling her against him.

He was pleased by the soft moan that escaped her and the almost reluctant thrust of her hips against him. He caressed the side of her breast, lifting its weight in his hand, flicking a thumb over the rough cloth separating him from her hardened nipple. He felt her intake of breath and repeated the movement, more slowly, pausing slightly to catch the peak between his thumb and finger, then moving back to her lush backside.

He deepened the kiss, thrusting his tongue against her, relishing the feel of her hands gripped tightly on his shoulders, as if that contact was all that kept her on her feet.

Slowly he began to raise her skirts, gathering the worn fabric above her bottom, exposing the back of her legs to the chill air of the room. She responded with another moan and a slow grind of her hips against his own hardness. Her eyes were closed and a dreamy concentration played across her features. He had never seen her so. It was akin to the concentration when she was healing, but this was focused completely on pleasure, not pain. She was focused entirely on him and what he was eliciting from her anything but cold body.

At last he had the skirts raised and his hands directly against her skin. He moved his hand around until it was between them, his fingers brushing the springy hair between her thighs. He wanted to lay her on the bed and bury himself in her, but it was too soon.

He dipped his fingers into the wet heat between her thighs over and over again, matching the rhythm of her movements with his own. He drew his fingers out and rubbed the dampness against that most sensitive nubbin, and she exploded in his arms, throwing her head back, gasping out his name and pulsating against his hand. Slowly she subsided, resting her head against his shoulder, which was still caught in her almost painful grip. He let her skirts drop, fighting with his own need, waiting for her to decide. He wrapped his arms about her, drawing her against him, relishing the almost pain of wanting her so badly.

He smiled, well pleased with the response he had drawn from her. "You did not answer my question, sweetling."

She blinked, focusing on his face. "What question?" she asked, her voice husky.

"Will you be my wife?"

"I don't think—"

"Do not think. Listen to your heart. What does it say?"

"It says I trust you, Symon MacLachlan."

Symon was humbled by the whispered admission. It was more than he had dared hope for, though not as much as he wanted. He kissed her hard.

• • •

E lena was shocked at the words that came from her own mouth. She trusted him. She knew the truth of her own words even as she reeled from the admission. She did not want to trust him, especially not a warrior.

But she did.

Fear tried to shake her, but the wonder of this new feeling rushed through her, layered over the heat his caresses and kisses caused, pushing fear aside like a leaf in a high wind.

Heat. She had been mortified at her own reaction to his pulsing fingers, but then a languor had overtaken her and she was lifted to a place of exquisite pleasure, the likes of which she had never before known. The likes of which she would do anything to repeat.

Heat pooled between her thighs and between her breasts. Each caress of his lips against hers tightened the coil low in her belly, preparing it for that cataclysmic release again. She could feel it building as his hands raced over her skin, weighing her breast, smoothing her hip, lifting her from her place by his side to his lap without ever relinquishing his attachment upon her lips.

Cool air wafted over her heated skin and she gasped as his hot lips enveloped her sensitive nipple, suckling, pulling, demanding, even as his other hand caressed her other naked breast. How had he done that? Her passion-muddled mind could not understand it, but her body did not care.

He stood, catching her in his arms and steadying her on her feet. His eyes on hers, he released his belt, letting his plaid fall to the floor. As he reached for his tunic, Elena stopped him. His questioning look had her blushing, but she wanted to see if she could make him respond as she was responding. Granted, there was ample evidence of his interest, but she wanted to make him gasp her name, even as she faintly remembered gasping his.

She stepped closer, her breasts tight from his attentions, a weight in her belly growing as if feeding on the heat they generated between them, and removed his tunic.

It was not the first time Elena has seen the naked male form. She was a healer, and as such, was privy to their wounds and their body parts. But this was different.

"Am I so horrible to look at, lass?" Symon asked quietly.

Elena looked him carefully in the eye and slowly shook her head, a sudden feeling of power and wontonness surging through her at the hesitance in his voice.

"Nay, Symon, you are . . ." She could not describe the powerful feelings his body fanned to flame in her. Hesitantly she reached out and gently ran her fingers over a scar on his ribs, and another at his collarbone. Slowly she traced the evidence of his years of fighting for his clan.

Symon groaned. Elena jerked her hand back. "I didn't mean to hurt you!"

"And you did not." He reached for her hand and guided it back to him. "Your touch may make my knees buckle, but certainly it does not hurt." His chuckle was eclipsed by another low, throaty groan.

Elena smiled, remembering her own groaning pleasure of a few moments before. Emboldened, she ran her hands over his chest, flickering her fingers over his own flat nipples. A sharp intake of his breath made her stop and linger there.

Her eyes locked with his, she lowered her mouth to his

nipple and suckled as he had at hers. When his eyelids flickered closed, she felt another surge of womanly power. All the pain in her life paled beside the pulsating pleasure that still echoed through her. All her fear of warriors paled when she realized that this mighty warrior quivered beneath her touch, moaned at the flick of her tongue over his nipple, trembled in his need of her. Yet he did not fling her to the bed and satisfy himself alone. He did not. Gently he laid her on the bed, taking back the lead in this dance he was teaching her.

He loomed over her, the look of a conqueror on his face, a look of exultation and expectation. She closed her eyes and tensed, knowing what would come next. Her mind circled the next step, but could not bring it into focus. Dougal had described the act in minute detail—the pain, the blood.

She felt the bed dip next to her, felt the length of Symon's body against the side of her own. Felt his need against her thigh.

"Elena-mine, if you do not wish to finish this, we will not."

Surprise had her opening her eyes to meet his worried look.

Tears welled in her eyes at the gentleness in his voice, the concern in his eyes. She reached up and ran her hand along his cheek. He turned into it and kissed her palm. Heat rushed through her once more, pooling between her legs, tightening her breasts. Her breath came fast and short.

"Heat," she said wonderingly.

"Aye. Heat, lass. You are a flame." He kissed her then, slowly, tenderly. His hand strayed over her belly, over her breasts, down to the tangle of hair between her legs. He cupped her there and deepened the kiss. Memory tugged at her hips, reminding her urgently of the pleasure his hand could bring her. She moved against him again, feeling the scalding heat of their connection.

He moved once more to her breast, suckling, nibbling, and suckling more, stronger, harder, pulling at her until she thought she could stand it no more. His finger dipped into her heat again, and she had the sudden longing for his body deep inside her own, joining with her, bringing her this potent pleasure even as she gave him his own.

"Please," she said. His hand stilled and she moaned. She kissed him desperately, unable to voice what she wanted. He moved over her, between her thighs. Never before had she felt this need, this driving, maddening want. Never before had she understood that pain was only part of life, that pleasure was just as powerful.

Slowly he entered her with excruciating care. She wanted him to delve deeply into her, raising the inferno, in that moment incinerating all that she had ever been before. She urged him further, murmuring words of desire. He held perfectly still.

When she opened her eyes, his face, just over hers, was one of complete and total concentration. He held her look and stroked into her. A flash of pain, and then he was filling her completely, creating such a rush of fire licking through her veins she cried out in triumph, the pain forgotten.

He held her in his arms, kissed her urgently, and began to move, sliding in and out of her heat, matching the motion with his kisses. Intensity spiraled through her, centering deep in her belly, coiling, wrapping around her limbs and grasping her mind. All was pleasure, potent, tangible pleasure. He tightened the coil with each stroke, fanning the fire, until she leapt into the abyss, flying free as he leapt with her, groaning her name even as she splintered into a thousand twinkling stars.

chapter 13

*S*ymon woke her near dawn, and they made love again,
exploring each other slowly, savoring the feel of each
other. Afterward he held her close in his arms, her back
cradled against his chest. He nuzzled her neck and she
replied with a sleepy, contented sound. He would have her
like this always, content, safe, his.

He tried to pinpoint just what it was about this woman
that made him so determined to claim her, body, heart, and
loyalty. He searched for something more logical than the
fact that she made the blood pound in his veins; that she
brought him to his knees with her trust. That she humbled
him with her courage, and made him fight to keep her safe
with her vulnerability. But more, she believed him to be
more than he thought he was, and he wanted to live up to
her belief.

He wanted her because he was a better man when she was around—not because she rid him of the devil—but because he wished to see her smile, to keep her safe, to hold her close.

Because he loved her.

Wonder spread through him. He loved her! And she would come to love him, in time, he would see to it. She held some passion for him, of that he was certain. Love would follow, given time.

He realized suddenly that marrying her was everything. Without that binding her to him, he would have to live up to his word and take her away from here in only another sevenday. Impossible!

"Elena-mine," he whispered.

"Hmm?" came her sleepy reply.

"You never answered my question." He slid his hand along her smooth hip and was gratified when she nestled her bottom closer to him.

"What question?" she asked, turning now to face him, her eyes only half open. She ran her fingers over his stubbled cheek.

" 'Tis clear we have some"—he cupped her breast and grinned when her breath shook—"affection for each other." He kissed her lightly, whispering against her satiny lips, "Will you wed me?"

Her eyes were fully open now, and she pulled back from him slightly, her brow furrowed and her mouth drawn down in a frown.

"Why?"

"You are my hope, Elena-mine. You have rid me of the poison. You have resurrected my soul and shown me that I can feel aught besides anger and grief."

"I am not any of those things," she said, rolling away from him and climbing out of the bed. She searched about for her clothes.

Symon could not help but appreciate her long limbs and full hips, in spite of the flash of anger in her eyes.

She slid her shift over her head, pulling it until it fell about her, hiding her body, but hinting still at what lay beneath. "I am a woman. Only a woman. 'Tis all I want to be. I am not responsible for your hope. I do not want that on my shoulders." She grabbed her gown and pulled it on.

Symon surged out of the bed, catching her hands, stilling them where she struggled with the laces he had so urgently pulled from the garment. He pulled her with him to the edge of the bed, where he sat, then silently fastened her gown. When he was done, he rose and took her face in his palms. Slowly he kissed her eyelids, her high, freckled cheekbones, nibbled on her lips until she melted against him. He folded her into his arms, grateful that she was so susceptible to his touch.

"Lass, you are a woman, first. 'Tis a certainty that I am all too aware of. But 'tis not all you are. You are also a healer. Whether you like it or not, 'tis a part of who you are." He pulled back just far enough to look into her eyes. "And you have brought hope to me and my people, whether you like it or not."

"Then we need not wed if I have done so much already."

"You will make me say the words, will you not?"

"What words?"

"Lass . . . Elena-mine," he said, raising her hands to his lips and looking deep into her eyes, "I love you."

"Nay, you need me, you do not love me." She slid her hands free of his and stepped back.

"Och, you're a stubborn lass."

"So my father often said."

Symon laughed, then sobered. "What if we have made a bairn this night?" He could not read her face.

At last she took a deep breath. "I do not think we have. But if it comes to be, we will discuss it then."

"If it comes to be, you will have little choice, Elena-mine. If you carry my bairn, you will be my wife."

She nodded, and hugged him tight. "But there is no bairn."

He smiled. Aye, there may not be one yet, but if he had his way, they would have a great many more opportunities to make one. She had given in to her body's need for him; soon she would give in to her destiny.

E lena led the way down to the Great Hall, Symon following close behind. They had said nothing more, but silently finished dressing, then left the chamber that had been their sanctuary through the night.

He loved her. Nay, it could not be. He needed her. He wanted her body. He did not love her. He was grateful. He sought to bind her to him for her gift.

But a voice deep in her heart decried that lie.

Lying in his arms had been . . . miraculous. Never had she felt so free, so cared for. She would not say loved. He had been a tender lover, careful, generous, and yet she had felt he held himself back somehow, as if he was afraid to hurt her. It would not do to hurt the woman responsible for your sanity. Again the voice complained.

And then he had thought of a bairn. Her bairn, and his. His eyes had lit with a soft glow, and she found herself wishing . . .

Elena had never let herself dwell on the question of whether she would become a mother or not. She was well past the age where most young women had their first children, and yet . . . if she did carry Symon's child, she would never be truly alone. She would always have someone to love, even if she lived as Auld Morag did, separate from society. But would she be enough for a child?

It did not bear worrying over just now. She did not believe they had made a bairn.

Wee Fia met them at the bottom of the stairs leading from Symon's tower. The child danced from one foot to the other in barely suppressed excitement. Elena couldn't help smiling every time she spied that elfin face.

"Good morn, sprite. Were you waiting for me?"

"Aye, mistress. Me mum. She's . . . the baby . . ." A huge gap-toothed grin spread over the girl's face. "It came!" she finally managed to say.

Elena squatted down and took Fia's hands in her own. "That's wonderful! You're a sister!"

"Aye, mistress, but me mum, she's"—the grin faded—"she's feeling poorly. She asked for you."

Elena looked over her shoulder at Symon, then stood and moved to the bailey door, Fia's hand in hers. "Let's go see how she fares, lass."

Symon followed behind. When they arrived at the chamber Mairi had been taken to in the night, Elena made Symon wait outside while she and Fia went in.

What Elena found inside nearly broke her heart. Mairi lay on the narrow bed, her skin gray, her eyes sunken. The midwife was helping her drink something. Elena squeezed Fia's hand, then turned to her, distracting her from her mum. "Sprite, will you go outside and keep Symon company? Tell him I'll be needing some things from the still-room in a bit."

"But—"

"Do not worry over your mum. We need to let her rest so she'll get strong enough to take care of you and your new . . ." She looked about for the infant, fear suddenly clenching her stomach when she did not see it.

"'Tis a fine boy-child," the midwife said. "Though I told Mairi here she shouldn't be having any more bairns. 'Twasn't prudent."

"My auntie has him," Fia said quietly. "She has milk for him and me mum does not."

Elena nodded. "Give Symon my message, then keep him company while we see to your mum." She gave the girl a little push toward the door. Fia looked back at her with big eyes. "Don't worry over him, sprite. You made him laugh yesterday, did you not?" Fia nodded. "Then you must be a fairy princess." A smile lit the child's face, and she scampered out the door.

When the door was closed and Elena could hear the low rumble of Symon's voice, she turned back to the bed. Blood stained the coverings, where there had been none but moments before. Memory surged into her. She was cast back into a similar dark, stuffy room, with another woman bleeding to death after a difficult birth. That bairn had not lived, and neither had the woman, though not before Elena had tried to save her. Tried, and nearly lost her own life with the effort.

But this was different. She was different. This woman

was not her own mother, and she was no longer twelve years old. She knew better than to let herself get dragged down with the dying, knew to do only what she could while keeping herself distant, safe.

She looked at Mairi, wee Fia's mum, and remembered what it had felt like to be cast adrift in a sea of men with no woman to guide her, to teach her, to comfort her. She would not see the same happen to Fia if she could prevent it.

She moved nearer the bed. Mairi slept, so she questioned the midwife. "Was it long?"

"Nay, indeed 'twas too fast. The babe was anxious and would not wait for her body to prepare completely. By the time I arrived, the bairn had been born and there was little I could do for the lass." She lowered her voice to a hoarse whisper. "I do not think she'll last the day."

Elena moved to Mairi's side and sat on the bed next to her. She picked up the woman's hand and let herself sink into the sensations that poured into her. Oddly, there was little pain, just a floating, boneless sensation and Elena realized that she, too, was probably too late to help. Still, she must try, for Fia's sake. She turned away from the dying woman to find the midwife eyeing her warily.

"I'll sit here with her for a while. Why don't you get some food and rest a bit?"

After a moment's consideration the other woman turned and left the chamber.

The midwife came through the door, took one look at Symon, and quickly crossed herself. She grabbed Fia by the hand, and he watched as she hurried away, pulling the child with her and muttering under her breath about devils visiting the dying. Quietly he opened the door and slipped inside the overheated chamber.

"You should not be here," Elena said without even looking up.

"How fares she?" he asked, moving closer to the bed.

Elena shook her head, then looked up at him, tears filling her eyes, threatening to spill over. "What will Fia do without her mum?"

"I suppose she'll do what all weans do when they lose their mum. Her da will be back in a day or two, and she's sure to have an aunt or a gran who will see to her."

She turned back to the sleeping woman and shook her head violently. "Nay, 'tis never the same. 'Tis never enough." She began rubbing her hands together as she stared at the woman's face. "I cannot let it happen."

"Lass, can you save her?" he asked, but she did not seem to hear him. He watched as she ran her hands over the other woman, letting them hover just over the bedclothes, near the bloodstain. He watched for any sign of pain in Elena, but there didn't seem to be any. He watched as she rubbed her hands together again and again, a little more frantically each time. At last she sobbed as she rubbed them together and Symon touched her. She was freezing, though sweat sheened her skin.

"Elena." She did not respond. "Elena!" He pulled her from the woman's side now, onto her feet.

"No! I cannot let her die!" She fought him, pummeling his chest with her fists, tears pouring down her cheeks.

He examined the face of the woman on the bed. The eyes were open, but no life sparkled there. "She's gone, lass. You did your best."

"Noooo!" It was a cry as much as a denial.

"Wee Fia will be all right. We'll see to it, you and me."

"But Mairi—"

"She's gone now. She'll suffer no more."

"I shouldn't have kept myself distant. I should have been braver."

"What do you mean, lass? I saw you. You struggled hard to save her."

"Nay, I kept myself distant, did not allow my gift to pull me deep where I could have saved her. I was afraid, too afraid."

She had quieted somewhat, resting her cheek against his tear-dampened chest.

"Why were you afraid?"

He did not think she was going to answer, but then she took a deep, shuddering breath. Her voice came quiet, almost a whisper, and her eyes were fixed on the dead woman. "Once before, in just this way, I tried to save a woman. I tried but did not know how to keep myself separate. By the time I realized what was happening, my gift had wound itself about her life, pulling me down into the darkness as she died. If my father had not pulled me from her when he did, I would have died with her. I have never allowed myself to get so close to death again. I should have today."

Symon cupped the back of her neck and kissed the top of her head. "You did what you could, Elena-mine. 'Twas not meant for this one to live beyond this day."

The door burst open and Fia entered, followed by the midwife and Jenny with a tray laden with food. Elena quickly stepped away from Symon. Fia stepped slowly toward the bed, her eyes big and her mouth solemn.

"Mum?" She stopped and looked from Elena to Symon and back, asking her question with her eyes.

Elena nodded, then knelt down and took the child's hands. " 'Twas peaceful," she said. "I tried to help, but 'twas not enough. I'm sorry, sprite." Tears rolled down Fia's face, and Elena pulled her into her arms. "I'm so sorry."

Symon shooed the other women out of the chamber, promising them quietly that he would call them when the wean had calmed a bit. He stood at the door, watching Elena rock the child in her lap, crooning to her and telling her how much her mum loved her, would always love her, over and over again. He couldn't help but wonder what would have happened if someone had done as much for him when his mum had died, or if anyone had done so for Elena when her mum died.

Sudden understanding rocked through him. The woman Elena had spoken of, the one she'd tried to save, had been her own mother. The enormity of it hit him, and once more he was amazed at the lass's courage. Once before she had attempted what she had today, and nearly lost her own life, with her mother's. And yet she had cared enough for Fia to overcome her fear and try again.

But had she not faced a similar dance with death when she healed warriors? He remembered the pain he had felt when she healed the burned lad. Perhaps the pain was enough to keep her separate. Perhaps. He would have to ask, later, when they were alone.

Soon Fia rose from Elena's lap and moved to her mother's side, Elena's hand firmly clasped in hers. She bent and kissed her mum's cheek, then Elena swung her up onto her hip and moved toward the door. Symon opened it, then followed the woman and the child out into the corridor. The midwife waited there with Jenny. He nodded at them, then turned to follow Elena.

E lena held Fia's hand as they walked back toward the gates of Kilmartin. It had been difficult for Elena to leave the relative safety of the castle's stout walls, but she had to do it for Fia. If she had only been braver, stronger, she might have saved the child's mum. A little voice at the back of her mind told her 'twas not so, but she tried to ignore it.

She had spoken with Fia's aunt, a sour woman with too many weans of her own. She lived in the hills east of the castle. She had taken the bairn, at least until he was weaned, but she did not want the keeping of another hungry mouth. Fia's da still had not returned from wherever it was he'd gone to. For now, at least, it seemed Elena was to be Fia's keeper.

In other circumstances Elena would have been thrilled to have such a clever child in her care, would have longed to claim her as her own, but this was not to be. As Symon's wish to wed her could not be. She could not stay here. True, since the discovery of Dougal's secret entrance to the castle, and the burning of the stable, he had not harried the MacLachlans further. He had made no demands, nor launched any attacks. But he would. She knew it, was certain of it. 'Twas as inevitable as winter snows or spring rain.

But she could not leave yet. Symon had not heard from his mother's people in the north, and Ranald had not returned from the errand he had been sent upon. He would have to be here to see to the clan's safety before Symon could leave for long enough to escort her north.

So if she must be here, at least she could offer some comfort to the lass, though she would have to prepare her from the beginning that it would only be for a short time, then she must look to her father, and perhaps Jenny, for her care and keeping.

She looked down at the unusually silent child and squeezed her hand. A lone tear trickled down Fia's cheek, and she smeared it away with the back of her hand. Elena stopped and hugged her, holding her close, wishing with all her heart that she could take this kind of pain from her. She remembered all too vividly the pain of losing her own mother. If she could not take this pain away, at least she could share it.

She held the child close. "I know, sprite, 'tis unfair. 'Tis painful"—she pulled back and touched her fingers to the child's chest—"there."

Fia sniffed and nodded her head. "How did you ken such a thing?" she asked.

Elena touched her own chest. "I have the same kind of empty hurt, right here."

"You do?"

"Aye. I lost my mum the very same way when I was only a bit older than you are now. Only I didn't have a brother to love for her when she was gone. You do. You're a sister, and the only thing that wee lad will ever know of his mum is what you and your da tell him. You need to keep those stories of her, the things you loved about her, the special memories you have of your time with her, and tell him, starting the next time you see him, and every time after. Your mum is here"—she touched the lass's chest again—"and here." She touched her forehead. "As long as you remember, she'll be here for you always."

"Does it ever stop hurting?"

Elena considered telling her it did, but could not bring herself to lie to the wean. "Nay, it never does, though 'twill lessen with time. 'Tis more of an auld ache now than the stabbing pain when 'twas new."

"But how did you get it to lessen?"

Elena looked out over the countryside, trying to remember those dark days after her mother's burial. She had spent hours in her mum's stillroom, putting things away her mum had never gotten to, arranging things to suit her own knowledge of the herbs, puttering with the things her mother had taught her. "I learned the herblore from anyone who would teach me. I kept my mind busy, so I would not dwell on what I had lost."

"Will you teach me the herblore?"

"Och, lass, 'twas what fascinated me. What fascinates you?"

"You do."

"Well, 'tis a passing fancy that. Before I came to this place, what did you play at? Did you help your mum with the ale brewing? Did you fancy yourself a cheesemaker?"

Fia just looked at her. "I fancied myself to be a fine healer, so I could help me mum when her time came upon her. I was no help."

Elena cupped the child's chin in her hand, lifting it until their eyes met. "Even I, with . . . with all my knowledge and skill, could not help your mum. Do not hold yourself responsible when you had no way to stop what would come. Wee Fia, your smile eased more of your mum's burdens than anything else you could have given her."

Tears streamed down the child's face. Symon moved close and scooped Fia into his arms. She laid her head on his shoulder, never taking her eyes from Elena, nor did she release Elena's hand as they moved through the gate. "Will you be my mum, now, Elena?"

Shocked by the child's request, Elena shook her head quickly. "That I cannot do, sweeting. When your da returns, he will need you with him. And I will not be here long enough to be a mum to you."

"Nay!" Symon and the child said together.

"Nay," Symon said again.

Elena glared at him. "We have a bargain, you and I. I will hold you to it."

"Things have changed," he said, barely suppressed fury thick in his voice. "I have changed. Circumstances between us have changed."

"But I have not." She looked pointedly at the child in his arms. "I'll take her. You can stay with me until your da returns, Fia. I'll teach you what I may of herbs until then."

The child said nothing, though she allowed Symon to pass her into Elena's arms.

"I have not," she said again as she passed him, heading to her original chamber, too close to his chamber for comfort, but the quiet would be good for Fia. Perhaps she could get the child to sleep a bit, then with luck, she might coax her into eating a little something. She would not see this child fall sick from grief.

S *ymon paced outside Elena's chamber, waiting until the* quiet voices inside ceased, waiting until he was sure the child slept. When he heard the thunk of a peat brick landing in the fire, he opened the door and stepped inside. Fia did sleep, curled up on the bed, her thumb tucked firmly in her mouth. Elena stood at the hearth, staring at him.

He told himself he had come to speak sense to her, bring her around to understanding that she belonged here, that wee Fia was but one MacLachlan in need of her gentle influence. It's what he'd come to do, but instead he crossed the room in three strides and swept her into his arms, his mouth descending greedily over hers. He was gratified when she molded herself to him, hugging him fiercely, kissing him with the same intensity, matching him as if they were made for each other.

Slowly the flare of heat between them calmed to a steady flame. Symon hugged her close, eased by her presence. "Do you ken that you need the lass as much as she needs you, Elena-mine?"

She said nothing, but rubbed her cheek against his shoulder. He smiled, sensing a softening in her, a yearning even. Yes, she would come around. Soon she would know how much they needed her and she them. Soon.

He kissed her again, then smoothed her fiery hair away from her face. Dark circles under her eyes marred her creamy skin. He ran his thumbs over her high proud cheekbones, marveling at the silky soft feel of her. "You need to sleep."

"Aye. 'Tis hard to sleep when guilt torments me."

"Ah, lass. You did your best. I heard what you told the wean today. 'Twas difficult for you to share that bit of yourself, I wager. I'm thinking you have not done so before."

" 'Twas not necessary before," she whispered. Her eyes

were closed and she nuzzled against his hands. If she'd been a cat, she would have purred for sure. He chuckled at the image, knowing that all sweet kitties had a wild streak and sharp claws to go along with the soft fur and quiet ways. He'd gentle this one soon enough, and enjoy the doing of it. They both would.

But not tonight. Tonight the wean needed her more than Symon did, though that was hard to imagine. Tonight Elena needed to sleep, to forgive herself, to understand. Wee Fia had worked her magic on Elena before; perhaps the fragile lassie would do so again.

"Sleep you well, love." He kissed her again, hoping she felt all the tenderness he had for her, the caring. He tried to hide the need, though he doubted such a strong need could be hidden completely. He left her there, by the fire, as he had found her. As he reached the door he turned back.

"I do not think Dougal of Dunmore can find another way in, but nevertheless, I'll be sleeping just outside your door here. Rest well and do not worry any more."

"I don't think 'tis necessary, Symon. Find your own soft bed this night. We will be fine."

"I'll sleep at the door," he said, unwilling to take any chances with her safety. He closed the door behind him, rolled up in his plaid, and lay down on the cold stone floor.

The next few days were frustrating and exhilarating for Symon. Frustrating, because Elena kept wee Fia with her through the nights, and through the days. Symon never got more than a few stolen kisses from her.

Exhilarating, because Elena truly had banished the madness—or the poisoning, as he had to keep reminding himself. He was clear-headed and even-tempered as he hadn't been in a year. Just watching the woman move about the castle, brewing teas for the sick, tending a wean's scraped knee, or taking a moment to soothe her shadow, wee Fia, made him think his luck had finally turned and all would be well for his clan.

At first, when he stopped and allowed himself these thoughts, people had scowled at him, skirting around their chief as he stood like a silly love-struck lad, gazing at the lass. But after a couple of days they began to look at him curiously, then they would glance at Elena and smile. By the end of the week he found them grinning at him, and he would grin back. There was a lightness about the castle that had not been there since his own mother died. Perhaps it was just a woman's touch upon the clan, or simply relief that their chief was no longer a threat to them.

Whatever it was, Symon did not care. The clan was more at ease and he was well. Now if he could convince Elena to marry him, all would be guaranteed.

Symon was leaning against the wall, accepting the passing grins of his kinsmen, when Murdoch appeared, grim-faced at his shoulder. Symon glanced to him, the grin sliding off his face. "What?"

"Ranald has returned. I think you will not like what he has discovered."

"You could not let me enjoy myself a few days longer, eh?"

"You should go now, Symon. 'Tis not a thing to laugh over."

Aye, little about his life was worth laughing over, except the last week. "Very well. Is he in his chamber?"

Murdoch nodded.

"Do not let her out of your sight," he said, pointing in Elena's direction.

Elena must have seen his movement, for she glanced up, concern on her face. Not wanting to burden her until he'd found out Ranald's news, he forced a smile to his lips, then signaled her that Murdoch would be watching over her while he was gone. She nodded her understanding, though the look of concern did not leave her lovely eyes. Symon gave himself a mental shake. He had other things to think about than the lass's eyes.

Moments later he opened the door to his brother's chamber. Ranald stood in the corner, his back to the door, pouring something. He glanced over his shoulder, saw Symon, and turned his attention back to his task.

"Close the door, brother. What I have to tell you does not need to be tonight's gossip in the Hall."

Symon did as his brother asked, then stood, arms crossed over his chest, waiting for bad news.

Ranald turned, holding a flagon before him. "Murdoch told me you'd been asking for my spiced wine. I didn't realize how low the supply was. I could've sworn there was another barrel in the storeroom when I left." He handed the wine to Symon, then turned to retrieve a cup. "This will not be as good as it might a sevenday hence, but 'twill be to your liking still. I think you may desire it, once you hear what I have to tell you."

Symon grunted as he took the cup from Ranald. "We shall see," he said, putting the wine on the hearth to warm, setting the cup next to it. "Well?"

Ranald looked nervous, which did not bode well for his news. "It took some doing, but I have discovered who exactly Dougal of Dunmore is."

chapter 14

A candlemark later the flagon was empty, and Symon was pacing the wall-walk atop the battlements, scanning the surrounding area for any sign of Dougal of Dunmore. The prophecy ran through his mind. *When flame and madness mingle.* That part had come true in more ways than one. *When cast out thorns grow strong.* That riddle was solved, too, though he did not see how there were any old wrongs that could be righted with Dunmore.

That part of the prophecy would make sense eventually, just as the others had. For now, though, at least he knew whom he faced. He would not be lax in his vigilance. 'Twas no wonder the daft bastard vowed to kill whoever stood between him and Elena, for he had ever been so.

Ranald had implied that Elena was in league with Dunmore, a spy of sorts, seeking out MacLachlan weaknesses, then feigning the violence of her encounters with Dunmore, when in fact they had arranged those meetings for her to pass him information.

For a moment Symon had been beguiled by Ranald's tale of deceit and disloyalty, but then he remembered all that Elena had done for him and for their clan during Ranald's absence. He had very nearly told Ranald of the discovery not only that he was being poisoned, but that the poison had been found.

But he didn't tell Ranald any of this. Nor did he tell him that Elena had cleared the poison from him, nor that they had become lovers. It did not sit well with him, this feeling of uneasiness with his brother, but he held his counsel, at least for now. He did however tell him he had asked Elena to marry him, telling Ranald only that it was necessary to keep her safe, not that he couldn't bear the thought of losing her.

Elena's laughter tinkled up from below. Symon peered over the edge of the wall to find wee Fia dancing about her, laughing and giggling. He smiled, realizing how everyone seemed to be laughing and smiling of late. 'Twas a wonderful change, and one he would ensure continued. No matter what Ranald suspected, or Dougal of Dunmore threatened.

Symon quickly found his way down to the bailey. He picked his way through the people, carts, and animals so that Elena would not see his approach. As he neared, he caught Fia's eye and quickly raised a finger to his lips, recruiting her into his game. The lass's eyes twinkled, though a tinge of sadness still muted them from their usual brightness. She continued chattering away with Elena and another child. Slowly Symon crept up to Elena, then deftly grabbed her about the waist and lifted her off her feet, swinging her around in a circle.

Elena squealed. Fia and the other child laughed and clapped their hands. Smiles met Symon from every corner, except for the glittering green eyes of his brother, watching from a shadowed corner nearby. Symon did not care if his brother approved of his choice of wife. He wanted her. He would have her, and together they would insure that laughter and joy always overcame sorrow and sadness within the walls of Kilmartin.

Elena pummeled his arms, laughing and demanding to be put down all at the same time. Symon obliged, then spun her in his arms and kissed her soundly in front of the entire crowd. There was hooting and hollering, whistles and impertinent comments, until Symon realized that she had gone still in his arms. Alarmed, he pulled back. Concern filled her brown eyes.

"Are you all right?" she asked.

"Aye, lass. Can't a man kiss his intended?"

He expected a denial, but instead she placed her hand upon his chest. Her eyes went hazy, as if she didn't see what was before her. At that very instant a vise twisted in his gut, sweat popped out on his brow, and the world went black around him.

E lena desperately tried to hold Symon upright when he doubled over. The pain in his gut echoed so strongly in her own she had trouble keeping them standing. The people who had gathered close only a moment before, scattered, putting as much distance as they could between themselves and their stricken chief. Sweat poured from

Symon, and he staggered, nearly pulling them both to the ground. Panicked, Elena looked around for help. Murdoch was loping toward her, concern etched on his face.

"Help me lay him down," she said when the giant reached her side and took Symon by the shoulders. Symon jerked, trying to break free of the other man's grip. "Wheesht," she said to him, "lie down, Symon. 'Twill be right soon." She murmured to him as Murdoch struggled to get him to the ground. When he would not lie down, Elena put her hand upon Murdoch's arm. "Sit behind him. Hold him still." The giant did as she instructed, pinning Symon's arms back when he would have escaped and wrestling him down.

Elena looked about quickly. Most people had retreated indoors, but she knew the doorways and windows would be crowded with anxious eyes. She regarded Symon; the wild-eyed expression on his face was terrifying, but she knew she had to help him. She could not allow him to suffer, nor could she allow the clan to believe he was mad any longer.

It would seal her fate, what she must do, but that was no longer important. This clan deserved to know their chief was sound of mind, that the trials that had befallen them were not Symon's fault. Indeed, that one amongst them was responsible for the calamity that had come upon them. Anger surged through her. Who would do such a thing to these people? To Symon?

Symon struggled in Murdoch's grip, kicking out and catching her in the shin. A gasp escaped her, but the fact that Symon, so gruff on the outside, but the keeper of a soft heart on the inside, could do such a thing just proved he was not himself. Murdoch grunted and hooked his own legs over Symon's, so that he was wrapped about his chief, restraining this man who only moments before had been swinging her in circles, laughing and carefree.

Elena ignored the throbbing in her leg and knelt in front of Symon. She took a deep, calming breath and began rubbing her hands together. She looked up at Murdoch. "Whatever happens, do not let him go until I tell you to, ken?"

"Aye, lass. 'Tisn't the first time I've held him down so an herbwife could have a go at 'im."

"I am no herbwife. Do not let him go."

At that Elena began burning the poison from Symon's blood once more. She was baffled at how dark the poison felt, how strong, how sinister, when there had been naught there an hour before. She pushed the torment from him, warming her hands again and again, smoothing her palms over his heart, resting her forehead against his. She battled the poison, imagining herself a great red dragon, circling a pool of bile, flaming it with her breath, slowly burning it away, revealing the man below, the whole and healthy man.

Again and again she struggled to rid him of the pestilence, moving her hands from his heart to his stomach to his head and back again, always finding wisps and traces, needing to eradicate every last drop of the noxious potion from this man she loved.

She paused, realizing just what that meant to her. Yes, she loved this man, and these people, this place. She was happier, stronger, since she had come here. Brightness filled her as she understood all that had been swirling about within her since she arrived here. She gathered that brightness and joined it with the heat of her gift, cleansing and purging, pouring the lightness of all that she felt into this man.

She knew she had won the battle when Symon's strength slowly wakened and joined her own. Together, they burned the last of the bane from him in a joining of their hearts that was as glorious as the joining of their bodies had been.

At last Elena opened her eyes. Her hands rested over Symon's heart once more. His eyes delved deeply into hers. She blinked and looked around. The crowd had regathered, mouths agape and the whispers starting. Fingers pointed at her and a kind of dawning horror washed the faces of those around her. Even wee Fia stood behind a woman's skirts, her thumb stuck in her mouth, uncertainty clouding her face.

Devastating loss crashed through the momentary joy, pushing Elena perilously close to tears. Never had she been so happy, nor felt so useful, as she had this past sevenday. Yet here, in the space of time it took to purge the poison from their chief, she had lost all of that.

They would never look at her the same again. They would never allow her that easy acceptance they had shown when they thought her a simple herb healer. 'Twas exactly as she had feared. She would have to leave here now, just when she'd begun to hope she might be able to stay.

But they would have their chief, safe and whole and able to lead them once more. At least she had given them that.

"You can release me, Murdoch," Symon said, his voice raspy.

Murdoch waited for her permission. She nodded her

assent. Even Murdoch looked at her differently now, she noticed. Not fear precisely, but not the easy camaraderie she had come to cherish, either. She rose to her own feet and offered a hand to Symon, who stood, with her help. He looped his arm over her shoulder and together they moved off toward the privacy of his chamber. Silence followed them until they slipped into the castle.

A tumult erupted behind them, feverish voices raised in question. The clan would debate what they had just seen well into the night, she was sure, and then they would come to one of two decisions. Either they would understand what she was, what she could do, and insist their chief use her as her own father, and then Dougal had, or they would brand her witch, banishing her from their midst, or worse. Elena found herself wishing for the latter.

S*ymon let Elena help him to the bed they had shared.* He sat, elbows on his knees, his head hanging, his mind still reeling from all that had happened in the space of an afternoon. He said nothing, for he couldn't seem to find the words to say, the words he knew needed saying. She would need reassurance, but he couldn't think how to begin. The poison was gone, but his body still was not entirely his own to command.

There was a sound in the doorway. 'Twould be Ranald.

"You were a great help," he heard Elena say, as if from a distance. The nasty edge to her voice made him wince. Ranald would not appreciate her tone.

"There was little I could do," his brother said, a sneer equally audible in his voice. " 'Twas best to stay out of the way. He has been known to kill when in the grips of his affliction."

Symon managed to raise his head, focus his gritty eyes on the pair before him. Elena stood, fists on her hips, between him and Ranald. He tried to smile at the image of her defending him, angry for him.

"So you bring him wine? You are a noble brother, worthy of Symon's loyalty." Sarcasm didn't sit well on her voice.

"Leave him be, Elena," Symon said.

She whirled around to face him. The anguished look on her face tore at his heart. She had revealed herself to the entire clan for him, and she was hurting for it now. He held out his hand to her, and she came to him, dropping to her knees and resting her head in his lap. She wrapped her arms about his legs, holding on as if she were afraid to let go. Gently he stroked her beautiful fiery hair.

"I would have some wine, brother," he said quietly, pleased that his voice was once more under his command. "The lass could use a wee drop as well."

Ranald filled the single cup he had brought. "I'll call for another cup," he said as he handed it to Symon.

"Nay, 'tisn't necessary."

Elena rose, unasked, and sat next to him on the bed, sitting close, so that their thighs met from knee to hip. He was grateful for the trust inherent in that contact, glad that he could offer some comfort.

It struck him that they were alone together, now. He, separated by the scene he had created in front of the entire clan. She, by revealing her gift in order to relieve him.

Symon handed her his cup. "Drink."

She took it, sipped the spiced wine, then handed it back to him.

"'Tis clear to me the lass is the key to your sanity," Ranald said.

Symon took her hand and squeezed it. "Aye, that she is," he said, more to her than to Ranald, "in more ways than one."

"Nay," she said. The cinnamon flecks in her eyes glinted in the firelight, and Symon found himself regretting the loss of the laughter that had made her shine like a shooting star. "Nay. 'Tis time you told him the truth." She reached for the wine and took a longer drink.

"Truth?"

Symon sighed. "Aye, truth. There has been blessed little of that for a long time." He broke his gaze with Elena and turned to his brother. "'Tisn't madness."

Ranald looked dubious.

Symon laughed, a sad kind of chuckle. "'Tisn't madness. The truth? 'Tis poison."

Ranald appeared confused, then angry. "Nay. How could that be?"

"Elena cannot heal madness, but this . . . you saw for yourself. This she can heal."

"With a touch . . . 'tis more like witchery than healing."

"'Tis healing, brother. Do not think otherwise."

"But who would poison you? And why?"

"We don't know yet." He took the cup from her and contemplated the bloodred wine. "Though 'twould seem to be an easy thing to do, slipping me the poison. It comes from mushrooms, we ken that much. We found a cache in the auld stillroom."

Ranald stiffened at that.

"Do not worry. We found your spice concoction, but we did not disturb it once we knew what it was."

Ranald nodded curtly. "Then where—"

"In another cupboard, mixed among bits and bundles. We know what it is, but we have not yet discovered how I am getting it." He raised the cup. "Could be anything, food, drink . . ." He sipped.

Elena went stiff at his side, pulling away the warmth where her body had been tucked next to his.

"What is it, Elena-mine?"

"The wine," she said, concentration marring her beautiful face. She took the cup away from him, sipped again, then closed her eyes as she did when she healed him.

"What, lass?"

Ranald moved closer, but didn't say anything. He glanced at Symon, but Symon just shook his head, waiting.

At last she opened her eyes, then spit the mouthful of wine back into the cup. Her eyes snapped with fire, her mouth set in a grim line as she stared at Ranald.

"The wine, Symon," she said without taking her eyes off his brother. " 'Tis the wine that poisons you. Your brother's spiced wine."

Symon's mind went numb as he took in what she said. Ranald? Nay, it wasn't possible. He rose and looked his brother in the eye. Ranald had been one of the few, indeed the only one to stand by him at first. Murdoch had come around quickly, but Ranald had been loyal, mostly, even when they did not agree over whether Symon should remain chief. Hadn't he?

To his credit, Ranald looked as stunned by the lass's accusation as Symon was. And yet he offered no defense for himself.

"What say you, brother?"

"I say she does not know of what she speaks."

Symon looked to Elena. She was determined, stubborn, her chin raised, hands curled into fists. He had the odd feeling she would have launched herself at Ranald if he threatened Symon. Slowly she rose to stand beside him.

"When was the last time you were beset by the devil— before today?" she asked him, but she glared at Ranald.

He had to think, and realized it was the night they became lovers, the day Ranald had left on Symon's orders, and Elena had discovered it was poison that plagued him, not madness. He turned and placed his palm against her cheek, gratified when she closed her eyes and leaned into his hand. "'Twas the day Ranald left."

"Aye. And you did not have his fine spiced wine after that," she said to him. "We drank ale the next morn," she whispered, cutting her eyes to Ranald and blushing slightly.

Ranald heard and Symon saw understanding flare in his brother. "You have already become lovers. Have you wed in secret, then? Is this some jealous lass's attempt to rid her husband of an adviser who does not wish her here?"

Elena lurched toward Ranald, and Symon caught her about the waist and hauled her so her back was to his chest. He held her close, enjoying the spit and fire of this unusual woman. "Wait, Elena-mine," he said, his mouth near her ear. "Let us get to the bottom of this before you scratch his eyes from his head."

"'Tis not funny, Symon. He has poisoned you." She struggled against him, but he held her firm, sorry he could not enjoy the situation better. "You said yourself he wished to be chief," she continued. "He did not believe you worthy of the position since the devil rode your shoulders."

He had said as much, but Symon had never thought Ranald would do more than fuss over the circumstance. No, he could not believe Ranald would be so disloyal. There must be an explanation—other than the obvious. There had to be.

"Could not someone else have put the poison in the wine?" he asked, more thinking aloud than expecting an answer.

"Then why were you not plagued while he was away? Did he not return today?"

Symon nodded, still searching for an answer. Ranald was not helping with his scowling refusal to defend himself. " 'Tis true. You were preparing a flagon for me when I entered your chamber. I drank it while we discussed . . ." He glanced down at the lass. He did not want to involve her in that business. "The flagon was empty when I left your chamber. Now you bring me more, and the lass finds the poison in it—" Sudden fear gripped him. Was her reaction due to the poison? "Elena, the poison—"

"I'm fine, love. Do not fash yourself. I had to cleanse it from my own body to make sure 'twas the same. 'Tis a subtle poison, that. It lurks about the body for a time before it starts to work. 'Tis another reason you would not suspect the wine, nor your brother. He could give you the poison, then make sure he was elsewhere when it began its work."

"Anyone could have put the poison in the wine," Ranald pointed out. "You said yourself you found my spice brew in the same room as the poison. 'Twould not have been difficult for someone to slip a bit of something more into my brew."

"Aye. True enough," Symon said, desperate to believe his brother.

A shout rose from the wall-walk. Symon rushed to the window overlooking the bailey and shouted to the men below. Their response chilled him to his bones. "Attack," he said, rushing past Ranald, who quickly followed him. He stopped at the door.

"Elena-mine, you must barricade yourself in here." The stricken look on her face tore at him, but he had no choice. His castle was under attack, and he would not have her exposed to the danger. "I am sorry lass, but you must."

He was gratified that she jerked her head up and down. He glanced at his brother, who was carefully watching the exchange, then the two of them left. The door banged behind them, and Symon heard the loud scrape of the lock turning.

Symon hit the top of the bailey stairs bellowing orders. Murdoch already had archers on the walls, and the gate and yett were closed. Guards were poised, ready to defend the bailey if the castle was breached.

E lena watched from the tiny window, trying to ignore the locked door, even as she squeezed the key so tightly in her fist it threatened to cut the skin. She could hear the deep, rhythmic pounding of a battering ram against the outer gate, and she tried to remember the short dark tunnel she had passed through on her way into the castle. The ceiling was lined with murder holes, where boiling oil or burning pitch could be dropped upon any who ventured through it. The walls were lined with arrow loops, where archers could stand protected inside the chambers that lined the tunnel, and easily shoot any invaders. 'Twould be difficult indeed for anyone to breach these walls.

But if 'twas Dougal leading this attack, then 'twas her own kinsmen who would suffer from the excellent defenses. And something deep in her gut told her Dougal was indeed behind this.

She struggled to breathe. If the man did not give up, then more people would be harmed because of her. More would come to pain and suffering, and even death, because she would not submit herself to Dougal's governance.

But she could not do that, even if she had the courage to allow it. For Dougal would only use her as he had before, to shore up the strength of her kinsmen so they could do battle more and more often. Dougal did not care how often they were hurt as long as they were able to fight when next he needed them. Nay, handing herself over to Dougal might slow down the pain he inflicted on others, but it would not stop it.

She had only the two choices she had had weeks before. She could take her own life, removing herself from all who would use her skill to their own purposes. Or she could find a way to lead Dougal away from these people, then disappear into the forest and travel deep into the Highlands, living as Auld Morag did, separate and alone.

But would she be alone? She placed her hands on her belly. Even now there could be a bairn there, deep inside her, growing out of the one night of complete joy she had ever experienced. If she followed the first path, she would be ending not only her own life, but perhaps, just perhaps, that of another. How could she deny the results of that joy, extinguish any hope that it could happen again, if not for her, then for her daughter or son.

She had not chosen that path before. She could not choose it now. Though she would have liked to thwart Dougal so completely, she would not let Symon believe he had any part in such a decision.

She glanced about the chamber, searching for items that would help her in her plan. She would wait until this danger had passed, for she would not be so daft as to run straight into Dougal's hands. She would gather those things that would help her in her new life: clothes, her herbs, a firekit, what tools she might glean from the still-room, and a knife. If she traveled north, she would head deeper into the Highlands. And of course, she'd have to find some way to make sure Dougal knew she was no longer within Kilmartin Castle, no longer amongst the MacLachlans.

It would take some planning, but she could accomplish this. She must, if she wished to keep Symon and Fia and all the others she had come to care for safe from the wrath of Dougal of Dunmore.

chapter 15

*S*ymon made a circuit of the guards, making sure everyone was in place and aware of the importance of vigilance. He had not seen Ranald in several hours, but he was bound to be somewhere, sorting out some mess that had slipped past Symon's attention. Murdoch waved to him from the wall heights, indicating that all was in hand. Symon waved back and signaled the man that he would be in his chamber.

He had not allowed himself to think about Elena, locked in his chamber all by herself. He couldn't or he would not have been able to do as he must, coordinating the defense, though, in truth, he did not think anything the MacLachlans had done was responsible for the retreat of the Lamonts. It seemed they simply gave up after charging the gate repeatedly. 'Twas as if they sought to distract—

Symon sprinted up the stair, then up the circular stairwell to his chamber. "Elena!" he shouted as soon as he reached the hall. He yanked the latch on his own door, only to find it still locked. Relief flooded through him, though it did not halt him from banging upon the door.

"Symon?" Her voice came softly through the thick wood.

"Aye, you can open the door now."

He heard her fumble with the key, jiggling it in the lock, then finally it clanked open and the door swung wide. Her face was tear-stained, but she was safe. Symon had never been so happy. He strode into the room, pushing the door closed behind him, and folded her quickly into his arms. His lips found hers, and the kiss they shared was achingly sweet.

All the fear and uncertainty of the last hours left him. He was desperate to experience the joy and abandonment they had shared in each other's arms once more. He swept her up and was gratified to feel her arms come around him, her lips nuzzling his neck. He groaned as her teeth nipped at his ear and her hands twined in his hair. At the edge of the bed, he let her slide down the length of his body. She could not miss his desire; indeed, she pressed herself against him, her kisses growing more insistent, her hands gliding over him as if she needed to learn every inch of him all over again.

He was not sure who removed the first article of clothing, but he knew he was the last as her shift puddled at her feet and she stood in all her glorious pale skin and long fiery hair in front of him. He remembered that moment in the stone circle when she had stood, chin raised, defiance in her eyes. He had thought her one of the ancients' priestesses.

That was nothing to the glory in front of him now.

He pulled her to him, kissing her hard, proud that she had protected herself, despite the need for a lock. Pleased that she was as eager for him as he was for her. Overwhelmed that such a woman could care for him.

As gently as he could he laid her back on the bed, trailing kisses down her neck, over her shoulders and down the valley between her breasts. Slowly he kissed her breasts, delighting at her gasps of pleasure as he brought each pink nipple to a tight bud, suckling, nipping. Slowly he slid his hand down her belly, slipping a finger inside her, unbearably pleased when he found her wet and ready for him. He moved over her, kissing her as she wrapped her legs about his waist, urging him to her.

Now she would be his. He slid into her, the heat and wet overwhelming him until he could barely form a thought. He wanted to let himself ride the wave of feeling, experience the total surrender, forget everything but this woman, and this moment. He held to one sliver of thought, waiting until she was ready, driving her slowly over the precipice until at last they raced together into the wind, their voices raised in triumph as their bodies united in joy.

Symon became aware of her hand sliding up and down his sweat-dampened back. He raised himself to his elbows and smoothed her hair back from her face. Gently he kissed her eyelids, her nose, her lips. When he finished she was gazing up at him, her eyes reflecting his own humbling emotions.

"Can you still say we are not meant for each other, Elena-mine? Can you believe we should not join our lives even as we join our bodies?"

She looked away, and a dark pit formed in Symon's stomach. "Elena?"

"'Tis my gift that makes you speak so," she said at last. The hitch in her voice scratched at him.

"Nay, lass. Can you not see how I feel about you? I cannot deny the need I have for your gift, but 'tis not why I wish you to be my wife."

He started to withdraw from her, but she held him close. "Not yet."

He smiled then, and moved slightly within her, settling himself in the cradle of her hips. He kissed her and knew, though she denied his feelings were true, she felt them. Returned them even, though she was not ready to admit it to him.

But she would. He knew it was only a matter of her getting used to the idea.

He had won, and the exhilaration rushed through him. He deepened the kiss and began to move within her again. She kept her eyes closed, and a sad smile played about her lips. Symon watched her, marveling at the joy and sadness that could mingle there, even as he saw passion rise once more, erasing all else. Symon closed his own eyes then, and rested his forehead against hers, remembering the joining they had shared when she healed him. Suddenly that same lightness swept through him, and he would have sworn at that moment that they joined completely—heart, mind, and soul—soaring into the bright sunlit sky, flying with the eagles high over the strife and turmoil below.

Symon arched into her, calling her name at the moment she called his own. Tears streamed down her face, and he knew she was as overwhelmed by the magnitude of the experience as he was.

The sky was just beginning to lighten when Symon fell asleep, Elena tucked firmly against him, his face in her hair, the smell of their loving surrounding them.

Elena lay, listening to Symon's quiet breathing, her mind in a fog of desire and despair. Symon's love-making was ardent, but her own reaction to him surprised her the most. Indeed, her own unrelenting response to him told her she would only hurt both of them more the longer she waited. And she couldn't wait much longer. Not only had she exposed herself before the entire clan, now Dougal had once more caused harm to this clan because of her. She could not allow that to continue. She would have to leave, and very, very soon.

She could hold Symon to their bargain, forcing him to take her away from here. Surely there had been time by now to get a message to his kin in the north. But if Dougal remained outside Kilmartin, he would see them leaving and either attack them or take advantage of Symon's going to wreak havoc on this clan that had taken her in, thwarting his plans.

Nay, Symon could not take her away. Either way he would be hurt, directly or indirectly. The only way to stop Dougal from harming Symon and his clan was to draw him away, draw his attention away. She would have to go alone. Somehow she would have to make sure he knew she had left the MacLachlan stronghold without allowing him to know exactly where she went. That would be tricky, a problem she would have to ponder.

For now, she'd enjoy the attentions of this man. She snuggled closer to him, content to bide with him for another few days. Her heart contracted. Another few days. 'Twas all she would get. It would have to be enough.

R anald was nowhere to be found.
They had stood, side-by-side, ready to defend their clan, as the Lamonts battered at the gate. Then, as suddenly as it had begun, the noise and commotion stopped. The Lamonts had withdrawn with nary a drop of blood spilt between them. Symon had hurried back to Elena, concern for her outweighing his need to learn the truth about the poisoned wine from his brother. Ranald could be questioned after he was sure Elena was all right.

But now Ranald was gone. Symon had searched the entire castle, but no one had seen his brother since the attack had ended. He hadn't been seen on the heights, nor in the bailey, not even in his own chamber, nor the Great Hall. Nowhere.

Symon could hardly allow himself to think about it. Elena had accused Ranald of the poisoning. He did not defend himself. And then he disappeared. Was it possible? Nay, it could not be. Ranald had been his one loyal kinsman since the beginning of this whole blasted trouble.

And yet, Ranald had disagreed about Symon's ability to lead the clan. Had tried to get him to step aside, let Ranald take over as chief. But there were simpler ways to take over than poison, and slow poison at that. Then why? Why would Ranald disappear just when the truth was coming out?

And where had he gone? The castle had been surrounded by Lamonts. If he left the castle, he would only land in the hands of Lamonts . . . in the hands of Dunmore.

Symon shook his head. It couldn't be. Ranald was loyal, despite his criticisms. He would not ally himself with Dunmore. He could not.

Symon's head pounded, though blessedly it was due only to the conundrum his brother's disappearance caused and not further poisoning.

He tried to think about the situation from a different angle. If Ranald had not disappeared purposely, then it was possible he was taken without his consent. This made much more sense. But why, and how? What use would Ranald serve to the Lamonts? To Dougal of Dunmore?

But Ranald had followed him . . . or had he?

Symon remembered his brother by his side as he crossed the bailey, but then, in the confusion and commotion, he could not recall Ranald's step, nor his voice after that. He had just been told of the poison, the connection with his spiced wine . . . had he gone to the stillroom? But why? It didn't really matter. He must have headed for the stillroom, not knowing of the tunnel, for Symon had not mentioned it. Could Dunmore—or someone else—have taken him, pulling him into the tunnel in spite of the guards posted there? Could he have been taken out of the castle with no one the wiser? But why Ranald? Perhaps he had been the first that Dunmore or his men had come upon. . . .

Realization slashed through Symon. Of course. That was why the Lamonts had retreated so easily. The attack had been a diversion, a ruse, but the tunnel was well guarded. Something was not right, but Symon could believe nothing else. Ranald would not have voluntarily abandoned his clan, and his brother.

He found Murdoch in the Great Hall, a lass giggling in

his lap. At the Devil's stormy entrance, she abruptly left her seat and headed to a table at the far end of the Hall.

"Did you have to scare the lass away with your dark countenance?" Murdoch said, grinning up at him. "I've been trying to steal a kiss from that one for a fortnight." He winked. "I nearly had it, too."

"She'll fall for your charms, lad," Symon said, sitting next to the giant. "But not today. I've a message needs delivering."

O*n the third evening after the attack on the castle,* Elena sat at the fire in Symon's chamber, awaiting his return. It had been a wonderful and a difficult three days. Wonderful because she had spent so much time in Symon's company, and in his arms. Difficult because where the clansfolk had begun to accept her, include her, they now kept a distance from her. She understood how Symon had felt that first time she had entered this place. Suspicion and whispers followed her wherever she went.

Even wee Fia did not dance to her side, pelting her with a dozen questions at a time. This hurt the worst, knowing that she had caused more pain for this child, when all she had wanted to do was help her. Fia kept to the shed where her aunt had taken up Fia's mother's task as alewife to the castle.

A few brave folk allowed Elena to tend their aches and pains, but even they were reserved as they had not been before. Finally she gave up, keeping to Symon's chamber or the stillroom, where she gathered together most of the things she thought she would need for her travels.

When the door swung open she jumped, startled from

her thoughts. Symon entered, smiling at her, but clearly distracted.

"Is there trouble?"

"Nay—aye, there is."

Elena rose from her stool by the fire. Somehow she thought she could withstand more bad tidings standing.

"Ranald . . ."

"Have you found him, then?"

Symon looked at her with unreadable eyes. "Aye. He's been found. Dunmore has him."

It took a moment for understanding to sink in. "Dougal? How?"

Symon shook his head. "It must have been during the attack, but I don't know precisely how. The tunnel was well guarded, but I cannot believe the bastard knows another way in."

"Dear God. But why would Dougal want . . ." Realization hit her. "He is held hostage in exchange for me, is he not?"

Symon pulled her close, and she wrapped her arms about him. The solid feel of him calmed her, gave her strength.

" 'Tis but one goal of Dunmore." He kissed the top of her head, then lay his cheek there.

"What will you do?" she asked, dreading the answer.

He sighed. "I do not know."

Fear shot through her. She pulled away, but he caught her arm, keeping her close.

"I will not turn you over to him, love. I could never do such a thing, and the clan would not allow it. Ranald would not wish me to give in to Dunmore."

"You believe that even though Ranald poisons you?"

Symon sighed. "I cannot believe he is the one behind the poison. Ranald wants only what is best for the clan. We differ in how to attain that, but nothing about my affliction has been good for the clan. He would not cause this suffering for our people."

"I hope you are right."

"I know I am."

She studied her hands for a moment, lacing and unlacing her fingers. "I suspect your clan would be glad to see me go," she said quietly.

"Nay." He raised her chin and kissed her sweetly. "I know they are wary of you just now, and I know too well how that wariness hurts you. They are overwhelmed with what you did for me, 'tis all. Give them time, and the auld women will be planning a celebration in your honor. They expect you to be my bride, you know. There is talk that we have already exchanged vows in the auld way and 'tis but a formality to announce our union before the clan. They would not allow my bride to leave."

"And you?"

"You know what I wish. I want you to stay here, with me. We should wed. 'Twould insure your safety, for even Donal would not—"

"Donal? You mean Dougal, do you not?"

Symon looked confused for a moment. "Aye, Dougal. Even Dougal would not steal another man's wife."

She pressed her palm to his cheek, quickly determining that there was no poison at work; just simple fatigue confusion had him mistaking the name. And mistaking what must happen.

"Marrying me would only anger Dougal. I ken him

well. If we wed, he will double his attacks. No one will be safe. Dougal does not ever give up."

"Aye. 'Tis why I must free my brother. I cannot leave him in Dunmore's hands. I couldn't live with myself. But first, we must marry, to keep you safe."

Elena didn't trust her voice. He could not wed her, though she could cherish no dream more. To do so would seal the fate of Clan Lachlan and their chief, whom she loved so much. Once more, Dougal controlled her life, though he was not even here. He would take all that she had come to love, all who had come to love her, and destroy them, and only because she thwarted him.

Only because she hadn't submitted to Dougal's will. And now he sought to bend Symon to his will, by forcing him to choose between Ranald and Elena. And Symon refused to bend at all.

If he married her, Dougal would kill Ranald, or worse. She was sure of it. She had seen his temper, his ruthlessness. If she allowed Symon to marry her, his brother would pay the consequences, and Symon would hate her forever for causing such a horrible choice, such a horrible outcome.

She would do what she must to help Symon retrieve Ranald, for she could do no less for the man she loved and the clan who had taken her in.

As soon as Symon slept this night, she would retrieve her things and slip out through the weans' bolt-hole once more. This time she would not be afraid. She would leave just enough of a trail south, to mislead Symon, and distract Dougal, making sure Dougal knew she was gone from Kilmartin and gone from the MacLachlans' keeping, drawing him away from Lamont Castle so the MacLachlans could retrieve Ranald.

Then she would head north, into the Highlands. When she was beyond where anyone knew of her clan she would find a place to live, making her living from simples or perhaps as a midwife, for women always had need of a midwife.

"We can tell the clan in the morn." Symon's deep rumble dragged her back from her plans. "We'll have to wed in the auld way, saying our vows before the clan. There is no time to call the banns."

"Are you hungry?" She kept her voice light, belying the sadness and despair that threatened to overwhelm her. "I had Jenny send your meal up."

Symon pulled her to him, kissing her until her head spun and her body ached for him. "I will eat, lass, for I fear I'll need my strength again this night." He grinned at her, and she knew she would remember this last time in his arms for the rest of her days.

chapter 16

❦

Symon reached for Elena, missing her warmth, but only cold bedding met his questing hand. He opened his eyes, searching for her. She was not within the chamber. He grinned. Of course. It was her wedding day. No doubt she was in the kitchens, selecting the wedding breakfast, or in Meggie's chamber, borrowing a pretty gown. Symon bounded out of bed, a weight lifted from his shoulders by the prospect of having Elena by his side for the rest of his days.

It was too bad he would have to kill Dougal of Dunmore—as Donal called himself these days. In some ways he owed his current and future happiness to the bastard. If he had not chased Elena from her home, she would not have ended up in his arms—and his bed.

His bride's ardor of the night before brought a huge grin

to his face. Aye, he owed Dunmore a thanks. And he would give it to him, gladly, as soon as Symon freed one of his brothers, and ran the other through with his claymore. Pity Dunmore would die before hearing the words from Symon's lips.

Symon took his time preparing himself. He brushed the dirt from his plaid and pleated it carefully, wishing to please his bride with his appearance. He scraped the whiskers from his face and even combed his hair, leaving it free as Elena seemed to prefer it.

As Symon went to leave the chamber, a quiet tapping sounded on the heavy door. He opened it, half hoping Elena had been unable to stay away longer. Instead he found Murdoch, his huge hand holding a tiny one. Wee Fia shrank backward and Murdoch squatted down.

"Do not fret, lassie. He is not near so fierce as he looks." But Murdoch looked worried as he stood and faced his chief. "The wee lassie saw something this morning you might have an interest in, Symon. I told her you would not be angry, since 'twas not her doing."

Symon motioned the two into his chamber. Murdoch lifted the little girl into his arms. "Go on. Tell your chief."

The child swallowed, then pulled her thumb from her mouth. "'Tis the mistress, Elena, she left, through the weans' hole." She quickly stuck her thumb back in her mouth and laid her head on Murdoch's shoulder, though she never took her eyes from Symon.

Symon heard the words, but could not understand them. Elena was preparing for their wedding, then he'd go off to the Lamont stronghold and free Ranald, end Dunmore's life. He'd be free to look forward to the future. With Elena by his side, he did not even worry over who had poisoned him. Eventually the culprit would slip up, and they would discover his identity and purpose. In the meantime Elena would keep him sane, free of poison. She must. She was the key to the future. She was critical to the prophecy.

She was his heart.

"When did you see her, sprite?" He winced when he realized he had used Elena's pet name for the child. She knew it, too, for she blinked, her eyes tearing up.

"'Twas just afore the sunrise, when the sky is still gray."

Which explained why the bed was cold. She had been gone for several hours by now. Numbness climbed into his chest, circled his heart, then breathed a chilling frost there. He nodded at Murdoch, who took the child from the room, murmuring something to her, gaining her smile.

Symon scowled and paced. He would have to go after her. She was in great danger all alone in the wood. Dunmore could find her, she would be frightened, running scared again. Why? He wanted to scream the question aloud, wanted to demand an answer. Why?

He had it planned out perfectly. Marry Elena, retrieve Ranald, do away with Dunmore. Together he and Elena and Ranald would discover the source of the poison, then that too would be finished, done. Life would return to the path it had once taken, only it wouldn't. Couldn't.

He wasn't the same man he had been before all this started—mad or not. He had experienced too much this past year to return to the callow lad he had been. And there was the matter of the lass he would spend his life with. No simple lass would suit him anymore. He wanted more than a pretty face and a willing body. Aye, he wanted a sharp mind. . . .

A sharp mind, one that knew their common enemy as well as he did, but she did not know the truth. Realization shook him. She had left to keep him safe. To keep his clan safe. It was her way. Dunmore would never stop in his quest for revenge on Symon, and Symon's taking of Elena was just the latest excuse. Symon knew this as well as he knew he would never give Dunmore what he really wanted. But Symon's way was to get rid of the man. Elena thought to rid Dunmore of his reason for tormenting the MacLachlans.

Guilt crushed him. If he had but told her the truth about Donal—Dougal of Dunmore—she would have understood that leaving would solve nothing, would only put her in harm's way, in Dunmore's way. Dear God, she had left the only safety she had found, and Dunmore was out there waiting for her. He was sure of it. Symon raced for the byre, shouting for Murdoch. He hastily saddled his horse as Murdoch slid to a stop in front of him.

"I ride for Lamont Castle. Gather any able to fight and follow as quickly as you can."

Murdoch agreed.

"Gather your mounts as fast as you may. I cannot wait!" He leaped onto his horse, shouting for the gate to be opened, then raced out of the castle and headed for the valley where he had first met Elena.

Elena pushed on, her steps faltering a little with fatigue. She had left before dawn, having spent her last hour with Symon watching him sleep, memorizing the details of his face, the sound of his breathing, the musky-sweet smell of their loving. She gathered her memories about her like a thick Highland blanket, holding them close to warm her in the days to come.

A branch pulled at her hair, and she stopped to free herself and listen briefly, as she had all morning, to see if anyone followed. No unusual sound came from the forest, so she continued.

No one had followed her from the castle that morning, she was sure of that. She had set off south, leaving just enough broken branches and a long red hair or two to entice any of the Lamonts lurking about to think she had headed that way. When she was sure no one was following her, she doubled back, passing near the castle once more, and heading north at last, toward a new beginning, though she did not feel she had ended this part of her life well.

Leaving Symon and his clan had been the hardest thing she had ever done. Leaving without warning or explanation chafed her. The MacLachlans had taken her in when she was in need, and allowed her amongst them even these last few days. She owed them so much more than to simply disappear into the early morning mists.

And yet it was the best thing she could do to repay their kindness. She could not let Dougal hurt them further. She would not be the cause of more suffering for them. Dougal would never give up until he had her back. A shudder ran down her spine. He would have to at least give up harassing the MacLachlans when he discovered she was no longer with them. She would have to keep moving until she was sure he was no longer looking for her, keep moving so as not to endanger anyone else.

Elena tried not to think about Symon when he awoke to find her gone. She tried not to imagine the depth of betrayal he would be feeling, the loss, the hurt. She had to remember why she was doing this, and keep going.

Otherwise, she would turn right around and beg his forgiveness, plead with him to marry her then and there so they would be together always. But she couldn't. For she knew if she did, he and his people would pay for her weakness. Dougal would make sure of it.

As the sun rose nearly overhead, Elena could barely keep her eyes open. She had not slept at all that night, wishing to spend every moment with Symon awake, aware. She stopped at the burn that ran down the heart of the glen and drank her fill, then pulled one oatcake from her small store of food and ate it. She looked about for a place to hide, to rest, just for a bit, but she was in the wide glen, and there was little beyond the trees and bracken. She walked on, looking for someplace to rest.

At last she came to a pile of stones forming a large hill. It was in an opening in the forest, oddly free of trees and bushes. Even the early spring wildflowers seemed reluctant to bloom within that circle of sunshine.

Elena skirted the edge of the stone pile, and when she reached the far side, she saw an entrance, a small tunnel built into the hill. When she bent down to look within, she could see sunshine streaming in to the center of it, illuminating what appeared to be an open chamber in the middle of the pile. Curious, Elena climbed the rocky mount and peered down into a small sun-filled, circular space. She would not be seen in there, she realized, unless someone troubled themself to climb to the top and peer in. Perhaps she could rest awhile here. She climbed down and then shimmied through the tunnel on her hands and knees. Once in the roofless chamber, she wrapped herself snugly in the blanket she had taken for her cloak and pushed her back to the wall on the shadowy side of the space.

"'Tis a fitting place you choose to sleep."

The harsh voice jarred Elena from a deep slumber. The shadows that had barely touched the floor of the space when she lay down now stretched to the middle of the circular space.

"There's not many a wench would choose to rest in the burial place of the ancients."

Elena gasped and sat up, looking about her wildly. It wasn't the words that disturbed her, but the speaker. At last her eyes adjusted, and she saw Dougal sitting on the rim of the chamber, where the roof once joined the walls.

"Ye do not have any words of greeting for your husband?"

Elena rose to her feet, her eyes firmly on Dougal. "I have no words of greeting for you, Dougal of Dunmore." She wasn't sure what he would do to her, now that he had found her, but she didn't care. The moment she had heard his voice, she knew her life was over. He might not kill her body, but her spirit would die swiftly.

He signaled her to crawl out of the cairn. For a moment she hesitated. What if he had others with him? They would grab her as she left the tunnel. And if there weren't others? Then Dougal would grab her. The alternative would be to stay put. She looked about and realized that if she forced Dougal to join her, she would be lost for sure. There would be no way to escape him except through the tunnel, and he would be able to keep her from that easily enough.

She cast him an uneasy glance, then stooped to exit her

temporary home. When she rose to her feet at the other end, he was standing there, a nasty leer on his face.

"So you've had enough of the Devil's staff, have you?"

Elena bit back any retort she might have thrown in the man's face, knowing it was better to hold her tongue, wait for an opportunity, than to give in to his baiting.

"You've caused great hardship to your clan, Elena," he said, reaching for a lock of her hair.

He let it slide through his dirty fingers, and Elena struggled not to let him know how much he revolted her. Once she had understood that other lasses might find Dougal attractive. But she could not see it any longer. Her contempt for him colored his appearance more strongly than any other consideration.

She looked at him carefully now, trying to understand how someone's attitude could so affect their appearance. He wasn't as tall as Symon, and Dougal was more whip-like in his build. But his hair was the same dark brown, though Symon's held a glossy sheen and was silky to the touch, where Dougal's appeared more coarse. And his eyes—

"Do you like what you see?" He used the lock of hair he had been fingering as a leash, pulling her close against him.

"You do not see what is plain before your eyes, do you?" He smashed his mouth against hers, and every instinct in her screamed in protest. She flailed against him, but he had her arms pinned to her side, his own wrapped vise-like around her. Desperate, she bit the tongue that probed her mouth.

"Arg! Bitch!" He backhanded her. She stumbled to the ground, her hand screaming in pain where she landed on a loose stone. "How can you go to his bed and not come to mine!" he screamed. Carefully she rose to her feet, the stone clutched in her uninjured hand.

"Do not touch me again, Dougal."

"I'll do what I wish." He lunged at her. She stepped aside, crashing the rock down on him, barely missing his head and instead hitting his shoulder.

Swiftly she moved away from him, keeping the cairn at her back. If she tried to escape into the forest now, he would have no trouble catching her. Nay, she had to stay and face him, here and now, somehow knock him out, then she could once more disappear. 'Twas her only hope of escaping him. At least now he knew she had left the safety of the MacLachlans. At least now they would be free of his harrying.

Dougal worked his shoulder, a deadly glare in his eyes, eyes that were the same as Symon's. The color was different, but the shape, the way the eyebrows slashed over them, they were the same. How could she have missed that before? The cool green of Symon's eyes, so full of love, had distracted her from the obvious resemblance to Dougal's hate-filled mud-brown glare.

Dougal began to move around her, obviously intent on moving her away from the cairn, into a less defensible position. But she would not give in to his bullying anymore. He had ruined her life, and done his best to hurt the MacLachlans.

"Why?" The question popped out before she knew she wanted to ask it.

"Why will I do as I wish?" He sneered at her.

"Why do you wish me harm? Why do you persecute the MacLachlans, when 'tis my gift you want?"

"If 'tis harm you think I wish you, then perhaps the Devil is far more stupid than I thought. I would have thought he'd taught you about a man's needs by now."

Elena felt her cheeks heat, but did not take her eyes from her foe. "Can you not answer a simple question? Perhaps you do not know why you are so evil?"

He advanced on her, murder in his eyes. Elena raised the stone, prepared to hurl it at his nose and run. He stopped and seemed to compose himself a little. "I am not evil, Elena. I am chief of Clan Lamont, and you will be my wife. You will secure my position by both your wedding me and through your power."

"So you cannot answer my question?"

"Aye, he can answer it."

Elena gasped and turned toward the voice she would know anywhere. Symon stood like an avenging angel at the edge of the clearing, his dark hair loose about his shoulders, his strong legs firmly planted on the ground and his eyes, full of vengeance, fixed on Dougal. Never had he looked more sure of himself, more like the powerful man he was. Elena's heart filled with love, and she took a step toward him.

Symon shouted. Elena whipped her attention back to the forgotten Dougal, but it was too late. He grabbed her, pulling her backward, pinning her to him, his dagger at her throat.

"Ah, now the tables have turned, Devil. 'Tis my dirk at her throat instead of yours at mine."

"I should have slit it years ago instead of letting you be banished, Donal." Symon stepped into the clearing, the bright midday sunlight glinting off his drawn claymore. "Release her."

She felt Dougal—Donal?—shake his head and his arm tightened about her. "Nay. Cannot you see you've lost at last, brother?"

"Brother?" Elena asked, confused and afraid.

"Aye," Dougal said, his hot breath singeing her ear, "did he not tell ye? Surely that whelp Ranald ran back to you with the news, Symon. But you did not think anyone else needed to know, did you? Ah, and I had heard you thought yerself in love with my lass, *my* betrothed. You've had everything else that belongs to me."

"I have naught that belongs to you," Symon said, moving around, forcing Dougal to turn with Elena in order to keep facing him. "You chose your path, Donal. You could have stayed at Kilmartin, even been champion, but 'twas not enough for you."

"Aye, 'twas never enough. 'Twas less than my due. But you, you have taken it all, always have. And now I will take what is mine, Elena, Lamont Castle, and even Kilmartin Castle, for I have earned them all."

Elena felt Dougal tremble, felt his breath come in agitated gasps, knew he barely held himself in control. Knew by the easy way Symon moved about them that he understood Dougal as well as she did, knew he would not back down, and only waited for him to snap, to attack, then Symon would be able to act, to save her once more. But he could not do it alone, for she also knew he would not risk her life.

But she could. It would be worth her life if it meant Dougal would no longer threaten those that she loved.

"You have earned nothing, Dougal, or Donal?" she said. "Which is it? You cannot even claim one name. You will never claim Castle Lamont. My cousin, Ian, will be chief.

'Twas always intended to be. I will not marry you and you will never be chief. I have already married Symon." The lie came surprisingly easy since, in her heart, it was no lie.

She saw a glint in Symon's eye, then felt the prick of Dougal's dagger at her neck. She closed her eyes then, hoping it would be quick. She was confident he wouldn't live long enough to see her body hit the ground.

When he did not act, she pushed him further. "I carry his bairn." 'Twas more hope than lie, but it served the purpose.

Dougal flung her to the ground and lunged at Symon, a guttural cry like that of an animal wrenched from him. The two men grappled, their blades quickly discarded in favor of fists. They rolled, too evenly matched to be sure which would prevail.

Elena rose and realized she still clutched the stone. Carefully she moved closer to the fray, prepared to crash her primitive weapon down on Dougal's head as soon as she could be sure it was the right brother. Brothers? It explained so much, and not nearly enough.

She watched as the two wrestled, landing thudding punches. Suddenly they were moving toward her. She couldn't scramble out of the way quick enough and found herself knocked to the ground, her skirts pinned under the fighting men. In danger herself, she quickly decided which was which and brought her weapon down on the closest head.

For a moment she wasn't sure if she had actually hit anything, then the man on top slumped and the one on the bottom shoved him off.

chapter 17

❧

"**D**aft lassie," Symon said, rising to his feet and pulling her into his embrace. "He nearly killed you."

"But he didn't. And now your clan is safe from him."

He was so stupid not to have told her the truth when Ranald first came to him. Symon glanced at Dougal, whose chest rose and fell, though all else would have indicated he lived no longer. "Nay, Elena-mine, as long as he lives, Kilmartin and Clan Lachlan will be in danger, as will you and your kin." He stroked her hair, holding her close to his heart, as he tried to figure out how to explain the complicated person who lay on the ground beside them.

"I will go far away," Elena whispered against his chest. "He will not bother you. He will come for me."

Symon sighed. "Aye, he will come after you. Donal is

not the type to forget someone who can further his grasp for power." He found her lips and tried to reassure her with his kiss. A crashing sounded in the wood. Symon pushed her quickly behind him. His claymore lay across the clearing, so he pulled his dagger and prepared to fight whoever would threaten them further.

Murdoch rode from between the trees and surveyed the clearing. "Och, lad, put that blade away. 'Tis only me and the lads, come to save you from yon thug." He grinned. "I never would have thought to see Donal again."

Symon sheathed his dagger, then reached behind him, wanting Elena safe in his arms. "How did you find out 'twas Donal?"

"And when am I going to learn why Dougal called you brother," Elena asked, "and why do you call him Donal?"

"I think I can answer both questions." Ranald moved into the sunlight.

Symon felt Elena tense and remembered the conversation—the accusations—the last time the two faced each other. "Not now, lass," he murmured to her.

Defiance flashed in her eyes, but she held her tongue.

Ranald moved closer, until he stood just on the other side of Donal's body. "Donal is, claims to be, our half brother."

Elena looked at Symon, who nodded.

"But how did he become Dougal of Dunmore?"

Symon took over the story. "I told you he came to us in his eighth year. By the time he had reached his eleventh winter, he began to persecute our mum, blaming her for our da not treating him as he deserved."

A snort sounded near their feet. Donal lay there, rubbing his head. "You are so stupid, still, brothers," he said, a sneer in his voice. Symon pushed Elena behind him again as Donal slowly sat up, looking about him with contempt clear on his face. "I did not persecute the bitch—"

Symon grabbed him by the front of his tunic and pulled him up until they were nose to nose. "You deny you bedeviled her, throwing your own mother in her face day after day?"

"Nay, but she did not die of persecution."

Symon's mouth went dry. "What do you mean?" He watched as pride glinted sharply in Donal's eyes.

"There are many ways to poison, Devil."

He heard Elena gasp behind him as Donal's meaning sank in. Ranald pulled the bastard from his grip, turning him around long enough to punch him in the face. "You killed her, poisoned her?" He punched again, but Donal ducked this time, and Ranald nearly caught Symon in the jaw. Murdoch moved his horse to block Donal's escape, but he did not interfere with the brothers' interrogation.

"You poisoned their mother?" Elena's voice was quiet, almost calm, though Symon could hear a hard edge to it that had not been there before.

"Aye."

"And my da?"

Donal snorted. "It took no poison to rid myself of that auld man. It took only a flagon of whiskey and a walk to the edge of Lamont's Peak. I thought 'twas a fitting place for the Lamont to end his days, don't you?"

Symon risked a look at her and was surprised at the cold hatred he saw there. Gentle Elena, skittish healer, glared at Donal, her fists clenched at her side. Elena wanted blood. He wanted some himself, but there was one more question to be answered before he allowed his blade the privilege of ridding the world of this evil.

"What is your preference for ridding yourself of me?" Symon asked Donal.

The pride was tinged with a self-satisfied smirk. "Ah, humiliation is the best revenge, do you not think so?"

"Nay, but I know you would."

"'Tis a nasty bit of poison, fly-bane. Drives one mad with pain. Muddles the mind so that everyone believes the madness. Brings the strong down into the mud with everyone else. And it is so easy to hide, in your food, in Ranald's precious wine. Especially in his wine." Donal laughed, sharp and jagged. "I humiliated you, and you never knew what was happening."

Symon nodded, but it was not a nod of agreement.

"The mystery is solved, then. Elena, Ranald is not responsible for the poison in his wine."

Now he saw the hate Elena carried mirrored in Donal. "If she hadn't interfered, Kilmartin would be mine by now, and you would be a raving lunatic, dead on the moor, or locked away in some dank hole in the ground for the rest of your days. Aye, 'twas fitting you should die of humiliation, since that was the fate your da gave me."

"He sought to keep your life, give you another chance to find your way. Were it up to me and Ranald, you would be long dead."

"Nay, those are pretty words, but they do not cover up the truth. You and that brother of yours hated me from the first day I showed up at your gate. You would not rest until I was humiliated, and banished, left to rot in the snow or beg for a louse-infested bit of straw to sleep in. No one would take me in, feed me, help me, until I reached the sea.

I had to change my name, for your blighted da had spread word of my humiliation."

At those words another crashing came through the wood. A dozen Lamont warriors burst into the clearing, weapons drawn.

"Ian, nay!" Elena shrieked.

The leader hesitated, looking from Elena to Donal, then taking in the gathering. "Are you all right, Elena?"

"Aye. I am fine. Do not harm these men, they seek to help us."

Symon turned to Elena, a question on his lips that did not make it out before he felt the sharp cold bite of a blade between his ribs.

E lena watched as first a question, then surprise crossed Symon's face. In a sudden flurry, Murdoch and Ranald ran their claymores through Dougal as Symon reached for her, nearly falling on her, collapsing in her arms.

"Symon!"

She helped him to the ground, vaguely aware of the commotion around her. She saw the carved hilt of Dougal's—*Donal's,* she corrected herself—*sgian dhu* sticking from his back at the same moment she felt the mirrored pain in her own. Quickly she laid him facedown on the ground and moved near the wound. Gingerly she pulled the small knife from him, feeling every slice of steel against flesh. Blood welled quickly, and she knew he had been mortally hurt.

Anger spiked into her, fear forced it deep. 'Twas exactly

what she had feared. Only Symon's whispering her name let her focus on what must be done and done quickly.

"Do not, lass, do not heal me. 'Tis too bad, too deep. You cannot—"

"Quiet, Symon. I can and I will. You will not die on me, I will not allow it," she said fiercely, meaning every word, even as fear knotted her belly. "We cannot let Donal win. Lie still now, let me work," she said, sending him a sad smile. "'Tis what I do."

Quickly she ripped the bloody tunic away from the wound, then warmed her hands, rubbing them rapidly together. Every ounce of strength and courage she had, she poured into that healing, every hope, and wish, and desire she had allowed to blossom in his company, she drew upon. Over and over again she forced the healing gift into him, over and over again she reinforced it with the depth of her feelings for this man. Still blood welled, and his skin grew more ashen.

Elena sobbed and began again. "You cannot die, Symon, you cannot," she whispered as she worked. "I failed with my mum, I will not fail with you. I love you too much to let you go."

Suddenly she felt the heat in her own heart, as if someone used her gift upon her, closing the old wounds there, the hurts and fears, the loneliness she had held close to her all these years. She used that power, poured it into Symon, letting all her love for him flow from her freely, like a clear mountain burn, rushing gaily down to the heart of the glen.

The bleeding slowed, then ceased, and before long, Symon's skin glowed pink and healthy once more. Relief coursed through her. She sat back on her heels, exhausted, but giddy. She was free of all that pain she had carried with her, the guilt, the fear. It had all washed clear of her in that moment of overwhelming love that had surged out of her, bottled up for so many years she had forgotten the power of it.

She reached to push the hair from Symon's face. He lay quiet, resting, not quite sleeping, she knew, but not quite awake. Somewhere in between, where all was peaceful, calm, serene. He would rouse soon, still weak, but whole, and alive.

She looked about her, suddenly aware of where she was. Circled about her were several dozen warriors, Lamonts and MacLachlans, all standing shoulder to shoulder, absolutely still, utterly quiet. Only the leaves rustling in the wind broke the silence. She took a deep breath, marveling at the fresh breeze that played over her skin, and brought the smell of damp earth, cold rock, and death to her.

Quickly she stood and looked about her. Murdoch stepped aside, revealing Dougal/Donal sprawled in the dirt, a bright red puddle gathering around him, turning the ground black where it seeped into the dirt.

" 'Twas up to me to stop him," Ranald said quietly. He rubbed his wrists absently.

Elena moved to him, lifted his hand away, and closed her eyes, touching her fingers to his abraded skin. She did not have the strength left to do more than take the pain away. "Murdoch, bind his wrists. 'Twill heal quickly."

Ranald nodded at her, his eyes wide. "And Symon?"

"He rests, but will rouse soon. He will need your help for a while, but he will be fine."

Ranald swallowed hard, then took her hands in his.

"Thank you for saving Symon's life. He is truly lucky to have your love."

She looked at him thoughtfully. "I am sorry I accused you of the poison. He was sure all along that you would not do such a thing."

Ranald squeezed her hands and released her.

Elena moved to her cousin Ian, standing nearby. "How came you here, cousin?"

"We were searching for you, and him," he said, pointing at Donal's body. "When we found his camp, we found that one"—this time he pointed at Ranald—"held hostage. When we freed him, he told us that you were safe with the MacLachlans. We were on our way to Kilmartin to find you when he"—he shoved his chin in Murdoch's direction— "came raging through the forest. He bade us all follow, promising answers when we found the Devil."

"And have you found your answers?"

"I do not know. Have we?"

Symon roused then, groaning, but insisting on sitting up. "You will be sore, but all is well," she whispered to him, helping him to his feet, then depositing him on a large rock.

"Dougal is dead," she said quickly. "Murdoch and Ranald can return you to Kilmartin Castle."

"And what of you, Elena-mine?" He lifted a hand to her cheek. "Will you not return with me as well?"

Elena looked about the gathered warriors, their faces full of respect when they looked at her. She glanced at Donal, lying in his own blood. He would no longer persecute her, but would the others?

She thought about the way the MacLachlans had treated her the past few days. There had been no fear, curiosity, yes, and—she examined the faces around her again—and the same awed respect she saw here, only she had not recognized it for what it was. Would her own clan see her the same way now that Dougal/Donal was not there to say when and how she could use her skill? She tried to remember before Dougal, but then her father had treated her nearly the same. Could it be different now that she was strong enough to control her own destiny?

"Why did you do it?" Symon's voice broke into her thoughts. "You could have died with me."

Elena touched his face, ran a lock of his hair through her fingers, and pondered his question. At last she understood the root of her own courage. "I did it because I would rather die with you than live without your love."

"Ach, lass—"

She kissed him, a smile tugging at her lips. Together they had changed so much. Together they would find a way. At last she knew exactly what she wanted, and she was going to get it.

"Ian," she said to her cousin, though she did not let Symon out of her sight. "By right, I am chief of Clan Lamont, am I not?"

"Aye."

"But my father wished you to lead the clan."

"Aye."

"Then so do I." She looked about at her kinsmen and planted her fists on her hips. "Is there anyone here who thinks otherwise?"

No one said a word.

"Fine. Ian of Lamont, as is my right as the only child of Fergus, chief of Lamont, I decline to become chief. I designate you to take my place, to lead our people well, and fairly."

"I accept."

"Not so quickly, cousin, there is one more thing you must do if you wish to be chief."

He cocked an eyebrow at her and waited.

"You must agree to abide peacefully, and as allies, with Clan Lachlan."

An uproar broke out, voices raised in disagreement, until Symon rose from his seat. "Silence!" Everyone stopped, tension thick in the air.

He moved toward her, and she felt his love as clearly as she had felt it when they had joined together in the healing, as clearly as when they made love. He took her hands and kissed them lightly. "Are you proposing something, Elenamine?"

She smiled up at him. "Aye. There was a wee lie I told, which I would make the truth."

"And what was that?"

She looked about at the mingled clans, enjoying the feeling of drawing these people together in peace. "I told Dougal, Donal, that we were wed."

A gasp flew through the Lamonts.

"I would make that true."

Symon pulled her close, kissing her soundly, as the MacLachlans cheered. The Lamonts were not so pleased.

"What has the Devil done to you to make you wish to wed our enemy?" Ian asked.

Elena went to him, stood before him, proud and sure of herself, her people—all of them. "He has made me love him, Ian. 'Tis no crime, that. If I understand what has happened here, Donal was responsible for the strife between our clans. He caused the madness in Symon by poisoning him. He sought to harm the MacLachlans, and did not mind harming Lamonts to do so. 'Twas he who killed Da."

Lamont voices rose in disbelief, and Elena let them rail against it for a moment.

"He killed Symon and Ranald's mother, too. He made sure the clans had reason to fight, then used my power— aye, my power of healing—to keep the fight going. We need not fight longer. I will marry Symon, you will lead Clan Lamont. Joined together we shall be greater than either clan was before."

She stilled, then turned to Symon. He stood before her, whole and confident, his love for her shining like a beacon fire.

" 'Tis as Auld Morag said," Elena whispered.

"She is seldom wrong, love."

"Aye, the prophecy, but she also told me I was stronger than I knew, if I but trusted my heart."

He smiled then, pride glowing about him. "I could have told you that. It takes no second sight to see you've a fine strong heart."

" 'Twould seem we've a wedding to prepare," Murdoch said, breaking the silence.

"The only preparation will be to bury that one there," Symon said.

"We'll see to that," Ian replied.

Symon looked about him, gaining his bearings. "Hmm, I know the perfect place to wed," he muttered as he grabbed Elena's hand and dragged her into the wood. Moments later they burst into the clearing of the circle of ancient stones where Elena had first run into Symon.

"'Tis the perfect place," she said, smiling up at him. They went to the burn close by to wash the blood and dirt from themselves. Symon borrowed Ranald's tunic and once more brushed what dirt he could from his plaid. Elena finger-combed her hair, then fashioned a crown of greenery for herself. By the time they were prepared, Ian and his kinsmen had caught up with them. Together with their kinsmen of both clans, Symon and Elena entered the circle and moved to the very center.

"Are you sure you want this, love?" Symon asked.

"Aye."

"Are you not worried I will try to use your gift as Donal did?"

She shook her head, laughter bubbling up within her. Joy spilled out, and she kissed him lightly on each cheek. "You could not do such a thing, Symon. You are too soft-hearted, and you love me too much."

"But what of others? Are you not worried that so many know of your gift now?"

"I know I am safe with you. I know our clans together will insure this gift is used as it was meant to be, to help those in need, not to advance any one person, or cause pain in any other."

"Then you are sure."

"Never have I been so sure of anything before, my love."

There, before warriors of their combined clans, Elena and Symon exchanged their vows of love and commitment in the auld way, in the place of the ancients.

"And that other lie?" Symon asked quietly.

"What?"

"The bairn?"

"Oh, well, we'll know soon enough. If 'twas a lie, we'll just have to try a bit harder to make it the truth."

Symon chuckled as he scooped his bride into his arms and strode out of the circle that had been the start of so many ills in his life, and so many blessings.